TIME'S MUSICIANS

TIME'S MUSICIANS

A NOVEL

Mark Paul Oleksiw

This is a work of fiction. Names, characters, businesses, places, events and incidents are either the products of the author's imagination or used in a fictitious manner. Any resemblance to actual persons, living or dead, or actual events is purely coincidental.

Cover Images © Adobestock, Stocksy
Cover and book design by Caroline Teagle Johnson

To everyone who searches, may a beacon lead the way.

CHAPTER 1

The Black Hole Down the Street

(Spring 1998)

"Billy, are you playing or not?" the voice shrieked over the schoolyard cacophony.

"What?" Billy replied, not even sure of the question anymore.

"Dodgeball, dummy. Go get the ball!" The child's legs pumped like impatient pistons, his voice stammering in frustration. "Shit, I'll get it." The child nudged past Billy and ran to the fence where a bright orange ball lay nestled against it.

Another boy strolled over to Billy, only to stop within two feet to study him. The boy reached out to tug on the short-sleeved shirt Billy had on. "What you looking at, Billy? Don't you wanna finish the game? We only need two more to win."

Billy never turned to acknowledge the boy. He tilted his head before speaking. "Something's going on over there. Look."

The boy squinted toward Billy's gaze to the far reaches of the schoolyard. He noticed a crowd of students, grade sixers, huddled in a semi-circle around a boy. The voices grew louder, almost shouting in tune with some melody. "Geez, that's that weird kid. Peter or Dieter or something like that. He's for sure making up another story."

"Weird kid? Why is he weird? What story?" Billy turned now to face his friend, a frown on his face.

"Sorry, I keep forgetting you're new. That kid makes up these crazy stories now and then. He just wants the attention. No one likes him."

Billy grew more and more interested. "Why don't they like him? Does he do bad things? Say bad things?"

"Naw, he talks about crazy things."

"Like what, Chris?"

"Oh, man, don't pay attention to that shit. C'mon and play the game with the rest of us."

Billy smiled at his friend but turned to walk towards the commotion's location. His pace changed from long strides to a sprint. Chris stood still, his mouth gaping open, then rolled his eyes before throwing his hands up and returning to his spot in the chalk-outlined world of dodgeball. He glanced over at Billy, who was now amongst the agitated crowd of six graders.

Billy reached the border of the throng of older kids. A fifth-grader himself, he respected the seniority of his schoolmates. He stayed close enough to hear, yet far enough to go unnoticed. Having spent time in a foster home and coming to a new school, Billy had mastered the art of schoolyard survival. A red-haired girl stood inches away from him by herself. He edged closer, invading her space before stopping at the periphery of her ear, then whispered, "What's the freak talking about?"

"He was talking about his latest trip."

"Oh, where did he go?"

The girl turned to Billy and laughed. "Not where—when!" She chuckled, bringing her hand to her lips to hold back the laughter. "He says he figured out how to time travel."

"Time travel?" Billy concealed his excitement.

"Yes. Listen, he's blabbing about it now." She turned her large green eyes away, ignoring Billy and giggling as she listened to the monologue taking place a few feet away. It surprised Billy that a pretty girl with the most gorgeous green eyes seemed so sarcastically wicked.

He stepped back to better observe the magic show. With arms flowing through the air, seeming almost detached from the boy's shoulders, the kid spoke to his audience with an ebb and flow of words. Each word exploded like fireworks from his lips. Dieter revealed that, while exploring in early spring, he stumbled upon a cave. Within the cave, he crawled through an opening that led to a different world and age. When he opened his eyes, he found himself on the cobblestone streets of a medieval village. He discovered a portal capable of transporting him back in time! As Dieter continued, ignoring the heckling and laughter aimed at him, speaking of multiple journeys taken. It didn't matter that he couldn't explain how he returned or how he had not emerged in a dangerous place. None of this mattered to the children surrounding him. They were witnessing a show.

With little regard for the mocking audience, Billy focused on the performer. Something seemed wrong—unnerving. The clothes Dieter wore were typical faded jeans with white socks and sneakers. However, he wore an oversized long-sleeved black shirt with large cuffs. Perhaps, Billy pondered, this would be an actual magic act, and those long sleeves concealed trick playing cards or even a dove. When Billy's eyes made their way up to Dieter's face, he realized what troubled him. The boy had thick, black, curly hair with matching dark brows. His nose was slender with a slight curve. Beneath his nose were thin lips. In rare instances, when Dieter smiled at his audience, Billy noticed two or three missing teeth. Yet it was the shimmering blue eyes that Billy kept returning to. No matter where Dieter's face looked or whatever expression on his face, the eyes remained focused on the horizon above the heads of the crowd. The look in his eyes struck a chord with Billy. That look was wretchedly familiar. These were the eyes of someone trying to escape, oblivious to his surroundings, but yearning to leap from his skeleton to some faraway world.

"On Friday, I will make another trip—my last one before the summer. Anyone wants to join me?" Dieter asked.

There were catcalls and snide remarks, each one muffled by the next to the point of being inaudible. Dieter appeared frustrated with the chaotic sound. A voice reached him from the fringes of the crowd. It was Billy's voice. Even Billy seemed surprised by it.

"Is it dangerous? Time traveling?"

Dieter's eyes opened wide—for the first time they scanned the crowd, looking for the source. "It can be painful. A few bumps and bruises." Then, like a true showman, Dieter pulled back his oversize sleeves to reveal, to the shock and horror of his audience, several bruises and scratches on each arm. "But I will time travel alone, at least this time. I want someone with me so they can vouch for my story."

Billy's eyes shifted to the marks on Dieter's arms. The enigma before him was too easy to solve. He suspected that his fellow students did not care. He did. Just as he was about to ask another question, the school bell rang and recess was over. The assembled crowd retreated, leaving behind shrapnel in the form of words like *weirdo* and *freak*. Billy stayed behind even as his own classmates returned from the dodgeball game he stopped playing.

Dieter shrugged his shoulders in defeat, assuming his show was over until he saw the younger boy shifting from side to side a few feet away. "Hi!" he bellowed as the smile returned to his face.

"Hi. My name's Billy. Um… I hope you didn't mind my question. I hate to interrupt."

"No, not at all. My name is Dieter. Are you in grade six, too?"

"Naw, I'm a grade fiver. This is my first year here. Parent stuff and all. I just moved here." Billy's voice trailed off, wondering if he had disclosed too much. Why would Dieter care anyway?

"Oh, that's why I don't know you."

"Yeah, this couple adopted me last summer."

"Adopted!" Dieter's voice chirped. "Sorry, I just never met an adopted kid."

"Yeah, it's no big deal. They're nice people. This foster mom raised me until then."

"So, your parents?" Dieter asked as he walked back toward the school in tandem with Billy.

"I do not understand what happened. I don't. They found me in a hospital lobby according to the story. My mom was an addict and died when I was an infant. No idea about my dad."

"Oh… I'm sorry for being too nosy. Look, if you are interested in time travel, meet me after school. Same spot, okay?"

"Yeah, sure. And I don't mind the question. Few people ask anyway."

"Few people ask about time travel either." Dieter laughed as he opened the doors of the school. "Black holes scare you?"

"Black holes?"

"Well, to time travel, you need a black hole," Dieter smirked. "We can talk about it later."

"Sure." Billy watched as Dieter raced ahead of him up the stairs toward his classroom. *A black hole? Now that is freaky.*

The afternoon dragged for Billy. Though attentive and curious to a fault, concentration was impossible today. He turned his notebook to the last page and began doodling. He imagined what a black hole looked like and drew small images of a child falling into a hole and appearing on the other side. Whatever lesson was being taught, drowned in the swirl of imagination pouring into his young, thirsty mind. The last bell rang at precisely 3:35 p.m., freeing him.

Billy moved out of the classroom, allowing his peers to clear out before him as to avoid an irrelevant conversation. Only one thing mattered now: learning about black holes and time travel. His parents worked and wouldn't arrive home for some time, allowing him to enter late unnoticed. He grabbed his lunch sack, tucked two books into his backpack, and sauntered to the schoolyard.

Dieter sat leaning back at the corner fence, his head immersed in what seemed like a small magazine. As Billy approached, he realized Dieter was reading—but not a magazine, a comic book. Billy stopped a few steps away, still undetected, and observed.

Dieter's eyes remained transfixed on the book. What intrigued Billy was the expression on Dieter's face. His eyes seemed to burst with color and emotion, almost as though the colorful book in his hands embedded itself within him. Billy had never read a comic book before. Not once. He had dismissed them ever since one of his older foster siblings announced years ago that comic books were for babies.

"Hi, Dieter. What you reading?"

For an awkward instant, Dieter did not respond nor even flinch. Dieter laughed. "Sorry, I just wanted to finish this page. This is so fricken awesome." He looked back down at the comic book, giving it a nod of approval when he noted Billy's crooked smile. "Oh, you're not into comic books?"

"Haven't read one in a while."

"Because they're for little kids, right?"

"No, not me. Someone told me that once. I just never got into them. My bookshelf at home is stocked with what my folks call the classics."

"Because of what someone said?" Dieter's face tilted to the side. "No, I get it. People talk shit and judge me, too."

"Judge you for reading comic books?" Billy crouched down and seated himself next to Dieter, mimicking his posture.

"I guess they consider me different."

"Different is good, different ideas better. Well, at least, I think so." Billy sighed. "Unusual thoughts lead one to wonder about mysterious things. Like black holes." Billy punched Dieter on the arm, laughing. It was a pure instinct that made him do it. "Shit, I may even read a comic book myself, one day. I enjoy drawing."

"If you enjoy drawing, perhaps you can be a comic book artist. I'm serious." Dieter laughed at Billy's skeptical expression. "I prefer comic books to regular books ever since I was very young. They help take my mind off things."

"I never considered them that way. I mean, I liked comic books before. Until someone told me I needed to grow up."

"Those are the worse people, you see. Not people telling you to grow up—although they're bad—the ones telling you what to like and not to like. I learned so much reading these things."

"Like about time travel." Billy grinned, thrilled by his deduction. "You read about time travel through a comic book, right?"

"But it's true. I *have* done it. I found out how..." Dieter's voice rose and then fell before trailing off. His eyes drifted, again zeroing in on the horizon.

Billy tried to get Dieter's attention again. "How do you time travel?"

Without blinking, Dieter replied, "You need to find a black hole. I did. Pure accident and a bit of luck."

"Black hole? I understand a little about that," Billy's face blushed with his admission.

"Oh, black holes exist but not like it portrays them in comic books. Believe it, though. If you can imagine it, for sure you will find it. Just like I did."

"Those marks on your arm. The bruises. Black holes hurt? Like when you fell in one, you got those bruises, right?"

Dieter's face contorted and his eyes reverted from the horizon back to his sneakers. "Yeah, I suppose. I woke up the next day and they were there. Time travel can beat up your body good. I don't remember too much about that part."

"I see." Billy changed the subject. "Um, you said you were going back Friday. Is that true? Can I go with you?"

"Yeah. I want someone who will show some faith in me."

"What about your parents?"

Billy noticed the twitch around Dieter's mouth and heard a sigh. Dieter did not need to answer, the hesitation gave it away. Billy did not pursue it. "My curfew is around nine if it's not a school night. Where do we have to go? Is it far?" Billy realized how foolish and childish he sounded. Sure, he planned to visit a black hole and time through travel—before 9:00 p.m!

Dieter laughed out loud, chuckling, putting Billy at ease. "Billy, we can go early, like around seven. I promise you'll be home on time."

Now unsure, logic tempered his excitement, Billy asked again, "Where is it? Please tell me."

"You believe me, don't you?" Dieter's voice grew serious. "You're not putting me on like this is a big joke?"

"I'm hardly that smart or am I here to make fun of you. Perhaps I can see the black hole and time travel, too. That would be something."

"Not this time. You can observe, but cannot travel. Maybe another night. I don't want you to get hurt. As you can see, scrapes and scratches are common when you move through time."

Remembering the marks all over Dieter's forearms, Billy interrupted, hoping he wouldn't show them again. Billy recognized the source of the marks, but his desire to continue the illusion overcame any reason. "Okay, I just want to see. So, where do we have to go?"

"Well, I live around the woods. You know the area?"

"That's where the big houses are."

"Yeah, I suppose. I live in one of them. The woods are just beyond my street."

Billy never imagined that Dieter lived in the more affluent section of town. The woods were the one wildlife area still untouched. They were off-limits because of the underground caverns discovered there. "The black hole is in the woods?"

"In the caverns. I stumbled upon the entrance a while back."

"How did you get in? I mean, the whole area is blocked off. It's too dangerous. They allow no one in those caves."

"They put up all those signs to guard a grown-up secret. Grown-ups are experts at keeping things hidden to control everything. I went exploring in there a few times and that's how I found the black hole. I escaped and traveled through time!"

Billy took a deep breath. Everything became very real to him. He knew Dieter sensed his fear, and it upset him. Dieter gently draped his hand over Billy's shoulder. "Don't feel forced to join me. I'm going on Friday, no matter what. I just was hoping to prove it to someone."

"No, I will go with you. I promise." Billy looked up at Dieter's shimmering blue eyes. He spoke with a resolve to convince both Dieter and himself of his conviction. He decided he would not let Dieter down. "Just tell me where to meet you."

Dieter began to tap Billy on the shoulder with enthusiasm, each tap harder than the previous. "That's great! Meet me here at six-thirty on Friday. But promise me one thing."

"Sure. Let me guess—don't tell anyone?"

"Please don't until after I prove it to you. People laugh at me enough."

Billy smiled. "Oh, they laugh at me from the inside too, sometimes. Everyone gets laughed at."

Dieter grew silent and then, like an illusionist, was up on his feet and headed home before Billy stumbled to get up. Billy leaned back against the cage-like steel fence that surrounded the schoolyard as Dieter disappeared down one side street, heading toward those larger houses.

Minutes passed before Billy headed home—to the opposite side of their town, with the modest bungalows and apartment buildings. Summer was on the horizon, signaling the end of the school year. An exciting time for most children, but this one child was incapable of concealing his delight. Not many kids have a black hole in their neighborhood, let alone one at the end of their friend's street.

CHAPTER 2

Houdini

Some cannot keep secrets well. Most adults cannot let alone a curious child. Billy differed from most children his age. Introverted, his adoptive parents found him almost too easy. Jake and Margaret Daintree were in their forties at the time of Billy's adoption, informed years early that their genes were incompatible with conceiving a healthy child. Both parents worked as high school teachers at the one public high school in town and bent over backward to feed Billy's hunger to learn.

Billy's foster mom had written a heartfelt thank you to both upon the adoption. In her letter, she clarified that Billy had enormous potential but had been through and exposed to more than many children his age. They wondered if there may be a medical reason for his positive behavior. He appeared to be well-adjusted, considering he had no past to cling to. Then again, he had no awareness of the past—or rather, of his birth parents' past. There was nothing to haunt him. Billy envisioned all history as his creation with no ancestors to contradict him. The possibility of moving through time on whichever path he chose intrigued him.

For the next two days, Billy daydreamed over and over about places, faces, and things he read about in books. Events that had happened were mere words on paper. The intervals between those events—everything that had happened but had gone undocumented or unspoken—that's what excited him. He longed to be part of an adventure, such as exploring the endless tunnels of time. Limits existed only at the outer fringes of imagination. His pure logic required that everything was possible. Why? Because if he thought it, it must exist somewhere.

Dieter epitomized more than an explorer with flights of fancy. He embodied the dream to forge a new path. Billy heard in Dieter's voice something he sensed inside himself—a desire to search. He made friends quickly at school because he didn't have an intimidating voice, nor did he demand much of others. Dieter challenged the social order of the schoolyard. He dared schoolmates to mock him and challenged them to call him weird in a way Billy seemed incapable of. Friday would not come soon enough, and Billy kept reminding himself to hang on to the promise and keep the secret.

He practiced in front of the mirror how he planned to solicit his parents' early dismissal from Friday's supper. Of course, he dared not tell them he was going there. He would end up telling them a half-truth: he would be at the schoolyard.

Jake and Margaret Daintree did not make much of Billy's request. They trusted him, for Billy had shown a great sense of responsibility and maturity beyond his years. Jake fumbled with his glasses before settling them on the table next to his dinner plate. He cleared his throat before grinning at Billy. "So, what event is taking place on Friday evening?"

"Oh, nothing too exciting." Billy almost choked on his own words. "I mean, just a game of dodgeball or soccer."

Margaret couldn't help but join the interrogation. "Well, don't forget your curfew. We want you back home by nine."

"I promise." Billy grinned, figuring the worse part was over. He threw a curveball at his parents to change the topic. "Would it be okay if you took me to the bookstore on the weekend?"

Jake grinned at Margaret. "Do you have an exciting adventure in mind to read?"

Billy smiled. "I wanted to go to a comic book store, not the regular book store."

Jake's head moved left to right, frowning. "Comic books? Why a comic book?"

"I wanted to learn about black holes."

"Black holes, from a comic book!" Jake began laughing. "If you want to learn about black holes, I have the perfect book for you." Jake walked over to the bookshelf in the adjoining room as he spoke. "Ah, here we are. Stephen Hawking."

Billy reached over to take the book from Jake. While four eyes zeroed in on him as he studied the cover, they might well have been a hundred thousand eyes, so powerful was the intensity of their interest.

"This is about black holes?" Billy asked.

Margaret nodded. "Oh, yes. It might be a slight challenge for someone your age. But it's a wonderful book, and it has a whole chapter on black holes."

"But, um…"

Jake did not wait to speak, stopping Billy as he suffocated on the words piling upon his tongue. "Yes. He talks about the theory of black holes."

"Theory of black holes? Don't they exist? I mean, can't you time travel if you find one?"

Jake started laughing, "That is why you shouldn't read comic books. Stick with things grounded in reality."

Billy frowned as he tossed the book between his hands. This was not the conversation nor lecture he wanted. "Oh, sure. I'll give this book a read. Never mind the comic book store, I suppose." Before Jake or Margaret commented further, Billy excused himself and retreated to his room with his new book in hand. He drifted slowly enough to hear them from the base of the staircase.

Margaret and Jake exchanged glances and rolled their eyes. "Where do you suppose he got that comic book idea, Margaret?"

She shrugged her shoulders. "So many kids read those things now. It's frustrating as an English teacher to see that garbage in class."

"I get what you mean. But, he'll grow out of it. I read a few of those comics back in my prehistoric days. That is until I discovered real science. He's still only eleven. Let's hope he gives Hawking's book a chance.

The book bounced off Billy's bed and plopped on the floor. Billy felt guilty for tossing it. He picked it up and began leafing through the pages until he found the chapter on black holes. With his fingertip gliding under each word, he read until his eyes grew heavier and heavier. Nowhere did this book mention black holes being found in caves. Deciding it was no use to him, he placed the book on the far left corner of his desk. He decided he would wait several weeks before sneaking it back to the living room bookshelf. If the plan worked, his parents would forget about black holes.

The bookshelf in Billy's room now looked bare. Sure, there were plenty of books, but he realized all of them were Jake and Margaret's strategic selections—none of them were Billy's choices. While he enjoyed most of them, he found his curious mind demanded more. His instincts told him there were more significant challenges and mysteries awaiting him outside the world of those books. Dieter had learned all about black holes and time travel through comic books and by exploring the woods. Billy kept his word and spoke no more of black holes until Friday.

School days always dragged on Fridays. On this last Friday of May, Billy became convinced time stood still. He agonized over every response to the simplest of questions. He even avoided eye contact with Dieter. They had formed an alliance that he dared not shatter.

At 6:15 p.m., Billy arrived at the farthest reaches of the schoolyard. The late afternoon sky grew cloudy with ash-colored clouds dominating the horizon. The rain was approaching. Never did Billy consider Dieter wouldn't appear. His trust was complete. It must be this way. He lied to his parents about venturing off into woods to search out some mythical black hole. Any doubt needed to bludgeoned by a hammer. A slight breeze caused Billy to untie the hoodie he'd fastened around his waist and hoist it over his shoulders. If it rained or if the cave was cold, he was ready.

Billy never ventured onto the other side of town even though it was mere minutes away. The woods were fenced off from the residential streets and extended to the farthest perimeter of the town. A running creek cut the woods in two. The discovery of an uncharted maze of caverns running beneath the woods fifty years ago demanded further investigation. However, these caves were deemed too perilous to navigate due to tight passageways and spring flooding. On the other side of the creek were trees upon trees as far as the eye could envision, leading to a distant mountain range.

Lost in his thoughts, Billy didn't notice Dieter entering the schoolyard until he was mere steps from him. "Hey, there. Ready to go?" Dieter asked, seeming almost surprised by Billy's presence.

"Yeah, but I only brought a hoodie. Do I need anything else?" Billy asked, noticing Dieter's beige-colored backpack.

"I figured you wouldn't have brought a flashlight, so I got one for you." Dieter unzipped his bag and pulled out two flashlights, checking each before tossing one to Billy. "There are no lights in the caves."

Billy felt foolish. Forgetting a flashlight was amateurish. "Thanks. I wasn't thinking."

"Don't sweat it. The first time I entered those caves, I didn't have a light and didn't get very far." Dieter started walking as he spoke, his pace quickening with each step.

"Have you visited the caves and traveled often?"

"A lot. I enjoy exploring, and they were off-limits, so they seemed like the perfect place to go."

Billy stopped speaking and grew breathless trying to keep up with Dieter, whose every step seemed more anxious than the last. As they wound their way through the residential streets leading to the woods, Billy noticed the homes appearing to grow larger in scale and luxury. He wondered which one Dieter lived in. Seeing Dieter did not stop to look at any house and seemed obsessed with reaching the woods, Billy decided against asking. At last, Dieter stopped just beyond the last house, climbed over some large cement blocks, and approached a fence with a barbed wire lining the top.

"Holy shit," Billy muttered, seeing the sharp protrusions.

"Don't worry. I cut out an opening where the pointed section is. Enough for us to climb over without getting impaled."

"Geez. You are well prepared." Billy realized how often Dieter had come here.

"Can you climb the fence on your own? Or do you need a boost?"

"I can manage."

"Start climbing. I'll stay behind, just in case. I almost killed myself trying once."

Defeat would not be acceptable, and Billy scaled the fence with pure willpower mixed with a triple dose of excitement. Within seconds, Dieter landed next to him and in one motion, got to his feet to lead the way into the woods.

Dieter stopped in his tracts without warning. He turned to face Billy. "Going forward, the woods become denser and the ground uneven. When you leave, make sure you have your flashlight on and a hoodie over your head so you don't get a bad scrape."

Billy grew confused. "What do you mean *when I leave*?"

"Pay attention to where we're going now. When you're

coming out, follow the glow of the streetlights, okay? Head in that direction." Dieter's cadence had taken a more sedate pace. He no longer sounded like a twelve-year-old. Billy sensed Dieter becoming apprehensive.

"Um, aren't you coming back with me? I don't understand," Billy stammered.

Dieter took a slow breath, composing himself. He paused and sucked on his cheek before responding. "Remember? I need you to tell everyone that what I did is possible. The thing is, I'm uncertain about returning. Sometimes it takes minutes, sometimes hours, even a day or two. You understand?"

"I guess so. What if you stay too long or lose your flashlight?"

"Been there and done it before. Don't worry about me. I need to test it to make sure it's safe for your turn." Dieter reached over and slapped him on the arm. "So... want to see a black hole?"

"Sure, would I ever!!!"

"Stop talking and stay close behind. Watch the low-hanging branches. In about ten minutes, we'll be there."

Billy reached and grabbed on to one strap that dangled from Dieter's backpack. Branches were slapped to the side by Dieter's slender frame. In no time, they arrived at a rock formation at the base of a mound. Kneeling, Dieter removed several stones until a black void appeared on the side of the hill. Billy moved forward with eyes wide. The crevice opening resembled a welcoming smile.

"It's the tunnel," Dieter announced. "Follow behind me and stay close. We need to crawl about ten feet, and then we'll be in an open area at the front of the portal."

"The portal!" Billy exclaimed. The belief that this was happening electrified him.

Dieter pushed his backpack forward and began crawling. Billy's head bounced off the tips of Dieter's sneakers until Dieter tumbled forward two or three feet, landing in an underground chamber. Billy fumbled with his light, creating shadows that bounced off each ashen wall before settling on Dieter's face. Dieter stared at Billy with only his face partially visible, and the rest lost in the shadows.

"Don't bang your head trying to get up because the ceiling hangs low." Dieter flashed his light at Billy and then to the nearest wall. As the light pivoted, the contrast been the blackness and the light unnerved Billy, who trembled. Dieter reached over almost and grabbed on to Billy's shoulder. "The opening is straight ahead."

The light shone upon another portal. An opening about two feet wide. Dieter crawled toward it with Billy at his side. When they reached the entrance, both set their flashlights into the hole. Billy witnessed nothing but vast space. The cavern seemed to go on forever—and somehow, nowhere except darkness. *Wow, a black hole!*

Dieter shifted his weight back on his hind legs and said nothing. His light shone in a chaotic and random pattern. Whatever thoughts were flowing through Dieter's mind, Billy sensed the sheer weight of them. He waited before tugging on Dieter's sleeve.

"Do you want to head back?" Billy's voice snapped Dieter out his stupor.

"No, no. I'm fine. I'm not turning back." With a monotone

voice, he added, "This is important to me." He adjusted his light and shone it on Billy's face. "I will go now, okay?"

Billy's eyes blinked. "Are you sure I can't go? Perhaps you'll need help."

Dieter shifted and leaned toward Billy. "Listen to me. Promise me you won't follow me. It might be unsafe for two people."

"I understand, but what if something goes wrong and you need help to get back?"

Dieter leaned closer. "I need you here. Tell everyone about my accomplishments. Promise me."

"Yes. Yes, I will."

Dieter reached into his backpack and pulled out a small booklet and handed it to Billy. It was a comic book. Billy grabbed it with enthusiasm and brought his flashlight close to the cover. *The Magicians of Time.*

"This is the comic book that got me into time travel," Dieter explained. "It's yours now."

"I'll give it back once I read it. Thanks."

"I want you to keep it."

"I can't. It's yours."

"I need you to have it. To thank you for following and believing me."

"Thanks, but I'll still give it back."

Dieter sighed. "How about giving it back the next time you see me?"

"Sure. Wow, I like the title."

"It's about these superheroes who use magic to fool time so they can travel to the future."

"Cool." Billy tucked it in his jeans while Dieter maneuvered himself to the opening. He turned around and had Billy recite the path he'd take to get out, making him repeat it three times. Satisfied, Dieter turned to the hole and began crawling through before his feet changed direction and shuffled back toward Billy.

Dieter pulled his head out and turned to Billy. "You're a good sidekick, Billy. I wish—" He cut himself off and turned back to the opening before Billy reacted. Within a few seconds, he had disappeared through the hole.

Billy flashed the light into the opening. The beam caressed the purity of the walls coated in charcoal but could not penetrate them. Soon silence married the blackness and surrounded Billy in an embrace. The weighty, humid air pressed against Billy's body. He surrendered himself to its force and leaned back against the dank cavern wall. As he sat alone, he awaited fear challenging whatever courage he had. Moving his hand along the tight confines of the cavern, the flashlight created bright images against the gray walls before the gloom returned. Billy's eyes followed the rays of light dancing at his command. Each brave beam of light met its demise within the sooty walls. Fear remained hidden. Billy brought the light close to his chest before flicking the switch to off and setting it by his hip. Infinite blackness swallowed Billy whole. Any second, he presumed, a great terror would spread over him. He awaited terror's arrival.

Without sight to guide and reveal what lurked around him, he only had his mind. Diving deep into the bowels of thought, he searched out whatever color or image possible. The foul air pressed heavier against him, and beads of sweat assembled on his brow, waiting to slide down his cheeks. Amidst the caress of terror all around him, Billy imagined Dieter traveling through a kaleidoscope of bright lights and landing in the greenest of fields next to blue running water in some faraway land. Billy laughed at the vision. As he did, his body leaned to one side, knocking the flashlight into the abyss and out of his reach.

Fear stood before him now, impatient, vengeful, and ready to pounce. Billy pushed off against the wall and fell forward onto his hands and knees, searching for the flashlight. Droplets of perspiration trickled down, creating tiny puddles all around him. The dense air began to soak up the breath from in his lungs, his heart beating faster with each passing moment. Billy stopped in his tracks and returned to the only safe place he knew, his thoughts. Summoning an image of Dieter again in the green fields, he reopened his eyes to find a faint light emerging from the far side of the cavern. It had to be the light from the emerging moon, finding its way through the tunnel.

Billy did not grin to himself in victory nor sigh in relief after surviving the tunnel. He emerged from the cave to begin the trek into the thickness of the woods. Once outside, Billy closed his eyes, acknowledging the awesome power of his thoughts to protect him from the unfamiliar.

With the path taken to find the cave memorized, Billy stumbled through the woods, using only the natural light of the moon as a guide. Upon his arrival home just before nine, he snuck back to his room with stealth. Billy reached into his pants, pulling out his prize possession, Dieter's comic book. He flung himself back onto his bed, his fingers caressing each word of the title page. *The Magicians of Time.* Billy would read the comic book multiples times over the weekend, each beautiful illustration tattooing itself in full color on his subconscious.

Because of every magic act Billy had ever seen as a child, he knew that the return of the magician was inevitable in any illusion. When he returned to school Monday, he would learn that fear came wearing many disguises, and reality often cut open the tissue of one's mind, allowing fear to penetrate and infect. Left alone with his thoughts in the cave, he demonstrated no concern. What awaited him would rock his core.

CHAPTER 3

The Last One

By the time he awoke the following Monday morning, Billy had memorized the comic book given to him by Dieter. Not wanting to raise the suspicions of his parents, he read it in secrecy. It stirred his imagination and fed his dreams each night. Although few words appeared in white bubbles, the colors exploded before his eyes on each page, engulfing them in images of worlds he had yet to explore. During the weekend, his thoughts turned to the whereabouts of Dieter.

He wondered how the world looked where Dieter had entered. He smiled, picturing Dieter as one hero of his comic book. All of this preoccupied his mind, shielding him from the reality awaiting him at school. Would Dieter reappear?

The one ill-fitting piece to the puzzle was the bruises and marks on Dieter's arms. Upon returning home from the cave, Billy examined his arms in painstaking detail: not one bruise or even a scratch. Apart from the dirt that caked his arms, he was uninjured. Saturday, Sunday, and Monday morning: still, no marks appeared. Ancient water had carved through the tunnels with such seductive caresses as to rendered the walls smooth and cold, like ceramic plates. Billy knew what may have caused such abrasions. He has seen fellow children bearing those marks. The weight of Friday night pressed mightily on his young brain because of Dieter's scars. The exploits of the magic man of Dieter's comic book distracted him from harsh truths.

In the minutes before the school bell rang, Billy stood still in the schoolyard with his grade five classmates. The overcast sky hid the blinding spring sun lurking behind. On most school mornings, backpacks lay discarded along the side of the building as a multitude of games continued outside. Today was different. Dieter's absence dominated schoolyard gossip. Small groups of children huddled together, speaking in whispers, eyes wide and mouths opened. Words wriggled into Billy's ears like *police*, *missing*, and *weird*. Billy's heart sunk. Unnerved by the scattered words, he twisted his face forward into a group of children. "Who's missing?" he asked before stepping back.

"The weird kid. Dieter. He left his house on Friday and never came back."

"Oh. Did the police… find him?"

"Naw. No one has seen him. No one. Strange fucking kid," chimed in another one. "Police searched the park on the weekend."

"It's possible he did time travel after all and hasn't come back yet," Billy offered in honor of his role as Dieter's witness.

"Are you fucking crazy, too?" screamed the older child, banishing Billy from the group with a deafening blast of sound.

Billy walked away as the bell rang, staring at his feet with each step. He had not noticed the police cars at all. He wondered if he fooled himself and just chose not to accept they were there.

Days passed, and with each passing one, the horror of the circumstances crept closer until the police arrived at Lindbergh Elementary School.

Class by class, they herded students toward the school gymnasium. Two policemen waited for the last student to enter before asking whether anyone had seen Dieter Brooks on the previous Friday evening. A photograph passed from child to child until it reached Billy. By then, the photo had become wrinkled and stained with the grease of today's pizza lunch. His first instinct was to hand off the photo to the girl next to him, but then he yanked it back from her outstretched hands. When he brought the photo close to his eyes, Billy recoiled, biting his lip. The impatient girl snatched the photo out of his hand, and the cold, impersonal journey of Dieter's picture continued. Once it completed its rounds, the officers thanked the children for their time and urged them to jog their memories. Billy returned to class wondering—not about where Dieter was, but about how he got the shiner in the photo.

Late in the day, as most students began arranging their desks and tucking notepads and pencils into their backpacks, Billy nodded off in the back row of his homeroom. It may have been a five-minute nap, but it was more frightening than any nap he imagined. He found himself in the dimness, figuring he was wide awake. He tried to open his eyes but failed, trapped in some nightmare. There were no scary images of vampires, headless horsemen, or vultures with elongated necks. Instead, Billy's dreamworld was devoid of color or sound, and worse,

Billy was alone in the middle of this place. *What am I doing in the cave?* Billy thought. He repeated "Hello" and "Help," yet nothing existed around him. To his relief, a classmate tugged at his shirt just as the school bell rang.

"Sleepyhead," Chris teased. "Wake up. Class is over."

"Oh, right." Billy slipped his books into his bag before scurrying past Chris. Within seconds he reached a sprinter's pace and raced toward the administration offices down the hall. He sighed when he saw the two policemen just outside the door of the principal's office.

"Excuse me," Billy said in a breathless whisper.

The officers turned to him and smiled. "Yes, young man. Everything okay?"

"Go to the cave. That's where Dieter is or was. The cave."

One officer moved to put the coffee cup he carried down on a desk while the other pulled Billy by his sleeve into an unoccupied office nearby. The coffee-drinking officer entered behind Billy, closing the door with force.

"What cave?"

"Near the edge of town there are caves. Dieter went there on Friday."

"The caves? You mean in the woods?"

"Yes, sir."

"Young man, those are off-limits."

"I understand, sir, but he and I still were there."

The officers wore grim expressions, notepads being pulled out of their back pockets as they scribbled furiously. "You were with him? Tell us what happened."

Billy remembered his promise to Dieter and told the officers the whole story of him having found a black hole in the cave and using it to time travel. The officers shook their heads dismissively as they listened and documented the tale. Impatient, an officer interrupted Billy's monologue. "Why didn't you tell anyone? It's been days!"

"Because he told me he'd return. He always came back."

"You were with him the other times?"

"No. Only this time. I mean, I waited for him for a while. A good while. But I figured he would come back… in the future."

By now, one officer had pulled out a walkie-talkie and stormed out of the office, leaving the other behind with Billy. "Look, young man. This is serious. You should have said something earlier. Your friend didn't travel through time or find a black hole. Those caves are no place for adults, let alone kids." The officer realized his tone had become severe and released his grip on Billy's shoulders.

"He found one," Billy insisted. "I am sure he did." His voice lost some of its conviction as he saw the look in the officer's eyes. No one believed him just as no one had believed Dieter.

In later years, Billy would not recall much of what happened in the days and nights following his meeting with the police. There were conversations with the school guidance counselors, more policemen, and his parents. No one asked him about Dieter's discovery. Not one person. With each discussion, Billy erased more and more of the details of that fateful Friday from his story, and with each interrogation, Billy grew more frustrated. He soon doubted anyone even cared if he knew Dieter, except for his parents.

Weeks later, on the second to last day of school and with

Dieter still missing, Billy was introduced to Dr. Simon Murphy, a psychiatrist. He would have regular sessions with him for the next few weeks. While classmates were enjoying the summer, Billy's eleven years of existence were placed under a microscope. By fall, Dr. Murphy found no more reason to treat Billy but advised his parents to be wary of any more instances of "delusional" behavior. Comforted that they had placed a bookend on the ordeal, Jake and Margaret decided not to speak further of it.

One morning, Billy stared at his breakfast of scrambled eggs and cereal, tilting his head to one side. Margaret reached over to Jake and nudged his arm while motioning with her eyes in Billy's direction. Billy maneuvered his fork to scoop off the last yellow traces of an egg before excusing himself to leave the table.

"Everything okay, Billy?" Jake asked.

"No one seemed to be interested in finding him. They didn't want to accept what I told them."

Margaret leaned over and stroked Billy's arm. "Are you referring to Dieter?"

"Yeah. I told them all about the marks on his arm. The black eye, too."

"I'm struggling to follow," Margaret declared.

"Dieter had marks on his arms—cuts and bruises. In the school photo, the one they passed around when he disappeared, around one eye, was this purplish color. It was faded, but I could tell."

"There was nothing for you to do. You told them everything." Margaret stated.

"They wrote it all down, but they didn't care."

Margaret pursed her lips. "Why is this bothering you now? I mean, I'm sure they care. What makes you assume they didn't?" Margaret looked at Jake, who appeared perplexed.

"When he crawled into the tunnel, I knew he wasn't coming back."

"Because of the marks and eye?"

"Yes."

"So, you understand that there was no black hole, right?"

Billy smiled at them, responding with his own question. "Do you have an idea what a black hole is?" Jake and Margaret shrugged, unsure of how to answer. He continued and answered for them. "It's a place where light can't escape."

"Oh," said Jake, his eyes growing wide. "You've been reading the Hawking book?"

"No. I got it from the comic book Dieter gave me that night."

Jake blinked. "You got that from a comic book?"

"Light can't escape from a black hole, right?"

"Yes. You're right in simple terms."

"What if you become part of the black hole? Don't you become light itself and escape from the other side? I mean, the end we can't see."

Jake shifted in his chair. "You have quite an imagination. No one is certain what would happen within the hole. It's all theoretical."

"Then Dieter found a black hole, for real. He never lied." Billy pushed his chair back to emphasize his point and end the discussion. "Dieter left to find the light, his light, and became part of the hole. We just can't see the light—and won't unless we become part of it, too."

Margaret now entered the riddle. "And this comic book talked about black holes?"

"Yes, except I didn't notice right away that the last page was missing. It had no end, which bugged me until I realized there was no back page."

"Oh. I see." Jake frowned, confused. "Are you sure?"

"I read it, like, a zillion times. I'm sure. Sorry, I guess it sounds dumb to bring it up."

"No." Margaret smiled. "Discussing your concerns is never dumb. You haven't talked about Dieter for a while. Talking is a great tool for dealing with it."

"I don't understand why, but I just wonder about him now and then."

"So, you were wondering why there was a page missing and why he gave you something so incomplete, right?" Jake added.

"I guess so—until I figured I could come up with whatever ending I wanted. That's why he gave it to me without an ending." Billy adjusted his jeans and exited the kitchen, not looking back.

Jake slouched in his chair and reached for Margaret's hand. "There's so much about him we don't comprehend."

Margaret tugged at Jake's hand, drawing him closer. "We've underestimated him, Jake."

"In a good way?"

"Yes. Does Billy understand—I mean *actually* understand—about Dieter?"

"Conceivably, he understands more than we will ever imagine. I'm glad he's, at last, talking about it." Jake nodded at his wife, trying to convince himself, let alone her.

"Well, he was the last person to see the kid before he vanished, according to the police. That must weigh on him." Margaret tightened her lips, remembering their final meeting with the detectives. After searching in and around the cave opening for days, they called the search off. Some searchers had gone into the cave only to be overwhelmed with its unchartered vastness. Like a jungle river, tunnels snaked off in many directions. Openings grew narrower, some leading into crevices, some leading towards large vertical drops, opening into an abyss. The musty and dank cave air offered no suggestion of life. The dangers associated with a search spread a virulent fear snuffing hope.

Jake looked at his wife. "I never understood why they stopped looking. I mean, well… until… I refuse to say it."

Margaret nodded, perceptive of what Jake wanted to say. *Until they'd found a body.*

"Yeah. I can't imagine Dieter's parents. They have no closure."

"And neither does our boy. It's something he always must live with. He was *the* last one."

After Billy finished grade school, Jake and Margaret decided a change would do wonders for him, so they moved farther into the forests and mountains of Vermont, where Billy attended a small community high school. Amongst his prized possessions was a particular incomplete comic book. In his quietest moments, Billy would imagine how the story ended and wondered if it ended the way Dieter may have hoped.

Over time, the past became buried under layer upon layer of new memories. Billy, now sixteen, inquisitive and bright, would go to his first summer camp. He did not expect the light to reach out to him from the black hole of his mind.

CHAPTER 4

The Boys in the Woods

(Summer 2003)

With each passing year, it became more apparent to Jake and Margaret Daintree that the introverted Billy needed more time with teens his own age. Not only had Billy been abandoned as an infant, but a childhood friend also disappeared while in grade school. As a gift for his sixteenth birthday, Billy's parents found an affordable, government-funded camp in the deep woods of New Hampshire. Most boys at the camp were from impoverished or broken homes.

The first two days were tedious. The rain had fallen most of the afternoons, which suited Billy since he preferred to immerse himself in the comic books stuffed in his duffel bag, though the purpose of the camp was to socialize. From the moment they assigned Billy his cabin, and he met his cabin mates, survival replaced socializing. Richard and Luc shared the bunk on the opposite end of the room. They were older and on the precipice of adulthood. Both had visible muscles, too much arrogance, and demonstrated great contempt for anyone less athletic. Billy was a good four to five inches shorter and forty pounds lighter than them. While not unathletic, he was different from these two boys. Their conversations were limited and came mostly in the form of grunts, and one-syllable replies. Billy took pleasure in the fact that the two older boys ignored him. He was not a threat to their dominance at camp. The fourth boy in their cabin was much different. He introduced himself as John.

John's height was comparable to Billy's. Whereas Billy's hair was straight brown with bangs that grew to his eyebrows, John's was thick and sandy colored with slight curls near the ears. His cropped hair framed his elongated face well. With a pointed nose, beady eyes, and skin with a hint of a tan, Billy looked muscular compared to John, who seemed malnourished. Yet John's appetite was more enormous than Billy, and John exuded an abundance of energy—nervous energy. Billy sheepishly took the bottom bunk on the first night, announcing his concern for falling from the top level. John grinned, said nothing, and threw his pillow to the top perch. Camp conversation was initially rare as camp activities physically exhausted the boys. Sleep overcame the campers without a fight with one exception. John seemed to awaken the moment the moon peaked.

That first night, Billy heard John dismount from the top bunk. With the moonlight blinding his eyes, he was not sure what he witnessed until he slithered out of his blanket and examined the higher bunk. Empty! John had abandoned the bunk and disappeared into the campground. Billy assumed that John had trekked to the camp latrine about forty feet from the shack. Fatigue overcame him, and he returned to his slumber. Just before dawn, with the first light of day entering, John jolted

Billy's bunk climbing back into place. When the older counselors woke up their cabin at 7:00 a.m., Billy rolled out of bed to find John, slight shadows beneath his eyes, yawning. John grinned at Billy in a manner that convinced Billy an interrogation would not be welcome. The day's activities, together with the wet conditions, painted over the events of the night, coating Billy's memory. Then, with the moon beginning its descent the following night, history repeated itself, and Billy became enthralled with John's behavior.

On the third night of summer camp, the great mystery captivated Billy to the point of obsession, spurring him into action. Without a watch or any electronics, Billy guessed it was before midnight as he lay awake, waiting for John to move. The musty smell of the sleeping quarters hovered around them. So dense was the aroma, gravity pulled it down. Each breath grew more labored. Anxiety hot-wired his heart into an erratic pace. He stared at the underside of the bunk above him, determined to honor the vow he'd made to engage himself in this new mystery. Wearing his light blue hoodie and clutching a tiny pocket light under the covers of his bed, Billy listened for any sign of life from above. John would not be alone in his adventures tonight.

The creak of the upper bunk crackled through Billy's patient ears. Within seconds, a figured descended the ladder. Billy froze and deadened each nerve in his body to avoid being found out. It took forever for John to make his way across the cabin, slip-on sneakers, and open the front door. Billy opened his eyes thanks to the playful jiggle of the door handle. A flash of moonlight briefly blinded him before the door closed again. Billy wondered if he could escape the cabin as discretely as

John. The massive, vulgar breaths of Richard and Luc grew louder. The consequences of getting caught overwhelmed him. Procrastination ate away time. John could be out of sight in seconds unless he took action. Curiosity throttled the fear of detection in a one-sided fight.

Billy shrewdly scooped up his sneakers. Putting them on the outside would be less noisy. He opened and then eased the door closed behind him. He bent to ties his laces with his head swiveling around, scoping out his environment. His surroundings were bathed in shades upon shades of black. He smelled the sugary aroma of pine trees after two days of intermittent rain. His eyes found the welcoming beacon of the moon, casting a spell upon a worshipping forest. His pocket light cut through the darkness. He searched, but no signs of John were detectable. Billy was dejected. He had been too slow and careful, and John had disappeared. His fingers squeezed the pocket light when a faint rustle of branches broke the silence. His body swung around towards the sound. Off in the distance, he got a glimpse of light shimmering in the trees about one hundred feet to his right. No doubt it was John making his way into the woods. Where was he going? With John's light serving as a guide, Billy gave chase, maintaining a safe distance. When he reached the edge of the campgrounds, just beyond the last embers of a dying campfire, Billy realized there was no turning back.

The light flickering ahead of him, combined with the echoes of footsteps, guided Billy through the woods. John's pace was frenetic, yet he seemed to follow a path—at least for the first few minutes. Suddenly, John veered off to the right, and the sound of crunching leaves and crackling branches grew exponentially. John had gone way off the path. Billy's heart raced. However, the fear of becoming lost was never a concern. Obsessed he may lose John, motivated him more.

As he zigged and zagged through the woods, branches struck Billy's face with higher frequency. A drop of blood beaded just above his eyebrow and trickled down along the plane of his nose. As Billy stopped to sweep his palm along his forehead, he noticed the light ahead no longer moved forward. John had stopped. Billy pointed his light to the ground to avoid being seen. Here, deep in the woods and no longer on the hunt, Billy realized the seriousness of his plight. Without John, trekking back would be futile and hazardous until dawn's light. Billy crouched down as he inched his way toward John. He urgently needed to keep him in sight, for his own safety. After a lengthy trek, he arrived at a spot overlooking a clearing in the forest. Not being able to see John clearly, he fixed his eyes on John's light, which like him, no longer moved.

Minutes passed, while an eerie calm and stillness swept over the forest. The only sound was the rustling of branches stroked by a sensual wind. Billy became hypnotized, gazing, and yet not seeing. Dawn remained far off, so what Billy perceived to be the humming of waking birds puzzled him. Billy traced the sound to one sole source by focusing on his sense of hearing. It was coming from John. He was humming! The sound grew brasher with his ears now properly tuned the source. No words were decipherable. It was pure sound. And mellifluous, too!

Insanity. Here, in the heart of the woods, hundreds of yards from camp, surrounded by thick brush and foliage, fear was not Billy's prime emotion. Total confusion was more like it. He'd been warned about teens at camp disappearing at night to get stoned, laid, or drunk. Not this. He strained to identify the sound invading his eardrums. While almost chant-like, it was not a tune he recognized. John remained obscured by the cloak provided by night. Billy crawled along the ground closer and closer until he reached the edge of the clearing. His eyes, fully adjusted to the lack of light like a cat, homed in on John. From between the foliage, he discovered a solitary figure seated with legs crossed. The hood of a windbreaker covered much of John's face. Two arms stretched out in front of the seated figure. John's hands appeared to open like a blooming tulip, palms facing the night sky. The voice hummed lower and lower in a rhythmic beat. The cry of a distant animal startled Billy and awakened him from his dreamy state. *Time to retreat.* Reaching for his light, he prepared to turn it back on and follow whatever path he discovered. About to turn, he did not notice the humming had stopped, and a voice wrapped itself around his head, holding him back.

"You never considered I was aware of your presence, did you?" the voice said with a chuckle.

"Um… shit. No. I… I…" Billy stammered, having been discovered.

"Fuck. I knew you were behind me the whole time. Next time don't flash that light all over." The voice seemed to mock him. "I mean, shit, you're lucky a bear didn't get you."

Billy turned to face the voice. "I thought you needed help or something."

"You didn't follow me for that!. Perhaps you were hoping I would smoke up and wanted to get some weed from me."

"Yeah, that's it. Sure. It's always a good idea to wander around a forest while stoned." Billy laughed.

"Hey, Billy? Why are you hiding amongst the pines? You taking a dump or something?" the voice continued in its playful manner, the figure remaining still.

"Naw. I'm like a loser stalker, hiding in the bush like this."

"I am used to being hunted. Happens to me all the time," John continued with sarcasm. "Since you came all this way, take a seat next to me."

Billy, on hands and knees, pushed aside the last branches before rising to his feet and venturing into the clearing. John remained seated like a Buddha with his back to him. Billy took a seat to John's left, unsure of what came next. "So, uh, why? Or, I mean, what?"

"What the fuck am I doing, right?" John's face remained hidden by a windbreaker.

"Yeah. I kinda was wondering."

"I'm doing the same thing you're doing."

"No, I was following you."

"Your intention was more interesting than following me."

"Sorry, but I don't understand. That's why I'm here." Billy shifted uncomfortably in his seat. "Curious, I guess."

"I'm not pissed at you. I just supposed you were out here like me, looking, searching." John's voice shifted to the sing-song rhythm of his humming.

Uncertain how to respond, Billy looked up at the sky, the same sky John's head tilted toward. Billy glanced over to notice John's head moving after being still for so long. John had turned to look at Billy. Even in the darkness, the smile on John's face was evident. Before Billy turned, John had twisted back toward the sky.

John's voice broke the silence. "You must think I'm super strange, eh? Out here by myself."

"No, I would never. I'm here, too, don't forget. I am just curious why."

"Let me ask you this. Look up at the sky and moon. How do you feel?"

"It's so quiet. I feel calm, I suppose. You didn't answer me, though."

"Out here, I feel part of something bigger. All of this out here." John's arms fluttered like butterfly wings motioning to the sky.

"Damn deep shit. You sure you're not high?" Billy laughed now.

"I like to be alone, yet when I'm here, I feel so not alone anymore. Riddle me this, Batman."

Billy giggled. "What? Are you riddling me?"

"Oh, everything is a riddle, a puzzle. The search for the pieces is the fun part, isn't it?"

"And that's why you're here? To be alone and not be alone?"

"Yeah, now you got it. I still appreciate the company, though." John laughed, adding, "Even if I don't."

Billy's eyes closed while pondering John's words. The trek to woods was exhilarating and fatiguing. Billy leaned back, his shoulders hitting the soft, thick wild grass. When his eyes opened, the pure infinity of the night sky engulfed his sense of sight. The moonbeam created shadows that danced, using the clouds as an ever-changing backdrop. Inexplicably, he understood John. He knew he did, which is why John frightened him. Then as a soft hum emanated from John, Billy used his elbows to leverage his body.

"John, what are you singing? Are you meditating?"

"Sort of. Take a nap if you like. I'll wake you when I'm ready to leave, and we can head back together."

"No. I was just relaxing. But, like, why are you humming?"

"I'm singing to the universe. It's my way of communicating with it."

"Oh, that's all," Billy remarked with deadpan sarcasm. "And how does it answer back? Does it sing? Does it strum a few power chords from a Tool song?"

"A Tool song? You're kidding me?"

"Yeah, I always thought if the universe were a rock band, they would play Tool." Billy paused for effect. "I mean, something heavy to mess with people's minds."

"Heavy-duty. That is fricken heavy." John laughed uncontrollably. "Not weird, though." His finger twitched. "Heavy. Never weird."

"Well, it's my universe, so it can play whatever music it wants."

"Clever. Now I get why you're here. My gut tells me I took *your* spot."

A brief silence followed the unabashed laughter. Awkward silence it was not. Each teenager enjoyed the empty quiet of the night and the protective blanket of the sky above. Billy returned to his reclined position. John soon continued his melodic but indecipherable chant.

They undoubtedly would suspect he was mad, Billy thought.

They being anyone observing these two boys in the woods. He imagined that, beneath the soggy grass, below the roots, and far below the mud, whatever lay buried below would surely consider him mad. No doubt, these were woods where bodies rotted after they ceased to be of any use. Or a sacred burial ground existed here. Yes, way out here, in this clearing, centuries upon centuries of past sins lay swallowed beneath nature's tapestry. And whatever lay buried beneath would hear the chants of the crazy teen at this hour and wonder if he were any more insane than the other boy who followed. Billy smiled to himself, opening his eyes to the infinite sky.

Why had each ventured here? Billy chose not to break the serenity with further interrogation. He feared to have to answer the same question, and what would he answer? *You reminded me of a kid I once knew. I worried about you getting lost by yourself.* Billy prepped himself to say that if needed. Lost in his thought, he had not noticed the chanting ending until John spoke, just above a whisper.

"So, what did the universe sing to you tonight?"

"Huh? You're the guy singing, not me."

"I guess you couldn't hear yourself, but I did." John leaned to his side, peering down to Billy.

Billy's head swayed. "Oh, very well. Yeah. I kinda made out the tune but, not the lyrics."

"And?"

"It sounds like the tune to song 'Schism' by Tool. The lyrics were in German, which messed me up." Billy looked up at John, scoping out his reaction.

"Well, naturally, the universe would play a Tool tune and all."

John started to chuckle, plunging himself in this riddle. "So, the universe would sing to you in a language you don't understand?"

"Then, the translation would be mine to make up, depending on how I feel." Billy's voice became lower in pitch with each word. "I'm not sure I want to decipher the song."

John raised his hands to his face covering his eyes before sliding them down his cheeks. He finally responded. "Young grasshopper, you reach for the pebble too fast." He leaned forward and tapped Billy on the sneaker before smiling back at him. "Now, you must return tomorrow, so you understand why I'm here."

"Grasshopper? Whatever. Sure, I'll come back with you tomorrow."

"Great. Now I hope we can find our way back."

"You're not serious. The way you moved through the bush. Now you tell me you're lost!"

"How are you certain I wasn't following you?"

"Oh, brother. This mountain air is messing with your brain." Billy laughed with hesitation, unsure if John was kidding or not.

The two teenagers rose to their feet, checked their flashlights, and trekked through the forest. Billy's breathing became steadier when he spotted the cabins in the distance. Stealthily, both boys slithered into their bunks, ever mindful of their two older roommates and potential calamity.

Billy, exhausted, threw himself into his bunk. Just about to doze off and enjoy a short but needed sleep, John's face emerged upside down from the top bed. "No prank, Billy. Thanks for joining me." His hand soon extended downward and outstretched. Billy reached out and shook it without saying a word before turning to his side to sleep.

The dark circles under their eyes the next day were the only clue suggesting their journey. The boys plodded their way through a day of camp activities. Their interaction was minimal, although both yawned in unison throughout the day. Billy grew pensive. The journey out into the forest seemed irrational once logic took hold, spurred forth by the clarity of the sun. He had promised John. Hell, he shook his hand, too. John was counting on him. Billy did not understand what drew him to the woods, why his need to track John was less about curiosity and more like real concern for him. Yes, he worried about John. Someone he had just met. Yet John was more than an unassuming, nondescript teenager.

The boys awaited night with the anticipation reserved for late-starting rock legends. Once it returned, the two partners in crime ventured to the bowels of the forest, armed with flashlights and a reverence for the unknown. With each step they took together, their destinies entangled into more intricate knots. The bond forming between them would mark their present and their future, much like a good tattoo, a reminder of something far more profound than mere ink.

CHAPTER 5

An Offering

The teenage tug of war between the need for sleep and adventure waged in Billy's world. The bright moonlight had long ago drifted through the cracks in the tattered cabin blinds and settled upon his bunk. He strained to listen for any sound from above, even a hint of noise would suffice. He wondered if John had succumbed to fatigue and if the previous night would be a humorous tale for Daintree generations of the future to ponder. The snoring from one of the cabin mates and the exaggerated heavy breaths of the other suggested the time was right to escape, yet John's bunk offered no trace of life. *Shit,* Billy thought in horror. John might have eluded him while he'd drifted off to sleep. It was possible. A sleepless night, followed by a day of physical activities and the wandering mind of a serial daydreamer, was a perfect sleep-inducing concoction.

Carefully, Billy slid his body at a sharp angle out of his bunk, balancing himself with his fingers clenched to the wood frame of the bunk above. The whites of John's eyes looked down upon him, like twin moons over an open field. A smile was invisible without the light, but Billy assumed one existed. Billy strained to listen to the trickling sound from John's lips. "You coming, sleepyhead? I thought you would never wake up."

"Christ. How long were you waiting?" Billy asked.

"Oh, since lights out. I'm not much of a sleeper."

"I guess not." Before Billy shifted back in his bunk, John had made his way down and shuffled his way along the dusty wood floor to the doorway. "Wait," Billy pleaded vainly, as the door creaked open John disappeared in the form of a silhouette framed by the moonlight. The snoring of his older cabin mates muffled his movements. He struggled to tug on his sneakers while maneuvering the door handled. Outside he deciphered John standing still at the fringes of the campground area, the dense forest providing a perfect camouflage.

"You sure you're good with this?" John whispered as Billy approached him. "I don't want you to be punished."

"I've been in worse trouble," Billy remarked. "Besides, you swore to tell me why you're out here."

"Oh, I guess I did," John said. "Try to keep up." With that, John took off at a quick pace, brushing back branches, and zigzagging before reaching a clearing highlighted by a hill that overlooked the forest. He stopped as Billy, head down, stumbled into him. "We're here."

"Great," Billy said hesitantly. "Um, where is here?"

"This spot. You can see the whole universe from here, millions of stars all in front of you. And it's quiet, too."

"Quiet? I suppose it was last night, too, until you started chanting." Billy laughed.

John ignored him and crept toward a flat area near the peak of the hill and sat down, staring at the sky. Billy remained still, observing him. Then John's body tilted from left to right, ending with him reclining back on his elbows, oblivious to Billy's presence. Confused, Billy looked back upon the forest, trying to find the path that took him here. He shone a light around hastily, only to find a dense array of bushes and trees shimmering back at him. The race through the woods made returning to camp on his own futile and dangerous. Embarrassed by his dependence on John, he hiked up the hill but sat cross-legged a few feet away in silence.

John stopped humming. "You will not sing or even hum?"

"Oh, you remembered I'm here." Billy quipped. "Don't mind me. Keep doing your thing."

"Sorry, I don't understand."

"I followed you here tonight because you promised."

"Well, you followed me yesterday. You must have had your own reason."

"I wondered what you were doing out here in the forest at this ungodly hour."

"But I told you, didn't I?"

"You mean communicating with the universe? I thought you were putting me on, so I went along with it."

John sighed and sat up straight. "I wasn't putting you on. I seem to recall you put me on."

Billy flashed his light, briefly blinding John before settling on a spot near his shoulder, illuminating his face. "Being out here is weird, right?" In the haunting light, Billy witnessed John's lips quiver and his body twitch. A heavy breath escaped him, followed by a gasp, as though John struggled for air. "John, is everything all right? Like, did you swallow a bug?"

John leaned forward and wrapped his arms around his knees as if a cool breeze seemed to find him and him alone. Without looking at Billy, he spoke. "Weird? I'm weird in your eyes, aren't I?"

The hurt in John's voice startled Billy. He replayed his last words before responding. "I just thought it must look weird if someone saw us here, singing in the wilderness."

John coughed and nodded his head, curling up into an even tighter ball. "I'm sorry you followed me. Perhaps you were expecting me to pass out some weed or even a mickey of vodka and drink until we puked." His voice became raspier, overcome by a spasm of coughing.

"You okay?" Billy crouched down.

John caught his breath and wiped his runny nose against his sleeve. "Don't worry about me. Go on back to camp. I've been called weird before. I'm used to it."

Billy paused and looked back into the woods before pushing off his heels only to topple backward on his posterior. Unable to find John's eyes through the dark, he shined his pocket light at the ground between them. "We've all been told we're weird at some point, John. I understand how it hurts as much as anyone. But, I don't consider it weird—you out here in the middle of the night, singing or rather humming, to the stars. Last night you were howling at the moon as opposed to humming. Heck, I kind of was hoping you would turn into a werewolf. Then I hoped against it, 'cause you'd probably bite or devour me. That'd be just my luck, getting killed on my first camping trip."

Billy heard a muffled laugh from John. "Be honest, you were hopelessly lost, so you stayed close by for dear life."

"That's just a detail. Now you *have* to tell me." Billy held his breath as he thought of his next words. "Please explain to what you are searching for because I care about the reason. I do."

"I hope to find it again. Out here in the wilderness, without people, just nature, I pray it would happen."

Billy leaned forward, pressing his knees into the wild grass. "Happen?"

"When I was a kid, I awoke one morning with a feeling that I understood everything." John paused, struggling to articulate emotions that once stirred in a child's heart. "My home wasn't a happy place. Kids I knew at school lived in far worse homes. I used to read nonstop to escape from the world around me. Just ten minutes here or there was all I needed."

"Comic books, too?"

"Yeah, those were the best. I visualized myself as a new character in them. I did all of that to escape. Then one morning, I understood. It came from a dream I had where it was as though my mind traveled everywhere. It was like I became part of everything around me, and no more was I just seeing a tree, I *became* the tree or the bird on a branch, all at once." John paused and stared down at his hands. "In that dream, everything living came from me."

Billy cleared his throat as his heart raced with excitement. "Wow, that's a fall-out-of-your-bed incredible dream."

"I realized that I can create the world I wanted once I learned to communicate my thoughts. No more pain or suffering or death. Everyone could find contentment."

Billy smirked. "Well, I guess it hasn't worked out. So I already get the punch line."

"But more than anything, it was the feeling I had from this dream, a feeling that's hard to describe—like I belonged to something much greater. No longer would I be alone because everything was me, and I was everything."

"That is an amazing epiphany. I guess there's more to this story?" Billy stared straight ahead, expecting the answer. "Nothing is that simple."

John's hands covered his face before sliding back to rest and dangle to the ground. "I went to school and told my friends and teachers about what happened. How I visited places in the universe, created by thoughts. How one day, I would teach others."

"You mean, learn again or remember how you created it."

"Yes. But with each day that passed, that feeling faded, disappearing. I grew frustrated and started having anxiety attacks, or that's what the teachers thought at first. They got worse and worse..." John's voice trailed off. "They sent me to a special place."

"A special place?" Billy's mimicked John's tone.

"They called it a 'special place.' An institution. My foster parents sent me to an institution. I was there for three weeks until this older doctor came to evaluate me. He encouraged me to continue believing, and that one day, clarity would return. I needed to be patient." John started to laugh. "Not a patient, but patient. He released me from further study."

"Patient. That's an adult word if there ever was one."

"Lucky for me, this one doctor seemed to understand. He explained to me that time is an illusion, and there is only a present, densely packed with the past and future. So that dream was like the sun piercing through the blinds before disappearing behind a cloud, giving me the illusion that the sun didn't exist. Eventually, the illusion will pass, and the sun will reappear."

"I'm guessing the sun hasn't come out again since."

John nodded his head. "I don't talk about it at all. The kids didn't understand, so they would just call me weird." He paused. "I'd hate to imagine what you must think right now."

"You were lucky, John." John fidgeted, trying to move closer to Billy. "The universe communicated with you in its own way. That's damn cool. I'm lucky if anyone talks to me at all. You had the whole shebang introducing itself to you." Billy reached through the night and patted John on the shoulder. "You believe the universe will respond to your hum or a song?"

"For some reason that I can't explain, it does."

"It's singing right back to you now, only in a frequency you can't tune into."

"Or I'm not listening properly." John laughed.

"Besides, John, being weird is a badge of honor."

"Now you've got me curious."

"When I was much younger, this older kid told me that *weird* means being supernatural, like a comic book hero who has a special power."

"Wow, you hung with a wise crowd when you were a pip-squeak. You were fortunate."

"I guess I have been lucky compared to other children. This older kid had a lot of shit to deal with, heavy shit, I'm guessing." Billy mumbled a few inaudible words while wondering whether he should tell the story of Dieter. John's hand reached through the darkness, grasping Billy's in a handshake.

"Tell me, Billy. Tell me everything, please. The night is

eternal—time doesn't exist in my universe."

"You sure you want to hear about the black hole in my hometown?"

"Like, how many kids have a pet, let alone a black hole nearby?" John said as he reclined on the ground to listen to Billy's tale.

Billy closed his eyes, sniffling and coughing, to control the emotions leaking through the memory he evoked. The memory blossomed in his mind, colors bled into one another to create images of people and places. The story ended abruptly as silence took over, interrupted only by crickets.

John cleared his throat. "They never found him? Like, did they even look?"

"They thought the cave was too dangerous, so I doubt they even considered what I witnessed that night. I suppose they thought I made it up for attention."

"And the marks on his arm? You deduced he was—"

"I've seen enough kids with similar marks to comprehend the stories are real. Most hide them or don't talk about them. I'm sure you've seen them, too."

"Worse, my friend. I've seen some nasty ones. Not scars, burns, or bruises on one's skin. The worst ones have the same look—like their soul escaped through their eyes, leaving the door open behind it."

"I guess we saw some shit, you and me. Yet, we've survived so far."

"Yep. Here we are at a camp for outcasts and daydreamers." John's voice grew deeper and seemed to rocket in pitch. "Holy shit!" John propped himself up onto his elbows and pointed.

"It's there. It's there." He sprang to his feet before feeling a tug on the hem of his jeans.

"What is it? What do you see?" Billy's pocket light sprang to life with a burst of white in the general direction that John faced.

"This freaky blue light came from the sky, and it settled behind the trees near that hill. A cipher!" John escaped Billy's grasp and began to run off into the woods in the opposite direction of where their campsite was.

Billy saw a faint glow emanating from the trees, but could not identify the color. Before being able to conclude, the sound of the first row of shrubs near the forest's gateway, disturbed by John's flailing hands, pierced his eardrums. The fear of getting lost, coupled with witnessing the light, shocked Billy out of his stupor and into action. Then he, too, raced his way through the dense bushes toward the luminosity originating within the bowels of the forest.

With each stride, the blue light flickered, at times growing more intense. The ground became more uneven, with a series of uphill steps followed by a downhill descent. Branches slapped his face, distracting him as he tried to steady his light on the outline of John's body ahead of him. A flareup of light, rays weaving between an opening in the trees, blinded him as the roots of an ancient tree clipped his toes and sent him off balance down a slope. As he struggled to regain his footing, his feet became entangled in a thicket of shrubs. Panicked, his shoes sunk into a cold stickiness as his body lurched forward. His forearms took the brunt of the blow, but rather than hitting damp, rough vegetation, the earth devoured his arms as the sickening sensation of mud entrapping his arms, overcame him. He closed his mouth in time, just as his face burrowed into the mud pit. Now desperate, he tried to lift his head as his lungs begged for air. He popped his head out, just enough for his nostrils to be free. However, with his arms encased in the mud, he gained insufficient leverage to lift his body up. With his legs entangled in the undergrowth, Billy's heart pumped blood faster and more intensely with each beat. His thoughts raced. His mouth opened, trying to find air, only to be filled with muck, suffocating him. He wondered what his body would look like when they found him, if they ever did. In the last instant of consciousness, he considered his life a sacrifice to the gods in exchange for John reaching the light. He hoped his death would not be in vain.

CHAPTER 6

Billy's Resurrection

There was no tunnel of light to pass through, nor did he encounter any biblical figure. Equally important, he didn't feel the eternal fire of damnation. Instead, he awoke to the cold slap of garden hose water. His eyelids burst open, as arms hoisted him from behind, propping him up. He struggled to identify the figure kneeling inches away and holding a hose. Nausea overcame him, and his body convulsed as the earth he had ingested spewed from his throat onto the ground before him. The tube moved closer to him, and soon the steel end of it pressed against his lips as water flooded his mouth. By pushing the hose back with his hands, he lurched forward, emptying the sooty contents of his stomach.

"Drink, Billy, force yourself," said the voice. "You will be fine. Keep drinking. We must flush that shit out of you." The voice was young but familiar. Billy rubbed the excess water from his eyes, and an image came into view. The curly blond hair and large blue eyes were unmistakably those of his cabin mate, Luc.

After spitting out a pebble, Billy coughed. "Luc, where am I?"

Luc reached for Billy's shoulders to steady him as another

person pressed on his back. "Quiet, Billy, unless you want to be in big trouble. You will live. He found you in time."

"Yes," said the voice Billy recognized as his other cabin mate, Richard. "Câlisse, you are fucking fluky. 4:00 a.m., and you decide to take a damn mud bath."

Billy looked around and found himself in the camp area, behind the back wall of one cabin, hidden from view.

"Look, if you feel you are dying, we'll get help, but you'll get into a lot of trouble," Luc said.

"You tell me if I'll survive. The last thing I recall, I was dead," Billy said.

"You're lucky. You fell into this sinkhole in the woods. A little longer—" Luc stopped.

"A few minutes and you were maggot grub," continued Richard in a heavy French-Canadian accent, moving to face him.

"Thanks for saving me, but how did you find me? You followed us?" Billy barely finished his sentence before he remembered his friend. "Where is John—has he returned?"

Luc and Richard were silent. Both lifted Billy up and led him back to the far boundary of the camp at the entrance to the forest. Luc aimed his flashlight at the ground and scanned the area. "Look, Billy. How many footprints do you see?"

Billy struggled to adjust his eyes. He saw enough to just notice the indentations in the hard, compact earth near the outskirts of the campground. "I see one set coming into camp." Billy looked closer. "John is missing. He is alone in the wilderness!"

Richard's face moved close to Billy's ear. "Those are John's footsteps." Richard hesitated, waiting for the message to sink in. "Your friend was the one who found you."

"And carried you back into camp," continued Luc.

"He carried me?!" Billy exclaimed.

"Yes, from wherever he found you. He woke us up and begged us to help him." Richard said. "My lifeguard training never included mud pools, though."

Billy's head swayed as though following a hypnotist's watch. "Where is he now?"

Luc laughed. "Once he saw we had it under control, he crashed, clothes on and all. You must have weighed quite a bit with all the mud everywhere."

Richard smiled. "We promised not to tell anyone. He never needed to ask. We wouldn't rat out one of us."

"Thank," Billy said, extending his hand to both of them. "I would have understood if you did."

"Adults are always looking for an excuse to give us shit. Can't tell you how many times Richard and I explored these woods at night." Luc said.

"Yeah, but at least we had beers with us," Richard said. "John wouldn't say—what were you guys doing out there? All this mud. We never noticed any area that muddy!"

"Oh, star gazing." A more rationale answer eluded Billy. "We saw this amazing light, a blue one in the sky that seemed to settle behind some trees in the woods."

Richard coughed. "Be careful with that star gazing shit. One minute you're looking at the sky and dreaming. Next thing, you want to visit the stars and realize you can't." Richard made a motion with his fingers around his ears. "It makes you crazy when you figure out you can't. Stick with a good Canadian beer next time you explore the woods at night."

"Hmm, don't mind Richard. He gets cranky at this hour," mumbled Luc. "We saw nothing out there. Might be a falling star, except you said it was blue. Probably just fireflies playing games with you."

"Whatever it was, I suppose John never reached it," Billy said.

"Good thing he didn't and found you instead," Luc said as the forest soon ignited in a faint aura of orange.

"Christ, the sun is coming up, and breakfast is in an hour. Since you're alive, we can go back to sleep."

"Yeah, I'm alive. Well, I assume so because I wasn't expecting you guys in my afterlife."

The three young men ambled to their cabin to salvage whatever sleep time would allow after changing out of their sludge soaked clothes. Soon the heavy breaths of Richard and Luc serenaded Billy as they slept. Billy lay in bed, unable to slow down the thoughts racing through his mind. Eventually, insomnia claimed victory, so he slid himself out of his bunk and looked up at John asleep on his back. The musty odor of the woods rose from him as he lay sleeping in the clothes he wore that night. Billy awaited the dawn after sliding back into his bunk.

The alarm ringing startled Billy as he lay wide awake. To his side, he had not noticed John staring at him, already conscious. "How are you feeling, Billy?" John reached over and poked Billy on the arm.

"I'll live thanks to you."

"Those buggers told you. I asked them not," John said. "You would have searched for me."

"I can't say that with certainty. I could never find you since you ran so fast ahead of me." Billy laughed. "How *did* you find me?"

"I lost the light, Billy. When I looked back, if you witnessed where it went, you disappeared, too. I tried to follow my path back, and then, by fluke, I saw a light coming from the ground—your pocket light. I ran toward it and almost tripped over you. Your body was half-buried."

"You carried me all the way back. I don't understand how you did it."

"Me neither." John laughed.

"I owe you, John. And I'm sorry the light disappeared before you reached it."

"I suppose it was a different light I need to follow, my friend." John rose and walked away from the bunk.

Two more days and nights of camp followed. Billy, exhausted from the ordeal, slept through both nights. John promised Richard and Luc he would not venture out anymore.

On the last day of camp, the boys boarded the bus to return to their respective hometowns. As the bus arrived at Billy's drop off point, he reached for his duffel bag, placed it over his shoulder and grinned at John. "One day, it'll come back to you again. I promise it will—whether sound or light, it will find you."

John's eyes squinted as the late afternoon sun obstructed his vision. "If you say it will, it will." Billy turned to leave as John reach across the seat and tugged on his T-shirt. "I believe your friend found the light, too. Outside the cave, it waited for him."

Billy bit his lip. "I'm sure he did. No one disappears in a black hole. I'm sure it's true because I can hear the music and distinctly his voice."

John nodded. "I guess you learned something. You are a wise man, Billy."

"I don't need to be a wise man, John, just your friend. You're the superhero. You saved my life."

John smiled as Billy walked off. His fears curled themselves into a ball, and he tucked them away for good, he hoped. John stared out the bus window at the endless blue sky before closing his eyes, hearing nothing but the din of a bus filled with teenagers. Under his breath, he hummed himself to sleep.

The two boys returned to their towns, their schools, and their separate lives. Two years later, on the campus of a small college in rural Vermont, their paths would cross again—or as Billy liked to think, each would bring their note into the next song about to play. Only the song would not be their own by the time their college years ended—its sound distorted by an unseen force—and the fragile hope of their youth would crash, scattering fragments everywhere, like the big bang.

Many years later, in a small Brooklyn apartment, the sounds of the universe would revisit Billy in the night, reminding him of a distant song searching for their audience. He would try to remember the sound of John's humming through the distorted screams growing in volume.

CHAPTER 7

The Strange File of Billy Daintree

(April 2008)

Carrie Woodson was no stranger to being called into anyone's office for a stern lecture. It began as a young student and continued until she obtained her doctorate degree. Many through the years considered her a brilliant troublemaker. Others considered her a "maverick" in her field. For Carrie, there were no rules. No rules *ever* when trying to help a patient. Dr. Charles Edelman surveyed the dossier on his desk. He replayed the phone call he'd received warning him it was coming before rifling through the pages in between the folder. Well into his sixties and having survived years of political battles within the university system, he recognized the need to keep his hands clean. He smelled the toxicity of the file. This would be a perfect test for Dr. Woodson.

Dr. Edelman had just shifted his weight in his chair when Carrie entered his office. The slightly open door was a clear invitation to bypass the customary knock. After exchanging pleasantries, Dr. Edelman slid the dossier across the table to

Carrie with a smile.

"You have a patient for me?" Carrie asked, trying to contain her excitement. It was not unusual to get referrals, but it was uncommon to get them from Dr. Edelman. Intuitively, she knew if it came from the dean, it had to be a compelling case.

"Yes, sort of, Carrie. It's not a patient of mine."

"Oh. I don't understand."

"A dustup occurred over at Hobart College. Somehow, I drew the short straw, and they came to seek my independent thoughts. They have asked me to present my findings and recommendations."

"Dustup? You mean a fight. Why does Hobart want you involved? Wouldn't it be an internal matter?"

While Hobart College was smaller and less prestigious than the University of Greater New England, current home of Dr. Edelman and Dr. Woodson's alma mater, Hobart was recognized for its avant-garde and progressive programs. Well-supported by private benefactors, Hobart built a reputation cemented by its more intimate class sizes and generous financial scholarship programs for gifted but less-privileged students.

Dr. Edelman started laughing. "Oh, dear no. I wish it were that. Nowadays, politics is far more subversive. A very old friend occupies a senior position at Hobart. Naturally, he asked me to perform an independent evaluation to take the monkey off his back. This is a case of academic rivalry, I am convinced. One student jealous of another and trying to undermine him."

"Undermine him?" Carrie knew political correctness. This was razor-sharp. "Why would they bring it up to you? These things happen all the time."

"Well said. My exact words. A simple case of punish, suspend, and even expel. That's what I thought."

"Obviously, there's more to it."

"Hobart despises academic jealousy and intrigue. From what I understand, this all culminated with an email sent by a student accusing Hobart of condoning or engaging in some very disconcerting experiments."

"Go on, Charles."

"Well. It seems the email was a hoax and sent by a rival student to make the other appear unhinged. The perpetrator came to his senses and confessed to hacking the email account."

"Since Hobart is involved, I presume they will expel this student, at a minimum." Carrie looked at Dr. Edelman's fingers as they rubbed against each other nervously.

"The file in front of you belongs to the accused student. They want you to interview him and get your professional opinion."

"You mean they wanted you to do it, right? Now, you're giving it to me."

"Discerning motivations are your passion, Carrie. Frankly, I struggle to find spare moments with all the shenanigans at this university."

"But I'm missing something. One student confessed. Shouldn't he be disciplined? Or even involve the police?" Carrie shook her in disbelief, given that the case involved privacy and identity theft.

"The victim refuses to press charges. He just wants to move on."

"Normally, the victim's opinion would not determine the

punishment. I mean, the college would want to set an example."

"Again, precisely what I thought. It seems the victim is quite a prodigy. As always, the college chooses not to rock the boat. To subject the victim to additional drama would be cruel."

"So he's important to them. Is what you're trying to say?"

"Bingo."

"And my role is to do what?"

"Evaluate this mischievous hacker and report back to us."

"What are they trying to ascertain?" Carrie tried to lock in on Dr. Edelman's eyes as he fidgeted in his chair, his head bobbing up and down.

"They require documentation a misguided joke occurred and not a campaign by an unhinged student."

"They basically want to understand the *why* part?" Carrie knew that was what everyone seeks to understand. Life revolved around 'the why.' Why did people do anything? Without motivation, anarchy would rule.

Dr. Edelman continued, "They want some clarity to make an informed decision about what they should do with this student. If he is unstable or even a sociopath, they want to commit him to a more extensive examination over a prolonged period. He, too, is quite the intelligent student from what I understand, which concerns them even more."

"He's intelligent, so they fear him enough to institutionalize him?"

"If it's necessary. It may sound radical, but we're talking about high-potential minds."

"They're scared of this student that much then?"

"Exactly, Dr. Woodson. You just confirmed to me why you

were the perfect choice for this assignment."

Carrie frowned, yet her curiosity riveted her to the cushioned chair. "My patient needs protection, too." A smirk cut through her face like a fine wire.

"Oh, Woodson. The college is our client, not your patient. A friendly reminder."

"I suppose I can't say no. This is not an option, I presume."

"Well, if your practice is so busy that you don't need the work or my referrals..." Dr. Edelman sheepishly smiled.

Carrie lowered her hands out of sight, so Dr. Edelman could not see them clenching. "I will take this on despite my reservations." The bottomless depth of her curiosity and cynicism overcame any reservations. She sensed this case had layers of thick fresh paint glossing over an image underneath. The search for *why* interested her.

"Good, Carrie." He got up to extend his hand. "The good academics at Hobart will want a report within two weeks." He overplayed his enthusiasm to usher her out. Carrie briefly rose, but then returned to her seat, flipping through the file. Dr. Edelman grudgingly settled back down.

"These students were studying what? I mean, what field of study, what department?"

"The Department of Universal Consciousness." He looked carefully at her, studying her response.

"That discipline sounds quite unconventional and interesting."

"Like Hobart itself, the program is very alternative, occupying a discrete faculty within their college. A new field of study."

"Hmm. The mind is a wonderful place to visit," Carrie stated.

"Well, to an old-school psychologist like myself, it's all funky new age stuff."

"I thank you for this." Carrie's eagerness precipitated the meeting's conclusion. She left her seat and headed for the door, leaving Dr. Edelman in pursuit.

"Um, Dr. Woodson. One last thing. The two students appear to have been friends at one point. I mean, the victim is the one who recruited the perpetrator to come to the school."

"You aren't more curious why one would turn on the other?" Carrie's eyebrows raised.

"Oh, I have lived through many academic rivalries."

"So?"

"Carrie, off the record—tread with utmost caution. Remember what I taught you when I was younger and wiser?"

"Yes. *The mind is a wonderful place to visit, but you would not want to live there*. I just never saw you in the role of Pontius Pilate." Carrie left the office without turning back. As she meandered down the hallway, she glanced at the student ID photo in the file and the name of the student: Billy Sinclair Daintree.

CHAPTER 8

Carrie's New Friend

Carrie slouched in her office chair, frustrated Dr. Edelman had cornered her. Sure, he had been her mentor and most trusted colleague, but this case tested her loyalty to him. While Carrie was a part-time lecturer at her alma mater, she also had her own practice, albeit a struggling one. While referrals were welcome, she wished to have the flexibility to decline them. The bright purple balloon with the faded Happy 50th Birthday remained stuck to her monitor screen. Over a month had passed since her party. She kept the balloon as a subtle reminder to herself of the things she wanted to accomplish still waiting and the outstretched arms of time tugging at her from behind.

Conveniently, she found a small office near the university. Here she sat with a mound of light brown folders scattered about her desk with one folder occupying her attention. The file containing the story of Billy Daintree seemed thin. She reviewed it to prepare for the first session with him. The life of a twenty-one-year-old university student condensed to a few sheets of paper in a folder. Carrie looked upon every file on her desk with the same determination—to add color, emotion, and a human touch to each case.

The mandate, as per Dr. Edelman, was a quick and dirty evaluation of Billy Daintree. They needed to ensure he was no danger to his fellow students and, informally, determine a course of action. The university would pay her for six hours of her time and needed a report within ten days.

The facts, as typed in black and white, stared at her. On April 7, an email was sent to all the faculty members at Hobart College.

To whom it may concern,

I beg you read this and please take the necessary action. This is not a trivial matter by any stretch of one's imagination. There exists within the college a program, the nature of which is beyond the bounds of human decency and morals. The research subjects are their very own students.

While I cannot name the professor leading this program and study, I have been a subject of these experiments. Please act immediately before more souls are sacrificed. It may be too late to save my mind and sanity, but someone else may be spared from this horror.

Sincerely,
John Adamson

Carrie sighed and leaned back on her chair. She had read the email many times. Nuclear warheads cause less fallout than an email like this within an academic institution. John Adamson's name on the signatory line intrigued her as Carrie had no file for a John Adamson. If one existed, she did not get it. Within twenty-four hours of the email heating the college servers, a student stepped forward to take responsibility for the chaos created—Billy Daintree.

Before noon that same day, Mr. Daintree arrived at the Dean's office at Hobart's College and declared that he had hacked the email of John Adamson, a fellow student. Regretful of his action and feeling remorse, he claimed responsibility according to the notes on the debrief in his file.

The only other documents in Billy's file were his academic transcripts and admission documents. Despite Carrie's objections to the scant details provided to her, she often preferred not having any information that would bias her impressions of the patient. Upon reading the offending email, she understood why Hobart was unwilling to go external for an investigation. The mere appearance of academic improprieties or secretive research so unethical would be scandalous and upset donors and alumni of the college. No publicity was the only acceptable outcome.

Carrie shuffled through the papers one more time, looking for something she suspected missing. The lack of any information about the victim troubled her. When she questioned Dr. Edelman about John, he represented to her that no further information was available.

The round schoolhouse type clock over her door read 4:00

p.m. Billy would arrive any second. She worried about being late for her dinner date with Marie and picked up the phone to call her when there was a light tapping on the door.

"Come on in, please," Carrie called as she placed down the receiver, swiveled out of the chair, and hurried to the door to greet Billy.

The only image of Billy had been his college identification photo in all its hazy glory. Carrie knew first impressions deceived and mastered the art of not reacting overtly to them. When she saw Billy, she stopped dead in her tracks. With a narrow, boyish face, wide brown eyes, and thick brown hair down to his eyebrows, Billy smiled meekly and extended his hand toward Carrie.

"Hi, Dr. Woodson, my name is Billy Daintree. Uh, they requested I meet with you… well." Billy stammered, unsure of how much Carrie knew.

Carrie greeted him with a smile and took his hand. "Yes. They debriefed me. Please have a seat." The young man's eyes searched the room to find an empty wooden chair in front of Carrie's desk. "No, I don't have a leather couch, if you are searching for one."

"Well, I kind of wondered," Billy said with a shrug before sitting.

Carrie stared at Billy before lumbering back to her chair. He seemed far too young and polite to be involved in anything so repugnant. Her mandate to assess the threat he posed seemed almost ridiculous. Billy sat patiently as Carrie rifled through the sparse notes she had before her, now and then raising her eyes to meet his before returning to the file. Billy wore a blue collared shirt, light blue jeans faded from the knee down, and white sneakers. He looked like an ordinary college student.

Billy grew unnerved by the silent observation, unsure of what was to come. To alleviate his nervousness, his eyes scanned his surroundings until he focused on the diplomas hanging on the wall of Carrie's office. Underneath the degrees was an oak cabinet holding numerous books. He strained to recognize any of the titles. Carrie noted his curiosity.

"By all means, take a closer look, be my guest."

"No, no. It's fine. Did you write any of those books?"

"No. The honest answer is I strategically placed them to intimidate people. Not you, mind you." Carrie laughed. "I do it to mess with the heads of any colleagues. I put the most academically obscure books there."

Billy looked at her, puzzled. Carrie continued, "This is why we're here, right? You wanted to mess with a classmate of yours. Same thing, right?"

The chair seemed to devour Billy. He pushed back on it, lifting the front legs up before rocking back and landing forward with a thud. "Yeah. I suppose so."

Carrie stared at Billy, trying to make eye contact. "Listen, Mr. Daintree. This is a serious action."

"Doctor, I do understand. I've apologized and... well, I am truly sorry."

"The email you sent is like a tidal wave in any academy institution. Sweeps everything in its path." Carrie pretended to look through her file as she asked her next question. "Who is John Adamson?"

Billy paused for an elongated period and then exhaled. "A

classmate of mine." Carrie expected a more detailed answer. After all, he went to great lengths to write a fake email from John's address.

"Just a classmate?"

"Well, he and I were friends, roommates, a while back until—" Carrie's eyes opened wide and instinctively reached for a writing pad. John and Billy were closer friends than Dr. Edelman disclosed! Billy noticed Carrie's reaction change. "Did I say something wrong?"

Carrie dropped her pen and pushed her notepad to the side. "Sorry, Billy, I wasn't aware you were roommates. That kind of explains some things, I suppose."

Billy looked at the yellow notepad on Carrie's desk while responding. "No one told you we were that close once? No one told you about Kate, either?"

Carrie went flush. She could feel the blood rushing to her cheeks. "Has someone interviewed you about this already?" she demanded, raising her voice slightly.

"Yes. Three or four men interviewed me. They refused to disclose who they worked for, but, I recognized two from Hobart. I was honest with them."

"Who were these other men?"

"They refused to disclose much other than repeating I faced serious consequences."

All this information was new to Carrie. The young man before her had already been through a more detailed interrogation than previously divulged. Why did she need to get involved? Dr. Edelman had withheld more information than she'd imagined.

"Well, I will be honest with you. They have asked me to evaluate you." Carrie decided that if Dr. Edelman withheld vital details from her, she would do things her way like she always did.

"I kind of figured," Billy said as he sat straight up in his chair.

"Evaluate you and recommend what they should do."

"Like calling the police?" Billy asked.

Carrie winced. "Not unless we need to—no, not unless *they* decide."

Billy looked past Carrie avoiding her eyes. "I only meant it as a joke."

Carried reached back into the file and reread the email before speaking. "These accusations you made in the email are not petty and don't sound like a joke."

"I meant it to freak John out. And he was freaking. I hoped Kate would see it and understand what a freak he was." Billy's tone had changed, but he continued to avoid eye contact.

"Fine, so, what is the punchline? Who is Kate?"

"Kate is the girl I liked, like, a lot."

Carrie's neck extended forward as she smirked. "Now, let me guess she is or was dating John."

"Yes, ma'am. That's what my reason was for doing it."

"Your pure Vulcan, aren't you?" Carrie grinned. "Yeah, I watched a little *Star Trek* in my day."

Billy rocked violently on his chair, his eyes now exploring Carrie's expression. "Vulcan?" he stated, almost in a whisper.

Carrie pushed her leather chair back, grinning at Billy. "You heard me. Pure Vulcan. Like no emotion and a logical bullshit answer."

Billy gasped. "I get the Vulcan part, but what's wrong with my answer?"

"No emotion, young Billy Daintree. If that were a stage production, I would have demanded a refund. Look, you can fool those administration geezers with some jealous boyfriend story. Not me."

Billy's feet began shaking as he shifted nervously in his chair. "I don't understand. That *is* why."

Carrie laughed aloud before rising from her seat and making her way to the one window in her office. She drew back the blinds, and the bright, late-afternoon sun illuminated the room before settling on Billy's face like an interrogator's light. "From this crappy office window, I can see a good portion of this university's campus and students. Students like you."

Billy squinted, trying to find a field of vision free from the light probing his eyes. Carrie then stood in front of the window, shielding Billy from the sun's rays with her back to them. "I love this university. Not the buildings. Sure, the trees are awe-inspiring as fall morphs into winter. Hell, I spent a lifetime under those trees, studying and writing. The way the sun illuminates everything out there is otherworldly." She paused and turned to meet his gaze. Like some biblical apparition, she stood before him with the unmistakable aura outlining her frame. "But that's nothing. All that is nothing. What makes it so beautiful are the ideas and thoughts of the students and professors here—the invisible ideas that create life, are life."

Billy leaned forward, entirely transfixed by Carrie's oratory and her reverence for wandering minds. Whatever perceptions he had entering the office were replaced with a sense of respect.

"That's why you became a doctor, isn't it?" He stared at his sneakers, worried about being perceived as too nosy.

She smiled at him. "The wonders of the mind are beyond a book's ability to explain." She pointed to the window. "All of those students have different thoughts, backgrounds, and come from different places. Each is unique, inspiring me to pursue my craft regardless of compensation." She started laughing. "Scratch that last part. I've spent too much time near a university."

Billy sat quietly, and he appeared utterly unsure of himself in this office. Once her laughter had subsided to a mere chuckle, he spoke. "The human mind is a wondrous universe."

She grinned at him. "Hence, this studying of universal consciousness."

"Yes. Of course. You're aware of that." Billy grinned.

By now, Carrie had retreated to her chair and settle back into it. She leaned forward, gathered the papers she had scattered over her desk, placed them back in the folder, and then extended her arm to Billy, offering him the file. "Here, take it. This is yours. I don't need this."

Billy hesitated before leaning forward and accepting the folder. "I don't understand."

"Well, everything in that folder tells me nothing about you. It tells me how you did in your courses, what you wrote in the email, and all the rest of the crap I don't need. Yet it tells me nothing about your mind's condition and your soul's intent."

Billy gripped the folder and scanned quickly through the pages before placing it on the floor at the side of his chair. "Doctor, I'm not sure how much trouble I'm in. What I did was mean, and if I deserve punishment, I understand that. It was a bad joke, done out of jealousy. I guess that's the best word for it, *jealousy.*"

Carrie rolled her eyes. "You're trying way too hard. It won't work with me. An email with those types of accusations cannot be retracted. You have panicked many people at Hobart. Spooked them sufficiently to enlist outsiders, including yours truly."

"I came clean. The next morning I confessed before it got further out of hand. After a restless night's sleep, I decided—" Carrie put her two hands before her, motioning him to stop mid-sentence.

"Look. We will devote the necessary time to discuss the details. I won't listen to any of it until I learn more about you. Why did you come to Hobart? You are bright and interested in something unique and fascinating."

"You mean the study of universal consciousness."

"I won't be dismissive and say it sounds New Age. Lord knows some students call me Old Age. I have been involved with this university for almost twenty years, but I can't say I am familiar with that field of study."

"It's a pilot project that started fairly recently. I'm part of the first group of students accepted into the program. It aims to marry the study of human consciousness with science—physics and biology, in particular."

Carrie nodded her head. "That would be heresy during the days of my youth. Everything has its silo. Heaven forbid anything being interrelated. Well, you must enlighten me. I guess this is a good start. We'll meet at the same time each day until we're done, okay?"

The meeting's conclusion startled Billy. Before he gathered his thoughts, Carrie escorted him towards the door. "Are there any queries for me? About the process, maybe?"

He looked back but not at her. His eyes followed the sunlight back through the outside window. Far off on the horizon, the university buildings became invisible to him. What he saw were the students scattered and drifting around the campus. He grinned, satisfied with the answer he was about to give. "Dr. Woodson, I'm thankful you are handling my case."

"Please call me Carrie. Our paths have crossed due to the workings of unseen hands. Let's dispense with formalities and explore our minds' universe." She extended her hand and opened the door. "One more thing, Billy. The next time we meet, bring one of your essays. Any work you presented in class or even something in draft form. Nothing plagiarized. One condition, though."

"I don't understand." Billy squinted and lowered his head.

"It has to be an essay you're proud of," Carrie said, before closing the door on a confused Billy.

CHAPTER 9

The Chalk Outline

Billy arrived for his next meeting holding a navy blue Duo-Tang. Carrie greeted him and ushered him to the chair in front of her desk. A large plate of chocolate chip cookies sat seductively at its lip. The trap sprung as Billy fixated on the offering.

Carrie smirked. "Please have a seat and a cookie. I limit visitors to one. If it's a good session, you can have two."

Billy eagerly reached for the closest one before settling back in the chair. "Thanks, doc—I'm sorry, Carrie. I'm guessing this is all a ruse for your cookie indulgence."

"You are too clever, young man." Carrie slid into her chair behind her desk. "Now, I see you did your homework and brought me some nighttime reading." Carrie reached over and pulled the Duo-Tang from Billy's hand.

"It's just an essay I recently completed. I haven't submitted it yet."

"Not yet?"

"No, ma'am. It's my final essay for a course. It was due this week until all this happened."

Carrie bit her lip and slid the Duo-Tang into her

russet-colored attaché bag. With each interaction with Billy, her stomach churned with a sense of uneasiness. Each new piece of information cast light on the human face at the center of the case. When she zipped her bag shut, she realized what had been troubling her. They expected her to pass judgment on the young man before her, a decision that would affect him for the remainder of his life. She envisioned one day, this young man seated before another psychologist, lamenting how he was judged instead of helped. Impulsively, she reached for a chocolate chip cookie, stared at an imaginary painting on the wall behind Billy, and slammed her left hand down in frustration.

"Sorry, Billy, I didn't mean to scare you." Stunned by her action and brought to earth by a startled look on Billy's face, an uneven smile spread across her lips. "That is some good cookie!"

"No worries, Carrie. The cookie is a decadent delight. You appeared a little distracted there for a second." Billy smiled.

Carrie's mind warped into overdrive, accumulating information, the subtleties of body language, the nuance of voice intonations, and observations. Dr. Edelman had coerced her, getting her agreement on a course of action she hadn't thought through. While upset, the challenge of finding an approach and a path, uniquely hers and morally satisfying, invigorated her.

Over the next hour, Billy orated his life's narrative leading up to the incident, including his relationship with John and Kate. She learned how Billy met John at a summer camp when they were cabin mates in their mid-teens and quickly became friends. They completed high school and found each other on campus one day at Hobart College, being interviewed for admissions. At the time, Billy was unsure of which field of study he should pursue. It was John who suggested that Billy should enroll in the newly created universal consciousness program. They kept in touch, and both were notified of their acceptance and scholarships on the same day. The two met again when classes began. Within a week, they manipulated dorm room assignments and were living together. Toward the end of his first semester, their paths crossed with that of an articulate, free-spirited women's rights activist named Kate. Billy described Kate as the female counterbalance to the male geekdom of Billy and John. By chance, Kate had an overlapping schedule with Billy during their first two years at Hobart College, and they often partnered on projects. Kate seemed to enjoy the intellectual dialogue between Billy and John. In short, the trio became inseparable on campus, with one caveat—at Hobart, boys were separately housed.

Events began to change during the summer preceding their final year, according to Billy's account. John and Billy had been amongst a select group of Hobart students invited to spend the summer participating in an intellectual retreat at the nearby Graduate Institute of Human Scientific Advancement. Billy declined—his adoptive father, Jake, had taken ill with an aggressive form of cancer. He returned to his hometown to be with him and stayed there until his passing late in August. The death of Jake made Billy realize he dare not wait to express his emotions, and he vowed to share his intensifying feelings for Kate. However, when he returned to Hobart that September, it was John who announced his intention to ask Kate on a date. Billy buried his emotions as John and Kate became a couple. But as the semester evolved, his feelings began to fester and percolate with each hand holding he witnessed, adding more degrees of heat to the smoldering cauldron.

Near the end of their final year, John announced they had accepted him for a full scholarship to the master's program at the Graduate Institute of Human Scientific Advancement. A week later, he announced that Kate would stay on at Hobart as an assistant professor and that the two would move in together in an off-campus apartment. The kettle whistle, signifying the emotions coming to a boil, was the infamous email. Each knew the passwords of the other, so Billy's hacking skills were overrated. Billy wanted to witness John ridiculed, at least for a while, and unnerved enough for Kate to have second thoughts. By the next morning, Billy, having witnessed the fallout, determined he had taken the joke too far. He woke up at 6:00 a.m, and after a torturous walk to the Dean's office, confessed.

"I can assume by then many within the Hobart community had read the email and were reacting?"

"Yes. John received over a dozen responses." Billy looked down at the ground. "I knew I hurt him and wanted it to stop. He wondered why someone would harm him."

Carrie reached for another cookie and nibbled on its edges in between words. "Was he mad at you?"

"Relieved that he knew who it was. Not mad. John doesn't get mad. That made me feel worse."

The crunch from Carrie's bite, deep into the soul of the cookie, startled him. "And how did Kate react? I'm guessing not so forgiving."

"Kate blew a gasket and vowed never to forgive me, even though my feelings for her caused all this. Her eyes banished me." Billy's chest heaved, and he swallowed hard. "Now, I'm here."

Carrie began flipping the pages in her notepad, returning to one of the early ones. "You accused Hobart of some horrible and specific things, like secret experiments. This is extreme stuff. You might have just painted the dean's car pink and signed it with John's name. Help me understand why you choose that accusation."

Billy hesitated and fidgeted in his chair. "Because I knew this would hit home and scare people. Hobart would not recommend John for any scholarship anywhere."

"You hated John so much, or did you love Kate that much? How much of each is it?"

"It no longer matters, does it? What I did was a momentary lapse of any logic or reason. I just don't want to…"

"Hurt anyone?"

"Kate's words were so vicious, I knew I hurt her. Coming from someone I cared about, they broke me into pieces."

Carrie slouched down in her chair and twiddled her pen in her hand. Billy had woven the tale of his life in a factual account. Every ebb and flow of his life became bleached of emotion and whittled down into a flat plane of events. A mere chalk outline around a life of fine texture and blossoming promise. The daily interactions between John and Billy persisted as an elusive mystery in Billy's narration. Hell, she wondered, what did he and Kate talk about when together? His story lacked hue or any hint of vibration, like an untouched guitar string. Despite so many trails to explore and expand upon, she wanted to trek down each one.

"I guess our time is up for today, Billy. We can continue tomorrow. Besides, it will give me a chance to read your essay. Is there anything you want to add?"

Billy inched forward and grabbed the last chocolate cookie, carefully sweeping up the errant crumbs that had fallen off the plate. "This may sound like a strange request."

"Request? I can play requests as long as you don't mind that I'm tone-deaf." Carrie laughed.

"Has anyone spoken to John?" Billy's elbows settled on his knees with his head hovering over Carrie's desk.

"Everyone in Hobart's academia will apologize to him for what he went through."

"I don't mean those damn academics or an apology. I mean someone like you, a trained professional."

"A psychologist? I kind of doubt it." Carrie's voice quivered, wondering where the question was coming from. "This concerns you?"

"A roommate and friend messing with your email and reputation. I imagine it would rattle a person. Even if it's nothing, someone should speak to him." Carrie noted Billy's lips press even more firmly together.

"You make a good point. I'm sure along the way, the right person will talk to him if they haven't already."

"Not now. I mean after, Carrie. After they punish me, I would feel better if they talk to him."

Carrie's eyebrows raised unevenly. "You're assuming a conclusion, young man. My modus operandi excludes judging."

"Dr. Woodson, we both realize you won't be the judge nor the jury." The words barely settled as Billy rose, leaving the room wearing a grim expression that lingered in Carrie's thoughts.

Carried began scribbling a few notes on a paper before picking up the phone. After multiple rings, a voice answered. "It's Dr. Woodson, I'm trying to contact Dr. Edelman." Carrie fidgeted with her pen while shaking her head, frustrated by the evasive voice at the other end. Fed up, she spoke again, "I must speak to him *now.*"

After a series of clicks, a male voice replied, "Dr. Edelman speaking."

"I want the truth, Charles. I want the truth!"

Dr. Edelman's voice seemed muffled, like a teenager calling his girlfriend from the basement of his parent's home. "I planned to call, Carrie. It's about the Daintree case. It won't burden you much longer. The ground and timing have shifted since we last spoke."

CHAPTER 10

The Exiled

Anger can be hidden, even locked away for years. Not for Carrie Woodson. The crash of ceramic against some solid object echoed through the phone line, and Carrie heard Dr. Edelman gasp as if a final breath was imminent.

"You threw a cup, didn't you, Carrie?"

"Don't worry, Charles, it was an empty ceramic mug. Probably the one you bestowed upon me when I turned forty. Anyhow, I would never toss a cup filled with coffee." Charles laughed nervously before Carrie switched from sarcasm to pure rage. "What do you mean the ground has shifted, or dare I demand an explanation?"

"Carrie, the Dean of Hobart called. They consider the matter resolved. All they desire is confirmation that Mr. Daintree is no further threat."

"Charles, I've met the young man twice. Despite this pre-emptive conclusion, I called you to ask for more time. My analysis requires further investigation. I'm convinced I can help."

"Help this young man? He's not your patient. His file belongs to Hobart. You should be pleased this is a closed file as far as Hobart is concerned. These rivalries amongst overachieving and ambitious intellectuals can get ugly. The aftermath is often worse than the actual incident."

"I presume you told them I was interviewing Billy and not you. I'm guessing they were not happy with my involvement."

"Well, that came up. If I may be blunt, your reputation for pulling out worms buried deep in the mud worries people. But that was not the clincher."

"Charles, the email had some serious accusations. Everyone is stepping away from them without trying to understand why, even as a hoax, they were made, as opposed to something less specific."

"Carrie, we are not Hobart. They can figure things out for themselves. They came to me, and now they don't need me anymore. The students involved resolved their issue, and if they reached a conclusion, far be it from me to swing at the flies with a straw."

Carrie's pen tapped rhythmically on the wooden desk. "Drop the bomb on me now, what is the conclusion reached by *your* friends at Hobart?"

"Well, there will be no criminal charges. That's good news. The victim, Mr. Adamson, has decided to move away with his girlfriend after he graduates." Charles took a large gulp of water.

Carrie understood where his train of thought headed. "They're expelling Daintree, aren't they?"

"Yes, and they want him to stay away from Mr. Adamson. That was a demand made by Mr. Adamson's girlfriend."

"So, Billy Sinclair Daintree has been blacklisted by Hobart, branded with this fucking *X*, and now must go into exile!"

"Carrie, don't forget what he did. He made a false accusation using his friend's email. He's no saint, Carrie."

"No saint, but possibly a martyr, Charles."

"Good lord, Carrie, you've only had two sessions with this character, and already you suspect he was persecuted. Stop projecting all the time."

Carrie did not respond. She knew her silence would suffocate her former mentor and the first person who support her years ago in her fight against intolerance. "I'm sorry, Carrie. I am just venting my frustration, too. Trust me when I say walking away is the best outcome for not just us, but Mr. Daintree. The stench of school politics is so nasty in this case."

"Charles, Mr. Daintree and I have a scheduled session tomorrow!"

Dr. Edelman interrupted, "You want to continue with that session? That's fine with me. Just be aware that this evening, he is being expelled and will have to leave his temporary dorm facilities."

"Still, I want to speak to him and get closure."

"Carrie, let's make this clear. For all our sakes, it ends after tomorrow. He can't be your patient."

"I comprehend that. You have made it abundantly clear. There is something, though, that puzzles me. It's about John Adamson. I was under the impression they offered him a full-ride in some master's program over at the Graduate Institute of Human Scientific Advancement."

"Yes, he's turning his back on all of that. My contact at

Hobart mentioned that the Graduate Institute is disappointed since Mr. Adamson was highly recommended after spending a summer there as part of a program they sponsor."

"Maybe, Charles, I've spent too long at this 'old' school, but the Graduate Institute intrigues me. That's that creepy looking research compound built down the road from Hobart?"

"Yes. It's about two or three exits from Hobart College. By creepy, I assume you mean modern."

"All privately funded, if I recall."

"Oh, yes, big time. Private industry and governments. It's the future for research. Groundbreaking research funded by those with the means."

"With no accountability to the higher good or to human ethics," Carrie muttered.

"To be honest, Carrie, it's not my business what they do in that playground for ideas they've built. I have my world to live in right here," Dr. Edelman announced. "Um, Carrie, there is one more favor I must ask."

"Why am I not surprised? Go ahead. You've already blind-sided me."

"I need a report from you on Mr. Daintree. One that I assume will say he poses no danger."

"I kind of expected you would need to cover your ass, or should I say Hobart's, with a memo to the file."

"Thanks, Carrie." Dr. Edelman was about to hang up when he thrust the phone back close to his lips. "Don't doubt my intentions on this. Please have your meeting tomorrow and then walk away. Your involvement was well considered. More than you can envision."

Carrie frowned as she hung up the phone without a reply. Marie would be home late from her shift at the hospital, so she double-checked her bag before leaving the office. She zipped it closed one more time after ensuring that it contained the Duo-Tang handed to her by Billy. Carrie thought of the essay as she stared at the pieces of her fortieth birthday mug scattered in the office's corner. She wondered if she would be the only person to read the last term paper ever written by Billy at Hobart. Deciding to leave the mug carcass on the floor as a memorial to her unresolved anger discharging beneath her steel exterior, she left the office.

In the stately administration building of Hobart College, sitting in the Dean's office, Billy Sinclair Daintree received word of his expulsion and his need to vacate the dorm facilities within twenty-four hours. About to leave the office, a final exclamation mark was added to the verdict—Billy was forbidden from contacting Mr. John Adamson or his girlfriend.

Billy said nothing as he left Hobart College one final time. It would surprise anyone gazing out of their campus dorm windows to see a young man alone in the darkened campus fields, lying on his back, staring at the night sky. A soft hum filling the air would entertain those close enough, if they listened.

CHAPTER 11

The Search for God

"I guess you weren't expecting me today," Billy smirked as he parked himself in the chair facing Carrie. "You got wind of what happened to me, I assume."

Carrie shifted restlessly in her chair. Under normal circumstances, words would come to her. At worse, some nugget of sarcasm would escape her lips. Today, words seemed lost inside her, unable to find the tunnel out.

Billy sensed her discomfort. "Dr. Woodson, I realize you don't own the decision. I'll survive being expelled. A price must be paid for my actions."

"I asked you to spend more time with you. I feel we've just started. In hindsight, I should have protested more, but they would decide no matter what. Your appearance today is voluntary." Carrie reached into her bag and pulled out the Duo-Tang before extending it toward Billy. "I take it you want your essay back, and that's why you're here."

"I didn't come here for that." Billy motioned for Carrie to keep the Duo-Tang. "I don't need it."

Carrie frowned. "Don't need it? You can use it at another

school."

"No, I doubt anyone would be interested." Billy grinned, making Carrie's fingers tremble. "I won't be needing it. Another scholarship is a pipe dream. I doubt anyone would accept me."

"Billy, I read your essay last night after hearing the verdict." Carrie held the document in the air. "How dare I ignore an essay entitled, 'God Does Not Make Noise'?"

"You can laugh, Dr. Woodson, if you found it amusing."

Carrie slowly rose from her seat shaking her head as she sauntered to the window before turning back at Billy. "I read a lot. Often for work and rarely for pleasure. There isn't much anymore that makes me pause and wonder." After taking a few steps closer to Billy, she returned to her seat and sighed. "I enjoyed this, Billy. It's a shame someone with your intellectual maturity, well, is no longer in a college or university setting to provoke discussion or debate." She shuffled through the pages and read aloud, "'Out of the silence, we created sounds to awaken the souls. In fear of the return of silence, God created musicians to turn the sounds into an everlasting song. Pity those subjected to noise alone or worse, silence.'" Carrie looked at Billy, "Ancient wisdom from a youthful voice."

"Carrie, leaving Hobart changes nothing. The thought of spewing philosophy in academic circles or trying to write equations that equal God—well, that just isn't me." Billy's eyes fluttered around the room, and his attention drifted to the office window. "People need help, Dr. Woodson. So that is my intention. We'll call it my penance."

"You're taking this far too well. I still don't understand why you showed up today. When I saw you walk in, I assumed it was to get your essay back."

"Carrie, you help people. I can tell. I came here to tell you I appreciate what you tried to do for me." Billy smiled and leaned back into the chair. "Not many people, aside from my parents and..." Billy stopped short.

"Who else, Billy?" Carrie leaned forward excitedly. "You were going to say someone else."

"Few people take a leap of faith." Billy sighed. "You didn't judge me, Dr. Woodson. I could tell you were searching for the truth."

"So you came back today to play a game of riddles with me. Fine, well, I set aside time for you today, and I'm willing to listen and take that leap of faith."

Billy's lips spread wide to reveal a grin capable of lighting up the dark side of the moon. "My intention wasn't to play riddles with you. I suspected you would worry, so I want to ease your mind. That's one reason I came here today. The other is to find out what happened to John." Billy paused when he witnessed Carrie's expression change. "Because I can't contact him, I'm wondering if he's staying on and going to that graduate school."

"After graduating from college, he's moving away and won't be going there. At least, that's what little they told me." Carrie looked deep into Billy's eyes as she thought through what else she would tell him. Satisfied with her conclusion, she whispered in a monotone voice, "They said his girlfriend will live with him."

Billy pressed his lips tight and nodded. "Thanks, Carrie. I just wanted peace of mind, especially after my misguided actions."

Carrie nodded, "Of course." When she told Billy about

John moving in with his girlfriend, she detected the slightest appearance of a grin. "I want to understand one thing you talked about in your essay, this part about the black holes in your neighborhood."

"A friend of mine convinced me they existed."

Carrie nodded. "Well, we have time, and I would love if you recounted the story of this friend. The black hole part is a bit over my head."

Billy's body unwound like a cobra released from a hatbox. He seemed to uncoil his energy and enthusiasm as he told the tale of Dieter. Carrie sat and listened intently at how the story of the tragic disappearance of a child, as narrated by Billy, evoked such warmth and humanism that a tear settled in the corner of her eye.

When the tale ended, Carrie maneuvered her head back to prevent even a single tear from trickling down. "So all Dieter wanted was someone to believe him. You gave him that gift."

"All I offered him was my belief. No one else did. What he wanted was an escape."

"From the abuse?"

Billy nodded affirmatively. "And he left me with a gift too—the comic book."

"Without an ending, though?" Carrie stated.

"That was the gift, Carrie. He left the ending to me. In life, what gift could be greater? For whatever reality to flow from your own imagination."

"Mr. William Sinclair Daintree, that would be some world." Carrie reached and tapped the cover of Billy's Duo-Tang. "If only God turned down the volume to let us enjoy the wonderful music being played."

Billy picked up the Duo-Tang and handed it to Carrie. "Please keep it. I don't need it anymore. Besides, my ideas are securely preserved." Billy pointed to his head and laughed.

"I may have to refer to this," she said. "I'm serious about that." Just then, her administrative assistant stepped inside the office to announce another patient would arrive shortly.

Billy stood up and stretched his hand toward her. "I appreciate you taking the time. It was an honor to be your temporary patient."

Rather than stand, Carrie pushed her chair back and studied Billy's facial expressions. "You were never my patient, young man. But I can't call you a friend because I sense you haven't told me everything."

"What haven't I told you?" Billy asked, sheepishly.

"The truth about the email and everything that happened with you and John." Carrie put her fingers to her lips for Billy to remain silent. "I also suspect you have a reason, and it must be a massive one. Whatever happened, Billy, don't bear that burden alone when you don't have to."

"Carrie, one day, the noise will succumb to harmony and truth." He walked around the desk and offered his hand once again. This time she grabbed it tight and got up and smirked at him.

"Promise me, Billy. If you ever need help, whenever or wherever, please don't hesitate. I can be quite the superwoman when I put my mind to it or when I am not overdosing on cookies."

"You would make quite the superhero. Don't concern yourself with my future. I will serve my penance with noble intent." He looked over at the Duo-Tang sitting at the edge of the desk. "What a horrible essay title that was. Good thing I never submitted it."

"Oh, it's not bad at all," Carrie said.

"*Time's Musicians*' would have been better." Billy laughed and turned to leave.

Carrie stood briefly, staring at the closed door. She assembled the notes on her desk and placed them in a new folder. She reached for Billy's essay and began inserting it into the folder when she changed her mind and walked to her bookshelf. Violently pushing aside various texts squeezed together, she made space for it at the topmost part of her shelf at eye level.

Just as she returned to the desk, her assistant entered to announce the arrival of the next patient.

"Do superheroes have to wear capes?"

"Excuse me?" her puzzled assistant thought she misheard.

"Wonder Woman doesn't wear a cape, does she?"

"Yes, last time I checked."

"Very well, I'll go with the cape."

"Is there are anything you need to fill me in on, Carrie?" she asked, glaring suspiciously.

"No, this superhero business is foreign territory. Just wondering if there's a certain look."

Her assistant stepped into Carrie's office and closed the door behind her. In a low, quiet voice, she whispered, "Carrie, you and I are both aware you don't give a damn about anyone's opinions, anyway." She reopened the door to summon Carrie's patient.

CHAPTER 12

Many Years Later: The Past Returns

(May 2018)

The past spoke to Billy, now in his early thirties, through a dream. It would begin with the promise of Billy's wedding.

Billy tried to understand his emotions as he descended from the bed. He had realized in short order that the feelings were new to him.

The surrounding room ached in antiquity. It was an old country home built many generations ago. So long ago, in fact, that Billy struggled to recall the names or even faces of his ancestors. He had seen the pictures a multitude of times, he supposed. This would be the first clue his subconscious bubbled to the surface. He rubbed his eyes and wandered around the room, conceding his memories were succumbing to his nerves. At least he deluded himself in that comfort for a little while longer. It turned out to be infinitesimally longer.

The dark mahogany dresser supported the most grandiose of oval mirrors. Billy succumbed to its lure. He positioned himself in front of it. The image seemed to leap from the glass and grabbed his lapels, pulling him closer. His hands secured his balance with his nails digging into the wood. Regaining his posture, he leaned back and straightened his stance. There he stood before the unrepentant mirror, clothed in a black tuxedo with a blue-and-red floral patterned vest beneath. Panic swept him up. He must have fallen asleep. The preparation for this day's festivities had taken its toll. Unsure of the time, he searched for a clock or a watch without success. From the brightness of the sun vulgarly crashing against the window, he surmised it was late morning. Strangely, the sun's glare seemed to stop at the window with nary a ray of light entering the room. Eerily, the room seemed to surrender itself to shadows. Billy rubbed his jaw and smirked as he held out his hand to gauge the extent to which it trembled in anticipation.

Silence can be frighteningly loud when unnoticed for too long. It caught Billy's attention. On a wedding day, frenzied activity rattling the corridors and walls was expected. Billy's pace quickened until he reached the door frame of the bedroom. His head poked through the invisible barrier into the hall. There was no sigil of activity.

"Hello, is anyone here?" Billy called with a slight stutter, not wanting to embarrass himself for not knowing anyone's whereabouts. He called out again after a few seconds of listening to only the hint of a breeze from an open window somewhere. There was no reply. He returned to the bed and plopped on it. His black leather Oxfords so shiny that in this reverie, they reflected his confused gaze. He cupped his hands to his chin, concluding they must be waiting at the church. He vaguely recollected the rehearsal and how he was to be picked up at his family's country home and brought to the church. A most intimate wedding was planned in this ancestral town. The ceremony would occur at an eighteenth-century church nestled within a forest.

There was but one picture, which sat on the dresser beside the bed. It was that of him and his love, Kate, taken at their engagement party. In the photo, he sported a light blue shirt with beige trousers as his hands entwined with hers. She wore a stunning yellow summer dress with her long, light blonde hair tied at the back. Her blue eyes sparkled with an intensity that threatened to melt the glass frame. Billy stared at the image, at how the surrounding light made him appear years older than her. He reached for the picture frame and caressed the silver border and the floral design embedded around its perimeter with his fingertips. From the first time he had met Kate—or, more precisely, when she introduced herself to him—he knew their destiny was forever connected. He carefully set the photo back down, convinced that today would be a great day, his happiest day.

He tried to remember when the car would pick him up for the church. No longer was he sure whether they were sending a limousine or one of the 1930s antique cars that captured Kate's imagination. Details were mundane on a wedding day, he determined. They would be married in this serene, natural setting, and that's all that mattered.

As he ventured into the corridor, a gentle tapping sound fluttered to his ear, seemingly from the floor beneath. Sound traveled well along the wooden floorboards and black knotted decorated walls. Billy stopped to listen, unnerved by the chaotic nature of the pitter-patter. The noise resembled the sound of small feet scurrying on a bare floor. In fact, it sounded like a child's footsteps. He became confident the sound was the overlap of children's steps. There were at least two children. Yet when he'd called out earlier, no one replied. Why would unsupervised children be scampering around?

"Hello?" he hollered again. "Is anyone downstairs? Your running gives you away."

The sound disappeared replaced by the low murmur of indecipherable voices. "Excuse me, I heard you downstairs. Please don't pretend you're not there. The noise you are making is a dead giveaway." He was almost pleading now. Still, his words disappeared into an empty void. "Look, it's my wedding day. They will be here soon to pick me up. We'll have time to play later." Again, there was no response. Billy's logical brain concluded they were part of the bridal party and accompanying him. Ah, yes, likely the ring bearer and flower girl. Pleased with his deduction, it dawned on him that they probably were left in his care until the groom's car arrived, and he must have dozed off when he should have been supervising them.

Feeling a spate of dizziness, Billy paused at the top of the staircase and gripped the solid wood banister with such force his hand went numb. He strained to decipher any whisper of words from below or even a faint breath. Nothing. In his head, he counted each stair while descending. His last step brought him to the foyer, and he turned to face the long corridor that split this home in two. At the far end of the corner was the open space, the large family room. No doubt, the children would hide there. With his first step down the hall, the silence surrendered to the sound of a high-pitched shriek followed by a machine-gun rhythm of footsteps. Two figures ran past the doorframe into one of the rooms further down the corridor. Their stature resembled two small children. Strangely, though, their hair seemed abnormally thick and bright atop their head, as though painted with the most buttery of colors imaginable.

"He can't hear us, can he?" one child bellowed to the other. "Impossible!"

"Shh. Something has gone horribly wrong. Be quiet!" demanded the second voice.

"Oh, my goodness, you don't suppose he can see us?" The voice trailed off as if muffled.

Billy resisted the temptation to call out again, took off his shoes, and glided down the hallway floor with just his socks on his feet. These children now appeared to be intruders. The logic behind their presence was beyond Billy's understanding. His immediate goal was to apprehend them. The murmurs stopped as he approached, and he sensed them holding their breaths. When he reached the doorway of the family room, he leaped past the imaginary line separating the room from the hallway. He landed like a cat and swiveled his body around to survey the entire perimeter. Two couches, an old television, a bookshelf, two windows with drawn checkered blinds—he scanned every detail of the room. His brain played back to him one image he'd skipped, two strange-looking, innocent creatures squatting next to a couch. Both with bright yellow hair. Both almost identical in appearance, except one wore a blue turtleneck sweater and jeans while the other wore a bright maroon sweater with similar jeans. Neither had shoes on. Both seemed confused, with looks of utter shock on their faces.

He found their location and turned to face them. Two sets of eyes stared back at him intently. Gradually, four eyebrows raised simultaneously in his direction. There was no fear in their glare.

"My goodness. He sees us," one voice whispered in a low tone to the other.

"Well, if we were not loud enough before, I am sure he can hear us now, you fool," said the other, irritated.

"Why would I not be able to? You're not hiding that well. I mean, you're right next to the couch. But I don't recognize you—are you from Kate's side of the family?" Billy smiled, remembering Kate had mentioned some eccentricities in her family. If not, someone needed to explain the yellow hair.

"You can see us?" said the child in the red sweater. "You're not supposed to."

"Yeah, I see you. Why would you be invisible?"

"Dear me," said the child in blue. "Something has gone wrong."

"Is it your hair? Is that what's wrong? Did you spill something, turning it yellow? I would guess it's the last thing you'd want to happen before a wedding."

"Wedding?" questioned both children in harmony.

"Yes, I'm getting married today. I presume you're with my fiancé's side of the family."

"There is a wedding today? Is that correct?" asked the blue child.

"Now, I am sure you're playing games with me."

"No, sir, we do not play games. We are also not aware of any wedding. This is all such a terrible mess."

"A mess?"

"Yes. You are never supposed to see us."

Billy inhaled, trying to maintain his composure. "I see both of you next to the couch."

The child in the red sweater moved toward him with his finger outstretched as if to make a point. "Just how many of us do you see?"

The other child looked puzzled. Billy looked to the high arched ceiling in disbelief. His patience unraveling ever faster. "There are two of you. Unless you have friends hiding somewhere. Look, just tell me how you're related to Kate. Little cousins?"

The child in blue staggered back and raised his small hands to his mouth. Billy noticed there were no fingers—his hands were similar to mittens. "But, sir, there are hundreds of millions of us in front of you. An infinite number." He started to laugh nervously. "Something has gone wrong. You must be joking."

Billy retreated to the staircase, positioning himself on the third stair. "Look, kids, stop messing with me. There are only two of you here. There aren't millions or infinite, as you say."

"Why do you say there are not? I am inquisitive."

"Because I only see two of you."

"Your eyes are telling you that, aren't they?" The child in the blue now moved toward Billy, looking much older with each step he took.

"My eyes? Well, my ears don't lie, either." Billy forced a chuckle, trying to hide his rapidly growing confusion.

"Wow." The child in the blue sweater turned to one in red. "He isn't ready to understand. And if he doesn't understand, how can he save them?"

"I'm not ready? Save who?"

The child in red smiled. "You have more senses than just hearing and sight."

"Yes, yes, I am aware of that. There's my taste, touch, and smell, too, but I will not get that close to you."

Both children shook their heads dejectedly. "We can't expect you to understand. With those senses, you were not meant to know we exist, whether it be one or an infinite number of us. Glitching happens but, never to us. Some sort of interference is occurring."

"Shh!" the other child demanded, flailing his hands haphazardly.

Billy's shoulders slumped, and he rubbed his eyes. "Look, whatever game you're playing, I have no time for it. I have to be ready when they pick us up." He turned around as his eyes explored the surroundings, searching the walls.

"What are you seeking?" said the child in blue.

"A clock. Where I can find the time? They should be here soon."

"For the wedding?" the two children asked as each took a simultaneous step toward him.

"Yes! Dammit, stop playing games. Get dressed, please."

The child in blue stared at him intensely. "Describe what you see. What do we look like?"

Billy's attention was consumed by two children standing before him. "You look like two children in red and blue sweaters. My first impression is your kind of look like Thing 1 and Thing 2—from Dr. Seuss." Billy smiled at this observation. His smile was short-lived, as the children looked back at him bewildered. "Yes, you look like the two Dr. Seuss characters. Oh, come on now! I'm sure your mom or dad has read it to you!"

The children retreated backward. They both spoke in a much deeper tone of voice, almost without moving their lips. "We are no such 'Thing' as the thing you see. We are what you can't see. Everywhere and everything. Nothing and nowhere. We are what you cannot see and... *you* created us, all of us."

Fear began to crawl up Billy's spine to invade his mind. "Created?"

"Yes. We are all your creations. Remember the music, Aeon. Remember your mission to save them."

"My mission? Aeon?"

The young child with more yellowish gold hair smiled. "You are so naïve. We are from *you.*"

"And who needs saving? Tell me, please," Billy begged.

"That is why we are here. To tell you to listen so you can hear them."

"Hear who?"

"Those crying."

"But besides you, everything is silent. Who needs to be saved? Is someone hurt?"

One child stepped forward. "They are calling for help. Their ears are in great pain. You can end it. The screams have to stop. You created us to warn you, and you can stop the screams once and for all. Silence masks the screams, remember that."

"Stay right here. I will find a phone and call your parents." Billy shuffled his feet and raced down the hallway into one of the four rooms that lined either side. As he walked, he became more confused, as it became apparent that every room he peered into was unfamiliar to him. *How can this be? This is my family's country place. I spent practically every summer here. Or did I?* Unable to find a phone or even a clock, he returned to the room he'd stumbled upon the children in. They were nowhere to be discovered.

Billy wandered into one room he previously explored. It was one with a rocking chair nestled in a corner. The events of the day and his own nerves were getting the best of him. The trembling in his left hand became uncontrollable. His sitting to collect his thoughts was an act of desperation. A hand-knit blanket, black with mustard checkers, covered the seat of the rocker and extended up to its back. He examined the walls surrounding him. An early 1970s-style boxed television set stood facing the center of the room. He doubted the set worked, the antenna sitting on top of its cabinet betraying its age. Overcome with confusion, he waited for someone to enter the house. As long as no more children! His brain settled in on the strange message of the children while his ears mischievously reminded him that, while they'd disappeared from his sight, they may still be roaming the halls.

One image poked its way through the murkiness of his thoughts. It was Kate's. Yes, this was the wedding she dreamed of and planned so diligently. Yet Billy only circled and surrounded the fantasy of this wedding. However, none of the details could be visualized. Everything appeared foreign to him. Everything, including the strange kids who seemed straight out of a childhood fairytale. Billy smiled at Kate's image framed behind his closed eyes with her blonde hair sporting a hint of a wave and ocean-colored eyes—the vision was identical to her appearance years earlier.

Billy shifted his weight back and built the momentum needed to topple the chair forward as it pushed his body out of it. With purpose, Billy sprinted from the room and ascended the staircase leading to the bedrooms. He knew he would see the limo coming to get him from the upstairs window. Truthfully though, Billy sought to take comfort in the image of Kate and him, hands entwined in engaged bliss. The stairs creaked with each step he took, announcing his arrival upstairs—or delivering a warning

Within seconds of entering the bedroom, his heart sunk long before his vision even reached the dresser. The photo had vanished. He dropped to his hands and knees, searching the ground for any trace of it—even the shattered glass of a broken frame upon the hard oak floorboards would suffice. Puzzled, he bent lower and stretched his hand under the bed, feeling every particle of dust along the way with his outstretched fingers. Success came when he touched a rectangular object with a glass covering one side. He pulled his hand back out from beneath the bed, prepared to bask before the image of their love.

He leaned back against the dresser as he brought the picture frame up to rest in both hands, balanced against the edge of the leather belt at his waist. It was with the unexpectedness of the image before him that pure horror punched him in the gut, winding him. It was not the engagement photo. Instead, it was the image of a man with a receding hairline, his hair silvering around his ears, eyes brown and encased with the shadows of experience and touched by the discrete lines of age. Billy wondered what a picture of his father was doing here of all places, under the bed. Only this was not Jake. And he had no image of his birth father. He examined the photo with forensic precision. Every detail probed by his disbelieving eyes. With a sigh, he concluded the picture was more mystery than revelation. This looked like *him*—an aged version of him. It had to be his father, though. Logic required it, however hard he tried to justify it, he knew intuitively it was impossible. Billy began shaking his head as he looked down to his left, away from the picture. He placed the picture carefully down on the floor to his side and summoned his hands to cover his lying eyes.

Slowly, logic reclaimed a foothold in his mind as his consciousness began erasing the sketched, pencil version of his fantasy. His dream unraveled. The photo could not be his father, nor could he be marrying Kate right now. His parents didn't have the means to own a country home. The two children he'd seen resembled two-dimensional images from a comic book created by him. Angry with reason, he summoned the courage to dive back into his reverie and make sense of it.

When his courage returned, his eyes opened again to see the same haunting image before him. He hurried to the oval mirror on the dresser and gazed intensely at the face staring back at him with equal ferocity. His trembling hands raised the picture up to face the mirror as he moved his face next to it to study. Each finger lightly traveled the outline of his face, stopping to probe any blemish or the wrinkles the photo foreshadowed. His visage lacked the etchings of aging. It was his eyes that appeared timeless, dusky, tired, and mournful in both likenesses of him. He forced a smile, one which pained his lips. The stunted grin in the picture was a perfect match. Lost in a swirl of data, his brain reached the only reasonable conclusion possible. He exerted a prolonged and hefty breath before bursting out in laughter. Naturally, the picture looked like him. He had a family, and it was natural that some relatives would bear a resemblance. He surmised that during his youth, he had not met all of his family, and this one particular relative bore a stunning resemblance to him.

Billy soon laid back on his bed, having thrown himself back with the relief at one riddle solved. Not wanting to consider how forcefully he had knocked the round peg into the square hole, he scarcely heard the voice burrowing through his ear.

"Billy, you were right the first time. Don't fret it, you have aged gracefully, I would say." Billy paused before embarking on a fervent search for the voice's source.

"You won't find where I am. Yes, Billy, I figured out how to do it thanks to your faith in me. You were the only one who followed me."

Billy's eyes detonated as if he had placed a grenade in each socket. He sprang up on the bed and swiveled his head, surveying the room. No one was visible. Yet the voice was familiar—John? It seemed almost as close as a mosquito circling for a landing.

"Yes, Billy, it's me, your friend—only not the one named John. I supposed you figure out I'm not physically there with you."

"For God's sake, stop hiding on me. Stop all these games! Come out from your hiding spot."

"If my feat was simply hiding, I would be the world's greatest illusionist. A magician, I would say, of the finest order. You surely realize what I have done? Only a magician can convince you I traveled through time."

Billy's head swiveled as he raced through the room, ducking to look under the bed and opening closets as he searched. The futility of his mission increased his frustration. He descended the stairs, skipping two and even three stairs with each stride. Darting through every room, his search proved futile. The voice, however, waited for his movements to pause before continuing.

"You are confused by all this. I'm so sorry." The voice's tone was somber. "I just thought you would be ecstatic that I did it. That I am at peace."

Startled but somehow comforted, Billy stopped and spoke while staring at a high ceiling above the stairwell. "Certainly, I'm thrilled. It's my wedding day, the most joyous day of my life. Everyone, however, seems to be playing these games with me."

"Your wedding day is today?"

"Please stop it and come on out from wherever you are. I'm sure the car will arrive at any moment to pick us up."

"Whose voice is invading your thoughts, Billy?"

Billy crouched down heavy in thought. The voice replayed over and over.

"Oh, my God. It can't be. That's impossible. Dieter, where are you?"

The voice grew low in tone and cadence. "You need to save them, my friend. The world you created is real. Their minds can be saved. The murmur hissing at the back of your mind is their screams, and they search for the one who will save them. Like they found John once and scream his name again." The voice trailed off as Billy's eyes tried to focus on the surrounding images, which merged at a quicker pace into a symphony of colors entwining.

"John!" Billy's head vibrated to the sound of his name.

The shrill, unholy sound of an incoming text message on his phone awoke him from his vivid slumber. He enjoyed the soft purr of his cat, who lay asleep on his lap, and his New York apartment surrounded him. Without looking, he knew the author's identity intuitively. Kate's appearance in his dream foreshadowed it. Kate's text messages became persistent.

I need to call Carrie, he thought as he covered his eyes with hands trembling. His heart pulsated.

Billy recognized he needed to take a chance. The only person who might understand the dream from which he awoke was Carrie. Only she seemed capable of understanding why he now heard Dieter's voice. The same boy who had found a black hole just beyond his street, or so the story went according to Billy. The boy who returned through a dream to warn him. It had been so long. Would Carrie even care or remember him?

His dream confirmed all his recent fears were frighteningly genuine, as were the cries that had yet to reach his ears. He wondered, though, if someone else had heard them. Soon he would not wonder anymore.

CHAPTER 13

Dr. Carrie Woodson, retired

An empty field of endless space stretched out before her. Not in a physical sense. No, the empty field represented infinite time in its purest form. Whether she had seconds, hours, or years to explore, it mattered not. Carrie Woodson hated boredom. She would devote every ounce of her being to trample it into the ground. Every speaker at her retirement party described, with impressive amateur acting, the excitement that awaited her. As she looked out the window of her study, she considered herself thankful not to be working with those damn fools anymore. She loved her work. Anyone telling her that boredom was better than working assuredly was an idiot of the highest order.

Yes, they told her she should write her memoirs, summing up her experiences and the cases she handled. The handful that slipped between her fingers overshadowed the multitude of people she helped. Each one, name, and face, indelibly etched in her memory. In the mirror of her soul, she swore each of their names were carved with barbed wire upon the faces that looked back at her.

Dr. Woodson, fresh from her sixtieth birthday lunch, found

a handwritten note on her desk. The Vice-Principal Academic at the university wanted to see her. She knew the purpose of the meeting. Weeks earlier, there had been cuts at the hospital where she spent seemingly every hour she was not at the university. Her position was abolished, and now she assumed that the university would elegantly push her over the cliff. They would call it early retirement. There would be no fight, nor vengeance from Carrie. Faced with the inevitable, she agreed to accept the package offered and retire early. Her conditions included retaining her files and notes and continuing to mentor the three young students under her tutelage. The university presumed she wanted to keep the records for her memoirs. She wanted the files just in case. Perhaps one of her old patients would need her, or perhaps some insight would come to her in a dream allowing her to save just one more psyche.

Finances were not a concern for Carrie. She did not live lavishly. She and her partner, Marie, a neurologist, lived the simple life on the outskirts of New York. Close enough to the buzz of chaos, but far enough away from it all to take hour-long walks in the woods with no chance of encountering any semblance of human existence. Marie was a few years younger than her—a love that found her just as she'd wondered if she was destined to live a life solely devoted to working. Marie coming into her life would not be the only blessing to sprinkle sugar on the blandness of her existence. There would be another.

Carrie closed her eyes, longer than a blink but not long enough for a nap to tempt her. When she reopened them, her vision turned to the trees, the antique oaks standing stoically along the border of her property. Beyond the oaks were miles upon miles of insects, plants, and life of all sorts, strategically hidden from her sight. The irony amused her. She took off her reading glasses, resting them next to her oversized coffee mug, and leaned back on her swivel chair. Like a twirling schoolgirl on a carousel, she glanced at the bookshelf, the aquarium, and the wood cabinets as she spun. The chair found its final resting spot facing the window. The oaks stood in majestic contrast to the thick Kentucky bluegrass that spread out from the walls of her home to the forest. Whatever lay hidden beyond the oaks remained in another world. She craved a long walk this evening. Yes, even if Marie were exhausted from a heavy schedule at the hospital, Carrie would venture off on her own. The forest never scared her. It teased her.

The late afternoon sun had succumbed to an encompassing cloud. Her study basked in the shadows now. The artificial light of her desktop monitor reminded her of why she had come into the study. It has been weeks since her last days at the school and her farewell party. During the intervening period, Carrie had ignored any outside communication like the plague. Converting the upstairs spare room to Carrie's personal study was Marie's retirement gift. The thorough Marie ensured that the stacks upon stacks of books from Carrie's office were not only sent home but positioned in almost the exact order as in Carrie's office back at the university. Carrie appreciated the gesture. Marie wanted her to feel continuity and purpose, so she surrounded her at home with what she loved so much. When Carrie saw the cabinet filled with all her handwritten files, she felt comfortable, if only for a moment.

Marie had let Carrie brood and simmer in her boredom until

the previous night. Finally, Marie reminded her of all those who cared for her and all the unanswered emails of the past weeks. People were asking questions about Carrie's mental state, and Marie grew tired of sheltering a moody psychologist. Carrie needed to buckle up and move on, even if it meant answering emails she'd rather ignore. Her keyboard taunted her. She hated technology. Although she'd adapted to using it in her day-to-day life, nothing provided a greater thrill than receiving a handwritten letter from an ex-patient, colleague, or friend. Over time, those became rare. Technology became a means to survive in her work environment. She gritted her teeth with each character stroke on the keyboard, resolving not to let the digital world defeat her.

The monitor displayed hundreds of unanswered and unopened emails before her. *Good lord, they are reproducing.* Once she perused the number of emails in her Inbox, she discovered many were spam. She skimmed over the subject lines hoping to find any that caught her attention. The ones from ex-colleagues bore striking resemblances to one another. Whether it be suggestions for subjects to write about in a future publication, anecdotes for the book she needed to write, or vacation spots she should consider visiting, all assumed she needed retirement guidance. Cynically, she scrolled down to the first unopened email and worked her way forward, pressing the delete button with delight. Halfway through her emails, a blood bath accumulated in the recycling bin of cyberspace. Carrie reached over, caressed her coffee mug, and smiled at the carnage. This was easier than expected, she mused. Within minutes and by the slurp of the last drop of her coffee, she reached the emails received that day. Now in an almost jovial mood, she responded to some of the latest emails. This would require more coffee. With her promise to Marie in mind, she chose to be dutiful. She'd ensure the last of the emails were answered or deleted, and then and only then would she allow herself not only another cup of coffee but two freshly baked chocolate chip cookies.

Thoroughly impressed with her logical shenanigans, she looked at the final unopened emails in all their black font glory. Not recognizing any of the senders' email addresses, she realized there were only one or two that were not spam. There was, however, one that stood out—from the hundreds of addresses she had perused this morning. The name seemed to glow, leaping off the screen to pull her eyes toward it: *Billy Daintree.* The email address was a Gmail account. Back and forth, she shifted her gaze from the email to her coffee mug, taking a sip from the long-ago empty mug and placing it absent-mindedly on the desk, only to repeat the sequence another time. The name never changed, nor did the coffee mug miraculously refill.

She convinced herself that it could not be *the* Billy Daintree—not the one from years and years ago. The possibility that he would reappear in the form of an email, a sequence of 1s and 0s pieced together in some source code, and transmitted via glass fibers to end up on some twenty-two-inch monitor, seemed too inhumane. It simply was not him. Satisfied with her conclusion of this being a strange cyber occurrence, she rose from her chair, coffee mug in hand, determined to not just refill the cup. No, three chocolate cookies would be sacrificed to the gods, and, upon her return, this aberration would disappear.

Carrie prided herself on her stubborn resolve, her instincts. By the time she reached the kitchen and raised the carafe out of the coffee machine, she realized that fooling herself would not last much longer. Sure enough, now distracted by doubt, the tepid black coffee slopped onto her bare hands. In pain, she let the mug tumble to the ground where it shattered into a handful of ceramic pieces on the gray stone kitchen floor. Angered by her own delusion, she bit down hard on her lip and focused. *Why now?* Sweeping up the broken mug and drying the floor with paper towels, she decided the smell of spilled coffee would have to suffice. And no, she did not deserve a chocolate chip cookie, let alone three.

She entered her study with purpose, the stingy pain in her hand an unnecessary distraction. Her mind began to try to connect the few dots. Dots, too far apart in time, to connect. She looked over the large burgundy cabinet, the sacred graveyard of her files. Did she keep Billy's dossier? Did she take it with her? She was not sure. Just as quickly as she moved forward to check, she stopped herself and almost threw herself back into the leather chair at the desk. The files contained antiquated information. New material awaited her only a click away. No longer did a doubt exist as to the identity of Billy Daintree. The feeling in the pit of her stomach told her it was him.

She grabbed a yellow-colored notepad from the side of her desk and a blue gel pen from the top drawer. Whatever information this email contained, she would transcribe it, word for word. Now ready, she clicked on the email, and the contents appeared before her eyes, short and sweet. There was only a paragraph.

Dear Dr. Woodson,

I hope you remember me, and I hope I have found you. You helped me a long time ago. I need your help again. If you cannot or don't want to, I understand. But, if you can, I would appreciate it.

Thanks.
Your friend, Billy Daintree

With all doubts dispelled, Carrie turned to the file cabinet. By the time she had finished reading the email, his whole dossier had flashed through her mind. She leaned forward to the screen and mouthed back the words: Your friend, Billy Daintree. Friend. She sighed and wrote Billy needs help on the notepad next to his contact information, which was simply an email address. For the first time since her last day of work, she cherished the excuse retirement gave her. It allowed her to run from the past—from the victories, defeats, and the uncertainty in between. Just as every detail of the dossier played around in her brain, her feelings toward Billy convulsed from her head down her spine. She was shocked by how much she had forgotten. With certainty, she reached for the notepad and began to crumple the paper when, at the very vista of her earshot, a key slowly turned in the front door lock. Carrie sighed and tossed the crumpled paper onto the desk. Maris was home from school.

CHAPTER 14

Friendships Do Not Retire

Carrie tolerated retirement almost solely because of Maris. She now spent more time with him and welcomed him home after school. Marie's schedule required less flexibility now. Both Carrie and Marie went to great lengths to ensure Maris was always a priority.

Carrie's attention diverted from her computer and the crumbled paper now sitting on her desk. She leaned back slightly, shifting her focus to the calamity taking place just a floor below. The swinging open of the hallway closet door and the loud thump of the backpack tossed onto the hardwood paneled floors echoed around the house. Maris's entrance required no vocal accompaniment. He was home. Carrie smiled as she vaulted out of her seat to escape her study. By the time she had reached the top of the stairwell, Maris was already pillaging the fridge.

"Maris, I saved you the last of the chocolate chip cookies over on the counter." Carrie grimaced at the lie she told. Her original intention was to have devoured all the remaining cookies and to justify it by arguing that a teenager should not have so much sugar in their diet.

"Thanks, Mom," his voice replied just above a whisper. "But I kinda thought you would have gotten to them by now. You must have had a busy day."

Smartass teenager thought Carrie. Yes, Maris was perceptive beyond his fifteen years. Too observant at times. Carrie made her way down the stairs only to stop before she'd reached the bottom. Through the archway leading to the kitchen, she studied Maris as he sat on a wooden chair, dipping a cookie in chocolate milk while reading a text message on his phone. The reality of time passing struck her. Now three years away from adulthood, no longer was he the child they had adopted several years earlier.

Carrie wondered if anyone would guess that the Maris standing in her kitchen was, upon a time, the life-weary little boy of years ago. The story of Maris began with the desire of Marie and Carrie to start a family together. When Marie had raised the idea with Carrie, Carrie feigned little interest in children, let alone adopting one of their own. Carrie was so immersed in the troubles of the children she treated that she didn't feel there was anything left in her tank when she went home at night. But for whatever reason, it all changed one day. The decision to adopt was a mere introduction to a more frustrating tale. A tale of a world gradually accepting the concept of same-sex couples adopting. Fortunately, Carrie and Marie found a supportive ally in Dr. Wes Shore and his work with Doctors Without Borders.

While performing work in the Middle East, Dr. Shore met a young boy who he estimated to be around five years old. The boy had wandered into a Red Cross refugee camp, malnourished and wearing worn sneakers, tattered shorts, and dirt-covered T-shirt. He did not speak, and no one cared to listen to his story just yet. The primary goal was saving the child. Once his strength returned, the boy described a life too typical of many. His village was caught in the crossfire of a fight between rebel and government forces. One night, his parents told him to hide in the nearby woods and if he heard gunfire to keep running as far as possible and not turn back. He did. His interviewers surmised that the boy had traveled at least ten to fifteen miles of rugged terrain before crossing a border and stumbling into the camp. The sounds of aircraft fire and screams were the last sounds of his village. The black-haired, coal-eyed boy called himself Maris.

Dr. Shore treated Maris's cuts and bruises from the days and nights spent wandering. He surmised the child had survived by eating berries and drinking stream water along the way. How he'd maneuvered through the thick brush was a mystery to Dr. Shore, who was a skilled hiker and amateur survivalist in his own right. While Maris spoke English, he spoke very little about the world and parents he left behind. After telling the story of his journey, he stopped talking altogether, as though the nourishment they now gave him had recharged the projector and played back the horror movie. Eventually, Dr. Shore determined that they had destroyed the nearest villages with no survivors left behind. Once Maris was treated physically, Dr. Shore knew the easy task was over. The more laborious task lay ahead. But he remembered a doctor he'd met years ago as a resident, a brilliant if somewhat arrogant psychologist who specialized in pediatric cases—Dr. Woodson. Yes, she could help.

Though he had treated hundreds of people, including children, throughout his journeys to war-torn regions, Dr. Shore sensed there was something special about Maris. One day, he pulled out a local map and ran his fingers over the path Maris had taken. The survival instinct thrived in this child. He would, at a minimum, place a call on his behalf.

Carrie closed her eyes and with vivid detail, recalled her first encounter with Maris. Within seconds, adoption became the only option. He needed her in his life. Marie was an easy sell. While the hoops and hurdles of any adoption are enough to shatter the hearts of most, Carrie Woodson was stubborn. Marie was a noted neurologist while Carrie was a reputable psychologist—they were the perfect parents for an emotionally scarred young boy. The adoption authorities agreed, and by the time Maris had turned seven, he was living with Marie and Carrie.

Despite all of Carrie's experience and research, the puzzle of Maris proved to be the most complex one. While well behaved, the almost eerie silence of his existence worried them. He communicated only on a need-to-know basis. In school, he displayed a strong academic work ethic but was socially distant from his classmates. Carrie would listen at his bedroom door for nights on end, waiting to pounce on any signs of nightmares that never came. The boy did no more nor less than just survive.

Carrie broke down at the kitchen table one late night, long after Maris had gone to sleep. Tears and Carrie Woodson were not acquaintances by anyone's definition. Marie heard the muffled sobs as she retrieved her milk from the microwave.

"Carrie! Are you worried about Maris?"

"Of course I am, Marie. My training should guide me. With all my experience, I should be able to connect with him. Crap."

"Carrie, you are the best at what you do. I've seen it with my own eyes, sweetie. It's what I love about you."

"Marie, I wish I could just cut him open and fix him." Carrie paused, playing back her words. "I did not mean it that way."

"Yes, you did. Just because I can cut people open does not mean I'm fixing everything for them. It's only the physical part. What you do is so much more. I acknowledge that," said Marie, smiling. "No, I am not mad. I get used to it." She smirked and brought her mug to the table. "It's possible we're going about this all wrong."

"What are you suggesting, oh, wise one?" Carrie said, struggling to smile back.

"We are both doctors."

"Yeah. I get that. I saw the diplomas in the den."

"Play along, Carrie. Play along."

"Sure. I'm not following, though. Yes, we're doctors. So?"

"Just suppose Maris doesn't need a doctor. Let's consider this as *parents* would."

"Shit, Marie. Now you're creeping me out. When did you become smarter than me?" She leaned over and kissed Marie on the cheek. "Now that you're so smart, you can take over my practice and make some real money." She started to laugh at her own joke.

That's when Carrie began to act less like a doctor and more like a parent. It was near his tenth birthday, and she'd brought him in for his dental exam. While waiting, Carrie noticed Maris's eyes studying a coffee table littered with children's books. She reached over and, one by one, offered them to Maris to read. The god, unhappy with the sacrifices offered him, became restless. Maris reached over to the table, brushing his mom's hand aside, and grabbed a thin, colorful-looking magazine from beneath the stack of books that hid it from view.

"Maris, that's a comic book."

"That's what I want to look at." Maris pulled the book out, rearranged himself in the hard, unforgiving plastic chair, and read. Never did his eyes stray. Carrie marveled at the hold this book had on him. She wondered if it was all an act—until she saw his face light up in a smile that lit the planet. *Who would have thought?*

Neither Carrie nor Marie questioned Maris's taste in books. Carrie's childhood was characterized by a brief obsession with *Archie* comics. Besides her conviction that Jughead would have been a dream patient, she never gave them a second thought, ever. If she did, she would have wondered why the understandable coupling of Betty and Veronica never occurred. To judge Maris's reading material would not be fair because of the significant turnaround in his behavior.

Marie and Carrie's son glowed with a bright light they had scarcely seen before. Soon enough, the local comic store visit became a regular family excursion. Carrie and Marie would drop Maris off with an allowance while they shopped in the mall nearby and returned to find him with two or three books in hand. Maris never looked back. He found his childhood bliss and outlet. His grades, ever steady though unspectacular, took off. Maris' smile became a portal to the wise and witty young child's heart.

Today, the smile remained concealed by a jealous frown intent to take possession of his face for good. The hazard lights blinking around Maris's aura were visible only to the ever-observing and doting mother that was Carrie. Maris tried to sneak through the kitchen, grab a glass of milk, and scurry to his room without an interrogation, but Carrie cut off his path at the stairwell leading to his bedroom. While Maris's hiding in his bedroom after school would not be out of the ordinary, today everything was amiss, and Carrie noticed the evidence.

"Running off to your room without your phone and iPad? This is serious!" Carrie feigned a laugh, hoping to lighten the mood. "Maris, is everything okay? Did something happen at school today?"

Maris focused on the ground until he reached the base of the stairs. Carrie stood perched like a vulture three steps up, blocking his path. He scratched his hair behind his right ear and gave a heavy sigh. "Oh, Mom. It's nothing you would understand."

Carrie Woodson and not understand in the same sentence! This was getting serious. Maris grew unnerved, seeing his mom's face burst with expression and turn the color of a ripe tomato. "Uh, shit," mumbled Maris, realizing his indiscretion and how his mom's brown eyes would morph into interrogation lamps.

"Maris, is it a girl? A grade?" Carrie started through the list of reasons, studying her son for a response.

"No, Mom. Nothing like that. Worse. Pretty crappy, the more I think about it."

"I can see that. You left all your electronics on the table. What were you planning to do in your room, anyway?"

"I decided to go off the grid for a bit, Mom. I just need some quiet time."

Quiet time? The kid is fifteen. When did fifteen-year-olds need quiet time? Carrie knew this was getting serious. Marie's return was two hours away, and Carrie sought resolution before Marie played the hero. She wanted this victory as she tried to look like she understood when, in fact, words were failing her. Her brain replayed Maris's words and became more confused. "Off the grid?"

"Yeah, Mom. Off the grid. Nothing but bad news today on the grid."

"Grid, huh? That means?"

"Social media, Mom. The internet. All the stuff you hate and ignore."

"Oh, yes, that grid. I still don't understand, though. Did something bad happen?"

"Bad? The worst, Mom. The worst. He's ending it. The main character is being killed off. It's over."

"Killed off? You mean on a television show?"

"No, Mom, my favorite comic book is ending. The next issue will be the last. It was all over the chat rooms today."

"That's what's bothering you? I mean, how certain are you?"

"Clues littered the last few issues. Dedicated fans pieced it all together. Besides, it's so obvious for us serious followers."

"Oh, I'm sorry. But there are other books, right?"

"It won't be the same, Mom. This was the best one. I've read every single one in the series."

Carrie saw Maris's lower lip tremble as he spoke. It didn't matter whether she knew what he was talking about, her son needed a hug, so she let her instincts take over. She stepped down the stairs to his level and ran her hand through his hair and kissed him on the forehead. "If you want to talk about it, I am always here," she said, winking at him.

"Thanks, Mom. I just need to lie down and read some older issues."

"Sure, go ahead, but as soon as Marie gets home, we'll have a nice supper." Carrie moved to allow Maris to pass. A man walking towards the gallows would have marched at a quicker pace. Carrie went through her laundry list of potential teenage boy issues and sighed. A comic book series ending, of all things. Oh, well, it could be a lot worse, she deduced. *Off the grid.* She committed that one to memory for future use.

When Maris reached the top of the stairs, he turned back to her. "Mom, just so you understand. I'm going through what it must have been like for you when Elvis died. I assume you were bummed when you got the news."

"Elvis? Um, Maris, I'm not that old. Elvis was in white jumpsuits by the time I started high school." Carrie, clearly flustered, hadn't noticed the widening grin on Maris's face.

"You take things too personally. I was just teasing."

Carrie shook her head and hollered back as Maris hurried his pace to avoid the retaliatory strike coming. "If you said John Lennon, maybe. Just maybe." Before the last syllable passed her lips, Carrie made her way back to the kitchen. Now she deserved those cookies. All three of them.

Suppertime shaped up to be more eventful than usual. Carrie's diminished appetite, fresh off her late afternoon cookie binge, did not deter her enthusiasm for mealtime. There were lots to discuss. In recent weeks, Marie's work had been the centerpiece of the mealtime discussion. Often Marie would arrive just before seven, first listening to Maris's recounting of his exploits in school, followed by Carrie's listing of grievances. Individually, each complaint represented a nuisance. Taken together, they were great annoyances. While Marie appreciated Carrie's now regular presence at supper, as well as her desire to prepare healthy homemade meals, Marie noticed how soon into retirement, Carrie's power of observation annoyed her. On a good day, Carrie's complaint would be about the mailman not passing by until after 4:00 p.m. instead of the usual 1:00 p.m. On a bad day, it might be about the landscaper missing a strip of grass with his mower. Today, both Maris and Carrie seemed preoccupied.

"My two most favorite people in the world are both strangely silent tonight," Marie quipped as she put down her fork to the side of her dish.

Maris and Carrie looked at each other. While Carrie longed for Marie's advice about her mysterious email, she remained silent to allow Maris an opportunity to vent. Carrie caught Marie's glance, and in an instant, the parental conspiracy was in motion. Marie shifted in her chair to face Maris. "So, sweetie, anything new at school?"

Maris frowned, realizing that if he said nothing, Carrie's sugar high would kick in, and she would babble on about comic strips. "Just learned my favorite comic book will release its final edition soon."

Marie looked over to Carrie, who nodded back, allowing her to continue the line of questioning. "How do you feel about that? It sounds upsetting."

"Yeah. I guess it depends on how he ends the series. It's the first one I got into."

"Well, I suppose it must frustrate you, but these things happen often. So many times, my favorite show or book series ended. The next cool obsession eventually took root. You can always reread the older ones when you miss it."

"Yeah. I will. Thanks." Maris smiled as Marie rubbed the back of his hand.

"Now, my dear Carrie, what has you so quiet and pensive?" Marie smirked.

"I'll tell you later. It wouldn't interest Maris."

Maris rose from the table to bring his dish to the dishwasher. "Can I go now? I'd like to go to my room and finish my homework." As he walked by Marie, he whispered with an intonation meant for Carrie. "Be careful if you bring up Elvis. She's kind of touchy about him."

"I am not that old, young man," Carrie protested to the retreating Maris.

Marie laughed and reached out to tug at Carrie's hands. "No, you are not that old."

"Hey, you're only a few years younger than me."

"But, I'm not retired." Marie sensed the glare from Carrie and added, "You strike me as preoccupied."

Carrie picked up a napkin and dabbed her lips with fervor. Her eyes followed Maris up the stairs and flipped the serviette onto her dish when his door shut with a thud. "Oh, I hope he's all right."

"He seems a little preoccupied, but it goes with the territory, doesn't it? I trust your judgment, so if you're concerned about it, I should be, too."

"He just seemed set off by some comic book series ending. He was despondent when he got home." Carrie sighed and then shook her head. "I'm overly sensitive. Too much going on in one day."

"Just recently, you complained about boredom. Your world became interesting today, from what I gather."

"Damn me for checking my emails. I knew I should just press Delete on the lot of them."

"Must be in the thousands, seeing how popular you are."

"Hilarious. I got an email today from someone who I haven't been in contact with for years."

"An old patient?"

"Patient… I prefer the term old friend."

"Now, you have my full attention." Marie pushed her plate forward and leaned toward Carrie with both elbows on the table. Her slender, elongated fingers tapped the embroidered table cloth nervously.

"Billy Daintree. I'm not sure if you remember him."

"Well, I recall a student you treated, ages ago, that you told me about."

"I forgot you had a terrific memory."

"If I'm correct, this one troubled you. Remind me."

"I never consider him a patient. He needed a friend above all else, not a doctor."

"How did it leave off with him?"

"I had to sign off on him. Move him on. They wouldn't give me more sessions with him. Bastards. They needed a decision that they made anyway."

"He went on his way, didn't he?"

"Sort of. If you call banishment and exile a happy ending for a brilliant student."

Marie frowned, rose from her seat, and moved around the dining room table to sit on the chair next to Carrie, pulling it close to her. "From what you explained, you treated him under bizarre circumstances. There was a professional risk. Your neck went way out there."

Carrie smiled and clamped down on her lower lip. Her brown eyes watered. "His story was incomplete. We played a game around a lie, and I put some pretty bows on the final product. That's the frustrating part. The truth was far denser in texture and complexity. The clock ran out before I could conclude."

"Carrie, sometimes you have to throw in the cards when your hand is not a winning one."

"Or when dealing against a stacked deck."

"Right. Now tell me, why did he email you?"

"All he asked for is my help. He said he needed my help."

"So?

"My first reaction was to delete the email and unplug the bloody computer. A good plan would be tossing it from the window."

"Let's go to your rational decision."

"Respond by email and tell him I'm retired."

"Wow. Progress. I take it the rational decision is difficult to digest."

"It keeps coming up on me. I remember how frustrated I was the first time I worked with Billy. Maris is not far off—I'm too old for this nonsense. It may be hard to digest, but I need to. I'm retired, whether I like it. When Maris came home, the choice was obvious."

"If you find an email to be very impersonal, may I boldly suggest something?"

"Sure. I married you for a reason, apart from your surgical skills."

"Speak to him face to face and offer him a referral. There must be an ex-colleague you respect?" Marie laughed.

"Now you're pushing it. I don't have the foggiest where he lives. Are you suggesting I meet him someplace?"

"No, just use technology. FaceTime, or Skype. Besides, I'm sure you're curious to discover what happened to him. You have files on everyone you ever met. I never doubt you care."

"FaceTime?"

"Maris can hook you up." Marie brushed Carrie's graying hair behind her ears and kissed her on the forehead. "I'm sure he'll appreciate the referral. Perhaps it's nothing at all."

"Nonsense. Even nothing is everything when it comes to my work."

Marie looked at Carrie. "Friendships do not end with retirement."

Carrie closed her eyes and then winked at Marie. "Yes, my old friend Billy Daintree." Carrie chose not to tell Marie any more about Billy. The stillness of his deep waters was capable of drowning the best swimmers or provoking a maverick psychologist to risk her career. Her heart longed for the truth, once and for all. With Marie and Maris in her life, the story of Billy Daintree would need to remain an incomplete tale in the handwritten notes filed away in her storage cabinet. Or so she thought. The truth, like a teenager, is often rebellious and arrives unannounced.

CHAPTER 15

Aeon, the Composer

Saturday morning coffee tasted different. Not that the coffee beans were ground uniquely, or that they used an unusual blend. Saturday marked a time of rest for Carrie Woodson—or at least it did when the rest of her week was defined by patient visits, lectures, meetings, or just plain old administrative work. Now every day became Saturday in Carrie's new world, the rest of her life. The end of her career ended the uniqueness of Saturdays, and the coffee would now taste like it did on all the other days of the week. But today, Saturday's coffee would be memorable. With the first cup from a freshly brewed pot perched within arm's length on her desk, Carrie waited for the call and the temporary return of Billy Daintree into her life.

With the willing aid of Marie, Carrie had crafted a straightforward response to Billy's email. Given that Marie was a master at probing and communicating, Carrie requested her methodical and frosty to-the-point skills. To exorcise Billy from her world, she needed the wordsmith skill of a surgeon. Marie's reply to Billy said no more and no less than it needed to. After highlighting her retirement, she requested that he

FaceTime with her on Saturday between 10:00 a.m. and 11:00 a.m. Carrie then would provide a referral to Billy. A shortlist of ex-colleagues, with phone numbers, and email addresses were scribbled on a note pad next to her laptop. The only reply from Billy was a curt, "Fine."

While Carrie expressed an interest not to get involved, it was more than curiosity which motivated Carrie. Marie was sure of it. The layered exterior of Carrie's persona did not fool Marie. Carrie Woodson had a vast but well-concealed heart. Marie knew Carrie wanted to see Billy face to face to satisfy herself that he did not need her help, and before she pawned him off to another person without regret.

Carrie tapped her fingers on the desk, the clicking sound of nails on wood taking on a rhythmic beat. The brilliant part of setting up a call on a weekend was Maris' availability just down the hall. Maris was not only her child, but he was also her own personal information technology support department. It was Maris who set up Carrie's computer with FaceTime, spending over an hour testing the setup to proof it from the clumsy fingers of the technology-challenged Carrie.

While waiting, Carrie's thoughts meandered to the absurdity of now treating patients over the internet. She quivered at the thought of data transmitted in one form to re-emerge on a two-dimensional screen. Cyberspace was pure spookiness to Carrie. A vast, undefinable entity filled with data. No one in space can hear you scream, but what about in cyberspace? Can 1s and 0s scream? What if cyberspace data had emotions—real emotions? *Oh, brother,* Carrie thought to herself as she emerged from her daydream, *now I'm tripping.* Perhaps the Saturday coffee had mystical powers.

Her eyes, now shuttered, flew open to the *Peanuts'* themed ringtone, signaling an incoming call on her computer. Right on time. She scrambled for her notebook, scanning her talking notes. Taking heed of Marie's advice, she would keep this short and sweet. With the flurry of activity in arranging her desk, she forgot to answer. Clumsily, she tapped on the phone icon to answer the call, noting the first three digits of the area code. The caller was also from New York.

"Hello, Billy. Billy Daintree, is that you?" Carrie spoke to the screen before her. An image cut in and soon disappeared, reverting to the azure screen. The sole response was a mysterious, muffled voice. A screen image emerged long enough to intrigue, puzzle, and frighten Carrie. The image she saw was of a disheveled, thickly bearded man with a gaunt, grayish-toned face. The discoloration under his charcoal-colored eyes was worrisome. His hair appeared thinning, protruding from a ragged royal blue baseball cap. While it had been years since she last saw Billy, she stared in perplexed horror, obsessed with the man on the screen. The years had been unkind to him. If his mental state approximated his physical, she wondered if she had chosen the right referral for him. He may have genuinely needed help all those years ago. Perhaps she had been entirely wrong in her assessment. She might have been lazy.

A voice, now perceptible, spoke directly to her. "Excuse me, the problem is on your end. Hello? The problem is on your end." Like the image, the voice sounded dire, hoarse, and gasping for air between syllables.

"Oh. I see. I'll try to fix it." Carrie spoke to the inanimate screen apologetically. A wise move to arrange a call on Saturday. Maris was close by. "Please be patient. I have a computer guru at my disposal. Just let me get him." Within seconds, Carrie raced out of her office and was down the hall at the entrance to Maris's room. Prepared to knock, she discovered the door wide open with him sitting upon his bed, frowning at her. "You were expecting me, weren't you?"

He slid off the bed and moved toward her. His bare feet dragged across the room. His pajamas hung loosely on him. He wiped his eyes and yawned. Carrie had forgotten that Saturday was Maris's one sleep-in morning. Even 10:00 a.m. qualified as early for him. "Yeah, Mom. I kind of figured you needed me, so I set my alarm for ten. Computer issue?"

"Yes. Please have a look. Someone just called. I got the audio figured out but only have a blank screen."

"Sure. It happened to me all the time… when I was nine."

"Smartass," Carrie whispered under her breath, ruffling his hair as he streaked by her.

A yawning Maris sat at her desk, and within a handful of keystrokes, an image appeared on the screen. Maris seemed uninterested in the picture that had spooked her and went about his business. "Can you hear me? Can you see me?" he asked the screen.

The figure on the other end, recoiled slightly, startled by the sudden activity. "Sorry. Like, dude. You freaked me for a second." The character lowered his head down, nodded to himself, and responded, "All good on this end. Thanks, kid."

"Oh, good," Maris smirked and joggled his head. Adults never ceased to amaze him. *Like, dude* and *freaked*? This guy needed his mom's help. Maris winked at his mom. She motioned with her hand for him to stick around for a minute. Maris moved to stand behind her chair as she slid back into her seat. "Don't worry. I'll wait here for a minute." Maris said.

Carrie typically would have pushed Maris out the door. Her work and family life were sacredly separate. However, given the circumstances, his presence reassured her. Besides, the face and voice coming at her were unsettling. Carrie's eyes shifted to her notepad. "Uh, Billy?" Something was off. The image teased her, demanding scrutiny. When she last saw Billy Daintree, he had thick, wavy brown hair. Introverted by nature, he nevertheless had an awkward handsomeness. When not smiling, Billy appeared severe, cold, and distant, as if his mind was off in a faraway place, leaving a facade behind. When smiling, Billy illuminated the universe. Even for a college student, he appeared young. He had the perpetual look of youth. That's what she expected to see when the image initially appeared. Instead, she saw a world-weary face before her. "Billy, are you all right?"

The face staring back at her recoiled and trembled. "No. I mean this—" The voice cut off as his head swiveled and spoke to an entity off camera. There was someone else in the room with him, she realized.

Carrie struggled to remain attentive. Her eyes stared at the file cabinet. She looked at the credenza holding the file with her notes from her time with Billy. Her folly was in not seeking those files before this call. How unprepared she was for this. She moved closer to the monitor, almost as if she tried to climb through it to the other side. "Billy? Billy?" Awaiting a reply, a pair of hands came into view over the shoulders of the man seated, patting them. Almost inaudible were the words, "I can handle this. Thanks so much. You don't have to stay." The figure on the screen vanished like a ghostly apparition, a supporting cast member in a show who, after reading their lines, needed to return backstage. In his place, appearing on the screen, was a younger-looking man with uncombed brown hair, noticeable subtle, and light brown eyes. The person wore a gray sweater with blue sleeves. Their face bore a hint of wrinkles and a solid dose of fatigue with lips lined up tight together before parting slightly. "Sorry, Doc. I had technical problems. My buddy helped me." An uncertain smile escaped. In an instant, Carrie knew. This was beyond doubt her Billy Daintree.

Carrie paused, letting the relief swim through her body. Instinctively, she retreated to her notepad. Her maternal instinct overcame her upon seeing Billy. She wanted to find the answers to the million questions she had. Billy looked fatigued and tired beyond the mere years. She sensed tiredness eating at him from within, not measured by wrinkles on a face or the shading under his eyes. A gut instinct. "Billy, I'm delighted to speak to you." Before he answered or offered further pleasantries, cold practicality took over. "You said you may need my help, but I'm retired now. I have someone I can refer you to."

Billy tilted his head, listening to Carrie. His mouth opened enough to flash his overbite before closing again. He bit down on his lips. "Carrie… please. It needs to be you in person. I understand I'm asking a lot."

"Since I'm retired now, it's best I not get involved. I promised my family. I have a son now." Carrie shocked herself by using her personal life as an excuse. The notepad slid to the outer edge of the desk, dismissed by her.

"Oh. I knew I shouldn't have. You're right. I shouldn't be bothering you—now, especially. I am so sorry." Billy's eyes blinked and were mere slits appearing to stare into an abyss.

A million more questions race to her mind. However, the exit from all this stood achingly close by. "I have some excellent referrals. Good people. Some I mentored myself."

Billy's eyes blinked while his hands fidgeted. "Sure, um, yeah. I guess just email them to me, please." His lips remained pressed forcefully together. The smile hid in a faraway place.

The coldness depressed her. Her voice responded on impulse. "I will do just that." With her index figure sliding the cursor over the orange icon of a phone, she prepared to click Billy Daintree out of her world, needing only to say the cursory "Bye" and "Take care" or perhaps "It was nice speaking to you." She came *that* close to moving on. However, festering inquisitiveness itched intensely. One question escaped: "Billy, are you in any trouble?"

Billy's oval face, punctuated by a pointed chin, inched closer to the screen. An aura of fatigue cast a shadow upon the once eternally youthful visage. Stubble, thick and uneven, cloaked his pale skin. "No, I wouldn't say I'm being expelled this time. I… well, I would appreciate the referral. Let's leave it at that." Carrie failed to understand why he appeared distracted until he continued. "Hi, young man." Briefly, flashing a smile, he waved, but not at Carrie. Confused, Carrie realized she had not been alone in her office. Maris stood patiently and quietly behind her.

"Oh, goodness. I am so rude." Carrie had ignored Maris. "This young man behind me is Maris. He's my son."

Billy smiled, and for an instant Carrie traveled back in time. "Hi, Maris. I'm Billy. Your mom is, well, exceptional."

There was no response. Carrie turned to find Maris towering over her shoulder with his mouth ajar, with an awkward expression, almost one of shock. Carrie nudged Maris, who waved at the screen. "Hi." He moved forward, nearly toppling over the back of the leather chair into his mother's lap. Carrie turned back to Billy. "Please, Billy, take care of yourself. I will forward those references to you."

"Thanks and… well."

"Well, what?"

"Nothing, I just remembered something you once told me about dreams. There is more to them." He winked with his teeth biting down on his lower lips, "Goodbye."

Before Carrie responded, the image disappeared as the screen flickered before turning pale sapphire. "Bye," she said to the blankness before her, pondering Billy's cryptic words. Maris shook her out of her stupor with his hands, one over each of her shoulders.

"Mom, how do you know him? It's *him*. Can you call him back?"

"Maris, that was Billy. A friend of mine from years ago. Why?"

"That is not Billy, Mom. C'mon, seriously, don't you get it? Are you messing with me?"

"Maris, what are you talking about?" By now, Maris had made his way around his mom's desk to face her. His feet shuffled sideways erratically, almost staggering.

"Oh my God, Mom. That was Aeon, the Composer. Aeon!"

"Relax, Maris." Carrie pushed back her chair. The emotional outburst and Maris's agitation unnerved her. "His name is Billy. That I am positive of."

"No. *No.* Aeon. Of all people. Aeon. That was him! You hung up on him! I am freaking out. I could have convinced him." Maris dashed out of the room, shaking his head incredulously before retreating to his quarters, punctuating his actions by closing his door.

Carrie stared down the hallway. Who the hell was Aeon? *Convince him of what?* Coffee would have to wait. Her eyes diverted back to the screen as if hoping for Billy to have returned. Since waiting was futile, she adjusted her slippers securely and marched down the hall to find Maris on his hands and knees with comic books strewn on the floor surrounding him.

"Maris, who is this Aeon, and what is going on?"

Maris looked up at his mother. His green eyes opened wide, his head tilted to the side as if pondering a difficult riddle. "You honestly don't grasp who that was!"

"That was Billy Daintree."

"Oh, Mom. Why were you speaking to him?"

"Look, Maris, it's an adult thing."

"Adult thing? Now I'm buzzing. Like, why was *he* speaking to you?"

"He needed my help, but I should not say anymore."

"Mom, you said he was a friend, not a patient, right?"

"Um, it's complicated, Maris. I haven't spoken to him in years. I don't have the faintest clue what he wanted, but I'm giving him the names of people who can assist him."

"He needed help. You don't understand."

"Look, Maris. Yes, he needed help. However, I am lost, so please be patient with me. What is all this about? Who is this Aeon?"

"Mom, it's *Aeon, the Composer*. The guy who created all this." Maris raised his hand and gestured toward all the comic books scattered before him.

Meanwhile, Billy Daintree began to hum before singing to the now faceless monitor. He sang a verse from "Flagpole Sitta." Neither was he sick nor well. He feared his dreams if he slept, so he sang to stay awake.

CHAPTER 16

Time's Musicians

Maris looked at Carrie with sad puppy eyes reserved for those moments when he badly needed to win an upcoming battle in the unending teenager versus parent war. His demeanor bore the burden of confusion. Carrie found room on the hardwood floor, choosing a spot free of the comic books.

"Maris, tell me, who is Aeon?"

The blacktopped head tilted to one side. Eyes rolled. *Time to educate the grown-up.* Carrie sensed that her question appeared absurd to him. "I meant to ask, why do you think Billy is Aeon?"

"Because he is. I'm sure."

"Well, I suppose that's progress. Sorry, sweetheart, I just don't understand. You will have to explain this. Step by step. I'm a little slow now with my age." Carrie winked.

"Aeon is the main character in the comic book. His name is Aeon, the Composer."

"I never was much of a comic book person. Besides *Archie* comics now and again. So, Aeon cannot be a real person then, right?"

Maris smiled at long last. "Of course not."

"So, how might Billy be a comic book character?"

"He is the *creator* of the comic book, Mom." Maris studied his mother's reaction. Now more confused, she bent down and rested her weight on her knees. "I'll show you." He leaned forward and handed her the closest comic book within reach. The cover art exploded with shades of blue and black blended together. The title was in bold: *Time's Musicians*. Carrie skimmed the pages looking for the credits. She did not find any. At the lower right-hand corner, the following words lay hidden in smaller type: "From the Mind of Aeon, the Composer." Any information about the author's identity was missing.

"I don't see any credits. Normally, they list the creator, designer, artist—"

"It's done on purpose. There's a number in the corner that tells you the book's series number."

"I see, but it doesn't seem a great way to sell a lot of copies. How did you discover this particular comic book?"

"Through social media. Someone posted stuff giving props to this cool new series, and the hype got around. There's a website, too."

"What's the connection between this Aeon character and…"

"Billy?"

"Without creator or publisher information, the connection eludes me."

"There is online. In one of the chat rooms, someone posted a picture of him." Maris spoke as though the answer was abundantly clear. "I'll show you. Hang on."

"Oh, honey, I am not moving from my spot."

Maris raced to his desk and returned with his tablet, typing as he walked toward his mother. Within seconds, he had found what he searched for. He clicked on a link, and a picture appeared on the screen. After examining it himself, he grinned and handed the tablet to his mother. "This is definitely that Billy dude."

With the tablet held at arm's length, Carrie's eyes widened with each passing second. The image was of a man wearing a black baseball cap, appearing to sign something. His grin gave away his identity: Billy Daintree. A caption under the picture confirmed it.

Comic Universe's annual convention was honored with the rare appearance of the reclusive creative mind behind the cult comic book sensation entitled "Time's Musicians." Above, the young creator is pictured signing autographs for his adoring and loyal fans.

"See, Mom. That *is* Billy. Right?"

"It appears to be."

"The forum I follow just calls him Aeon after the main character."

"How many comic books exist in this series?"

"He does about ten a year. He is up to twenty-nine now. But the thirtieth will be the last. I cannot believe it. Like, I should have asked him. Is this why he needs your help, Mom? Is he ending the series because he has a problem you can only solve?"

Carrie's brows furrowed. Rambling was rare for Maris and caught Carrie off guard. She placed her fingertips together and pressed them to her nose in a triangular shape. Satisfied she'd assembled enough information, she shuddered. "This is *the* comic book. The one that has you all upset."

"I thought you knew already."

"How positive are you that thirty is the last one?"

"It's all over the place online. Aeon, the Composer, will be defeated in the last episode. That means he'll die, and it will be over."

"Die?" Carrie inhaled and held her breath as she thought. She looked at her son and noticed his unhappiness. "Maris, is this Aeon a good guy? Like Superman, for example, fighting evil."

"He is the ultimate good guy. Not strong like Superman, though."

"You're sure he will be defeated—that he's going to die?"

"The chat I follow is never wrong, Mom. In the last episode, Aeon had a premonition about succumbing to the forces he's been fighting." Maris stared as his mother rose, almost not listening to him. She struggled to contain her heartbeat, which vibrated into the spinning vortex of her brain. "Mom. He asked for your help, didn't he?"

"Yes, he did."

"You're going to get someone to help him? The best person you can find, right?" He pleaded with her in a childlike voice.

"Oh, he will get the best doctor. Gray hairs and all. Wrinkles, too."

"Mom! Are you serious? Don't mess with me."

Carrie smirked and reached out her hands, offering Maris a lift, yanking him toward her, and hugging him. "How did you guess?"

"Gray hairs and wrinkles! Who else could it be?" He winked at her. "Besides, the best has to be you, doesn't it?"

"I suppose you understand me too well, young man." Carrie

laughed. Reality gradually sunk in. This whole bit of retirement became tricky. She leapfrogged that issue with the logic that a friend needing help was nothing to scoff at.

Marie returned from her journey to the grocery store, expecting to find Maris in his room, either reading or with headphones while Carrie sipped coffee while perusing a periodical on the back deck. Instead, both waited for her in the entrance, dutifully grabbing the groceries out of her hand before stocking the cupboards and fridge. The bounce in Carrie's step and the energy in her movements caused Marie's suspicions to grow. A good tale surely awaited her. Reminded of the scheduled call with Billy, Marie assumed Carrie dispatched him. The ever logical and methodical Marie misread the buoyant enthusiasm of Carrie and Maris.

Although not entirely understanding the relationship between some Aeon character and Billy, Marie took pleasure in the vigor and enthusiasm emanating from Carrie as she spoke and saw the gleam back in her brown eyes. After reassuring Maris that Carrie would aid Billy, Maris returned to his room.

Once safely out of earshot, Marie pulled out a kitchen chair and positioned herself facing Carrie. "Let me see if I can connect these dots. This person, who you helped years ago, reached out to you. He's also the creator of this comic book series Maris adores that's about to end—the one he's so bummed out about."

"Well, that's about three hundred out of the five thousand pieces of this puzzle. Trust me. That's all I have figured out so far."

Marie reached out and grabbed Carrie by the hand. "You are not just doing this for Maris, are you?"

A rosy hue appeared on Carrie's cheek. "My dearest Marie. I often have said you need to quit the cut-and-paste world of surgery. A bright future awaits in my world."

"My question is awaiting an answer. You spoke to Billy. Now, you *do* want to get involved?"

"Marie, he looked so tired from what I saw… and sad. Now with this comic book thing—the main character, a do-gooder, faces doom. It seems connected, and I'm worried now."

"I can tell you are. What do you want to do?"

"He lives somewhere in New York City. I must go for a few days. Our former nanny has availability this week when you are working."

"Carrie, I can take vacation time. You've done it many times for me when I had emergencies."

"No, Marie. Patients depend on you. Anyway, she already confirmed."

"That is good. Look, I never pried too much into your work, Carrie. What is it about this Billy character? I can sense something bothers you."

Carrie paced to the sink and emptied her coffee mug before rinsing it in cold water. She returned to the kitchen table and pulled out a chair on the opposite side of Marie. "It's what I've always been missing, Marie. I never got the truth from him. They didn't want to give me the time, nor did I want him to be a martyr. He was a kid hiding the truth."

"I'm just worried, Carrie. What if you were wrong then? This may be dangerous for you."

"If I'm right, I'm worried I may not be able to assist him after all these years."

"Did you not consider him a friend rather than a patient?"

"Yes."

"Then, it's simple." Carrie smiled as Marie leaned over and kissed her on her forehead. "Besides, you're the best, anyway."

Carrie laughed before excusing herself to pack. As she prepared lunch, Marie heard the flurry of activities up above in Carrie's office. Cabinets opened with reckless abandon as footsteps were audible scurrying about, including the heavy sound of teenage steps that echoed down the stairs and rushed into the kitchen.

"So Mom is planning Aeon's rescue?"

"Yes, she is, dear."

"I'm thrilled. Besides, it will keep her busy."

Marie spun to capture the pleased look on Maris's face. "Yes, I agree with you." She turned and opened the curtains above the sink. Her head shifted from side to side as she extended her torso over the sink and pressed her face close up to the window.

"What are you looking at?" Maris wondered.

Marie reclined back on her heels while shaking her head in disbelief. "I am so disappointed in myself I did not see it sooner."

"What?" Maris, now immersed in Marie's drama, moved toward her and peered out the window in the direction she faced. "I see nothing other than the sun."

Marie placed her right hand upon Maris's shoulder. "Look carefully, Maris. If you observe close enough, you can see the Bat-signal way off on the horizon. It's kind of hard to see because of the daylight. What else could it be but the Bat-signal?" Just as she spoke, Carrie emerged at the bottom of the stairs with an oversized backpack in tow.

Maris smiled. "Oh, now I get it."

Marie laughed and caressed Maris's cheek. "I may not read many comic books, but I recognize a superhero when I see one."

Nestled in Carrie's backpack were her notes from her encounters with Billy and the nondescript Duo-Tang that she had placed with reverence on her bookshelf upon retiring. Her meetings with Billy happened a decade ago, but her mind easily retrieved the memories.

CHAPTER 17

All Musician's Welcome

The silence surrounded him. Billy ended his impromptu singing to languish in it. The screen flickered sporadically. Despite the graying hair and the creases forging a path from the outskirts of her eyes to her temples, Carrie Woodson remained unchanged by the years. Billy briefly had comfort and hope. This was a Hail Mary pass, a last-ditch effort to find an ally and build a trench around his modest fortress. His stomach gurgled with uneasiness. He regretted sending off Riley, the man who helped him with his technology issues. Though he wasn't expecting any heroic actions from Carrie, he nevertheless felt a tinge of disappointment when she only offered a referral.

The footsteps in the hall caught his attention. Paper-thin walls did not shelter him from much noise, but the steps were louder than usual. Riley had not closed the door shut. Billy shuffled his feet, peaking outside into the hallway and searching right and left before shutting the door. Billy leaned against the wall, worried. Should he have let Riley go? So caught up in his intrigue, Billy clenched his fists feeling he should have given Riley his attention, especially after getting his assistance.

Hopefully, Riley would be fine. Billy's eliciting Riley's technical support on the call with Carrie was merely a ruse. He wanted Riley to feel useful again. In truth, he needed Riley—the friend, not the recovering addict.

A faint red light flickered on the kitchen table. A magazine covered Billy's smartphone, yet the beacon of an incoming text message still caught his attention. It could have been anyone texting Billy, but he knew it was not *anyone*. He ignored the light and repositioned the magazine to better suppress it. The attempt would eventually be futile. Billy needed time to get his thoughts together. He surveyed his apartment in all its unpretentious splendor. The polite word to use was cozy. It served his purpose. Billy walked over to his favorite refuge in the studio apartment, the window frame and its sill, which provided ample space for him to sit. He referred to this place as a studio, and visitors viewed it as minimalist.

He leaned his back against the wall, both feet up and extending across the sill. The overcast sky hinted of rain. From the fourth floor, he had a view of a nearby park and trees. The hustle and bustle of the neighborhood below relaxed Billy. He watched people in the streets, moving in and out of alleyways and weaving through traffic like experimental mice. No treasure appeared waiting for those who conquered this maze. Not even from this elevated vantage point was any prize visible. He pretended not to be part of the organized chaos below. Some days, fooling himself for just a while, he felt keenly aware that somehow and somewhere, someone looked down upon him with the same dreary fascination. How ironic, he thought.

A high-pitched whimper pulled Billy from his meditative

state. His three-year-old cat, Amber, leaped up to the sill to join him. Landing on his lap, she made her way down to his shins, where she stretched out for an impromptu nap. Amber's raccoon-like tail, with black-ringed markings, quivered across his chest, moving from left to right before settling in one spot. Amber had become his closest confidante over time, a loyal, trusted friend, demanding only food, shelter, and an occasional rubbing of her ears. In return, she offered all Billy needed: friendly, nonjudgmental companionship.

Billy shut his eyes. However, sleep was neither craved nor needed. But Billy feared what was beyond his control—his dreams, or, more particularly, his thoughts of recent nights and weeks. Amber shifted her position on his legs, the sound of birds and a barking dog coming in through the window beside them. Her pointed ears perked up, followed soon after by her torso. The filtered sunlight highlighted the auburn and amber tints to her fur. He had not named her Amber. It was the name given to her at the animal shelter where she was found. His exile need not be a lonely one. Such was his rationale for accepting her without question.

The smartphone lay well hidden, though not from Billy's thoughts. At some point, he would read the texts upon texts piling up. If it were Kate, the real one and only Kate, the texts would multiple like digital zombies. Anticipating her motives was impossible, so he refused to allow his mind to mosey down foreign paths. Eventually, her knock would play a beat on his door. His one defense: a referral in an email he would delete.

Billy's attention turned to a commotion on the street below. A homeless man wearing a green camouflage overcoat was flailing away at another man, a patrolman. The homeless man, appearance hidden behind facial hair, turned away and moved toward the oversize cardboard box, presumably his home the previous night. He dragged the box with him as he meandered farther down the street with the patrolman following nearby. How far would the patrolman follow him? Billy knew the homeless man could ramble forever. Wherever he stopped would be his destination. Billy's squinting eyes burst with expression. The man reminded him of the time he first met Riley.

Amber leaped from Billy's leg, allowing him to slide off the windowsill. He raced over to the magazine, flung it to the side, and reached for his phone. The phone beeped with digital delight as he typed a number, and within seconds a female voice answered.

"Hello?"

"This is Billy. Cass, please—I mean Cassandra. Is she there?"

"Sure, Billy. I'll find her. Is this an emergency? Just in case she's occupied."

"No. I'm just checking on someone. If Cass is busy, just have her call me, please."

"Sure." An indistinguishable flurry of sounds followed. Billy moved the phone away from his ear. He could make out faint screams in the distant. Sadly, this did not startle him. Soon enough, a reassuring voice entered his ear.

"Billy? It's Cass."

"Hey, Cass. It sounds like you're swamped. I just needed to ensure Riley showed up there."

"No, I haven't seen him. How's he doing?"

"Seems to be fine, but I will always worry. I tried to find

things for him to do today. He may be heading your way as he is due to start soon."

"I appreciate that, and I'll keep you posted. What about you?"

"Been keeping busy."

"You sure? We haven't seen you in a while. I haven't seen you. Yeah, I realize we have not been working the same hours lately."

"Not sure you would've appreciated my company the past few days. I look a little ghoulish." Voices in the background erupted all around. Billy overheard Cass being called. "Sounds like they need you. Don't worry about me. Keep an eye out for Riley, please."

"Sure, and thanks." The soft voice disappeared, followed by the phone's dial tone. Billy held the phone close to his ear, letting the voice echo for a time. It soothed him. Cass had that effect. His thumb slid over the phone, scrolling through the unopened emails and texts, and paused. One name soon caught his attention. Carrie Woodson had emailed him. Undoubtedly, with the names of referrals.

Dear Billy,

Please give me your address. A person I trust will be in your neck of the woods (Manhattan). They will visit you at your home or wherever you prefer. I assume it would be more convenient. By the way, you cannot delete this email and pretend you did not ask for help.

Your friend,
Carrie

Billy frowned, reread the email, and then smirked. Typical Carrie. Resistance was futile. As he moved toward his saved texts, he knew he owed her this much. He could not avoid the inevitable. She would send in her version of the marines, likely some young hotshot psychologist. Carrie would fill in this person and tell them the story. Only Billy possessed the most critical piece of the puzzle, the truth as he perceived it. He dutifully responded with his address and thanked her. The minute their conversation terminated, he knew he'd demanded too much of her to begin with.

There were almost a dozen texts from Kate, each one longer than the next. The messages stopped, with the last one at around nine that morning.

"Look, if I found you, Billy, I need to see you. If not, I am sorry for bothering you. I won't send you any more texts. Must be the wrong number."

Billy placed the phone on the table. A million thoughts raced in unison in his mind. He did not mind the thoughts; it was the feelings trailing the ideas like cans attached to a beat-up second-hand car. The emotions clanged with an ugly, deafening sound. Living a reclusive existence ceased being an option. With the exiled man discovered, lines were converging at a common point, as foreshadowed by a dream, of all things.

The phone illuminated as Billy pressed Reply and typed. "Yeah, it's me, Kate. It's Billy." He tapped the Send button as he held his breath. If Kate had found his number, she would soon enough find where he lived. Billy clicked the phone out of mute mode in preparation. A mosh pit of feelings simmered inside him. He wondered if he could describe Kate to anyone.

Did his dream do her justice? Is that what she looked like now? Woven beautifully before him was a tangled web, each memory a silken thread.

His eyes shifted to the chaos of the walls, one wall in particular. A bulletin board dominated most of it and hovered ominously above a simple desk. A handful of illustrations peppered the board, hanging by multi-colored pins. The pictures and characters were hand-drawn, some crude, some bordering on museum-quality pieces. The drawings had been mailed to him, mostly by children and teens, representing the world of Aeon. Billy never expected the world he created would catch on with a cult-like fervor. While never expected, acceptance was the goal. He moved closer to a radiantly colored drawing in periwinkle blue of a new character. It was a monkey-like creature with fur and three arms. Around the character's neck, a red guitar with swirls of black slung down low near its waist. A dialogue bubble over its head proclaimed, "I want to be in your band!"

Billy's strong suits did not include resting on his laurels. His eyes focused away from the bulletin board. The rumors of the impending end of the *Time's Musicians* series were like pickax swings chipping at a rock. *Time's Musicians* had served its intent, he supposed. It seemed logical to end it. While an announcement never was made, the voracious fan base reached a conclusion already. Billy rested his eyes wondering what the next frame of the strip would portray, let alone the last. Just as his thoughts lined up at the start line for another race, his phone vibrated in his hand.

"Billy! I'll call you right now. Please answer. Please."

While holding the phone in his hand, Billy returned to his bulletin board and the small poster in its upper right, the original cover from the first *Time's Musician* book. It was a young girl looking up to the sky. A spacecraft with musical notes vibrating around it extended overhead with a banner along the bottom. "We seek musicians. All instruments welcome, only imagination required." Below the first set of characters were depicted, both sporting yellow hair and an eerie semblance to the children from his dream.

The distinctive ringtone emanating from Billy's phone brought reality home. Kate was calling.

CHAPTER 18

The Ghosts of Hobart

Kate and Billy's conversation was short compared to the endless stream of thoughts that raced through Billy's mind before he answered. Normally, he would toss his phone onto the nearby couch after a call. For this call, there was no pacing back and forth, nor multitasking. After ten years that seemed to border on forever, Kate's voice would float into his ears like a timeless symphony. Every second on the phone with her would both elate and torture him. With the final syllable of her words clinging to his ear, he placed the phone down only to pick it back up to get the dial tone, confirming he could press the End Call button.

After several minutes of staring through the still air before him, seeing nothing but the thoughts twisting and turning in his mind, he settled in on the conclusion—Kate was in town and desperately need to see him. She did not explain why, and her tone remained monotone throughout. She spoke in a calm voice, not permitting Billy much opportunity to contribute to a conversation. Her intent was clear. She needed to confirm whether he would see her.

Billy's thoughts drifted back in time. He closed his eyes and recalled the day he met Kate on campus, his first day at Hobart College. Her flowing blond hair, bright blue eyes, and that beaming smile. She wore an oversized jacket with faded jeans and mud-stained sneakers. He could not remember what Kate protested that week or what petition she was passing around. Later, he would sit next to her in his introductory philosophy class and many other classes soon after. When she asked him to join her study group, he nearly suffocated on his tongue, trying to respond. For years they would study together, drink and eat together, and share their thoughts and dreams. Kate was the free-spirited activist that Billy only wished to be. What Billy thought about Kate did. Yet there were things Billy struggled to share with her, including his feelings for her.

The inferno that burned in his soul interrupted the serene musings of his past with Kate. His last conversation with Kate, years ago now, replayed itself over and over as it had ever since he received the first text from her. He could explain everything in the universe to her, except those emotions he kept buried deep in some mineshaft of his being. *Why now? Why does she seek me now?* He knew the answer full well. The game now played was against himself.

All Billy could do was await Kate's arrival. His clumsy attempt to tidy up his apartment kept his mind occupied. With obsessiveness, he returned to his laptop and phone to check for any incoming messages. He reread the last email from Carrie and sighed. Ten years later, it was too much to expect her to drop everything for someone she'd spent less than a week with.

Billy had drifted off to sleep on his couch, his cat sprawled on his legs. Amber's presence gave him the comfort of not being alone when Kate arrived. And when she left, he knew Amber would rub against his leg, regardless. His apartment bell buzzed. Then a second buzz followed, much more menacing and impatient.

After struggling to his feet, he slid his palm along his chin to wipe the sleep-induced drool off his face. His apartment screamed out for more mirrors. After ten years, what thoughts would invade Kate's mind when the door opened? He pulled his hand back from the door handle and swept it from his forehead up into his hair. One last profound breath was needed, so he inhaled before opening the door. He closed his eyes and forced his lips to press together, not smiling unless she did—and he knew that would not be the case.

"Um… hi, Kate. Sorry for keeping you waiting. I, well…" Billy stumbled to find the words.

Billy searched hard for a hint of a smile, even a twitch of her lips. Nothing. Kate walked by him, and if he had been in her direct path, it would have been through him. In the center of his living area, she stopped and pivoted in abrupt, one-hundred-and-eighty-degree turns, surveying his apartment without saying a word. He watched, unsure of how to even communicate with her, let alone stop her. He followed her eye movements until she focused on the desk in the room's corner. From a distance, she squinted her eyes, trying to magnify any document on the surface. Only the thud of the door as he closed it broke the silence. Yet she ignored the noise.

Over the years, rarely did moments pass when Kate was absent from his thoughts. The Kate he knew was independent, courageous, and outspoken. Now, witnessing her investigating his surroundings, he sensed her anxiety, which he could never imagine radiating from her. The multiple texts from her foretold the frantic behavior occurring now. Kate took a heavy breath before sighing and turning to face him.

Kate wore blue joggers, dark sneakers, and a bulky hoodie with its sleeves rolled back to the elbow. Her blond hair was neatly trimmed and short. Her eyes were a darker shade of blue than he remembered, and her cheeks slightly rounder and fuller. What struck him most about her appearance was the hollowness of her eyes and the prominent creases around them. He had seen her pull all-nighters and never look so exhausted. He knew aging and work-related stress were not the causes. His instincts believed something more ominous was afoot.

She spoke in a hushed voice. "Billy, I'm sorry for barging in. I..." She seemed uncertain of what words should follow. Billy nodded to put her at ease. "Promise me something, okay?"

"Sure, but what's going on?" Billy moved toward her as he spoke, then stopped himself. "Yeah… I forgot. I should keep my distance."

Kate looked at him, surprised. "Oh, I won't get you in trouble. I promise. I remember what I said the last time we spoke."

"That I'm not allowed to speak to you, let alone be in the same room, remember?" Billy declared.

"I didn't forget, Billy. I still recall what I said. Anger follows a different calendar." She waited for a reaction, but all he could do was stare down at his feet. "I texted *you*. So you're off the hook. Answer me."

"It would help if I knew the question."

"Are you involved with what's going on?" Kate's voice rose.

"What's going on, Kate?" Billy, pursed his lips, worried about the answer.

"It's John. Tell me if you are at the heart of his turmoil."

Billy stepped back and closed his eyes and immersed himself in thought as he tried to understand. "John?"

"Yes, my John. My husband, John." She pulled her hands from the pouch of her hoodie, where they had been hidden. A gold wedding band glistened on one of her fingers.

"You and John got married?" Billy said as he ambled over and sat on a nearby chair, bracing himself for the onslaught of thoughts and emotions he expected.

"Yes, we married a few years ago."

"I didn't know." Time had passed, leaving Billy a bystander. Multiple sentiments overwhelmed him, each wanting attention. "I'm sincerely excited for you. But an announcement was not your visit's purpose. You mentioned turmoil." Billy hesitated as he spoke, fearing the response.

"If you instigated this... I cannot control my actions." Kate moved toward Billy and stood over him. "I'm serious, Billy."

"You assume I am hiding something, don't you? But I promised to stay away. I promised to stay away no matter what, and I did—I had to. Trust me, please." Billy looked up at her, watching her facial expressions.

Kate grew silent and began looking around the room one more time. "Your apartment is a tad understated, isn't it?" She walked away from Billy, moved over to his desk, and hovered over it, searching. "I didn't tell John that I came to visit you. I devised a story about a nearby conference."

"Kate, tell me what's going on. You can look through my whole apartment if you prefer. The fridge has frightened the bravest souls, so proceed with caution." Never had he seen Kate so frazzled that even humor seemed useless.

It pained Billy to learn Kate and John both abandoned their studies at Hobart right after Billy's unceremonious exile. She told him about how they moved hundreds of miles away to complete their studies at another university. John set aside his craving for esoteric knowledge and pursued a degree in education and found work at a nearby high school. Kate obtained her veterinary medicine degree and now had her own practice. In a nutshell, their lives had moved forward, uneventful until recently. Billy smiled and nodded with keen interest, but with each story Kate told of the life she lived with John, his heart shredded. He had once been part of both their lives and now realized just how cold it was living the years hidden in the shadows.

She stood at his desk and put both her hands on the chair before leaning against it. With her lip bitten, she turned to face him. "Billy, John is sleepwalking, and I suspect having nightmares."

"Since when?"

"He left our home about two weeks ago, well after midnight." Silence followed. An independent observer could measure the time passing in eternities. Kate watched as Billy reclined, testing the ability of the chair to support the weight pressing against it. She grew impatient. "Billy, are you paying attention? He walked out of the house and onto the street before coming back."

Billy escaped from his stupor and leaned forward. "Did you confront him?"

"No. No." Kate began shaking her head. "I should have, but, in the morning, he was fine. The way he was acting like nothing happened, I hoped it was an aberration. But it's happened a few times. He tosses and turns like a wounded animal each night. I hearkened back to Hobart."

"Kate, what are you trying to tell me?"

"Things were happening like back in school. Like the last time. It just sounds so much like how you described it to me back then. I ask him if he remembers anything from his sleep. He responds with a blank stare. Damn, I've convinced myself I imagined it."

"How is he acting when he is awake?"

"Strangely. I'd say preoccupied and pensive. He has that look all the time like he's trapped in his thoughts."

"Kate, I swear, I'm in the dark. However, for you to come and find me—you hoped I'd help after everything that happened."

"You are the last person I'd visit." Kate turned away from Billy as her eyes began to moisten.

"Why?"

"Why I am here?" she blurted as she sniffled. "Because he talked in his sleep. When I followed him one night, he mentioned your name. Because it was your name, I wrote it down." She slid her hands into her jeans to pull out a torn loose-leaf sheet. She stared at it before turning and moving toward Billy as he rose from his chair to meet her halfway. "I transcribed word for word what he said."

She handed Billy the paper, which Billy read aloud, "I can

hear them, Billy. Help me find them. We can save them this time. Don't you hear their screams?"

Billy's hands trembled as he read the words. "Oh, shit," he muttered. "Kate, I am confused by what this all means, but he has to get help."

"What does he mean? Enlighten me, Billy. What screams?" Kate reached out and grabbed Billy by the wrist. "I can't forgive you yet. Only if you help him, I will. You understand?" She squeezed his wrist one last time before releasing them. "Whatever is going on in his nightmares, you are there with him, Billy." She looked at him to study his reaction. Again, he was in deep thought. "You don't know, do you?"

Billy lowered his head and buried it in his hands. "Kate, make a leap of faith and believe me. This is all new information."

"What is haunting John?"

Billy ignored the question while walking over to his fridge. He poured a glass of orange juice and brought it over to her. "You must be thirsty."

"Thanks." She hesitated before continuing, "I haven't told you everything. There's more going on." The last words seemed to fall from her lips. Her eyes gauged Billy's reaction.

Kate looked up past Billy at the drawings hung up on the walls, trying to immerse herself in the world Billy had created. Suddenly, her expression changed. Billy could see her eyebrows flinch ever so slightly before she snapped out of her stupor and responded to him. "In some ways, I hoped you wouldn't know. In other ways, I kind of hoped you did. Does that make sense?"

"I guess so. Kate, is it like last time, his behavior?"

"You mean what you told me about him rambling about

things and people I've never met. No, not like that. Aside from the one time I just told you about it, he doesn't talk much in his sleep. One night, he was yelling at some doctor to stop. Like he was pleading for this doctor to stop the noise. Everything else was muffled."

Billy's heart raced. His left hand clenched as his right tried to steady the paper, now shaking in his hand. "Kate, this is jarring to absorb. I wish I could give you some insight. Did you tell him about these nightmares?"

Kate turned and walked towards the window. She sighed. "No. I kept praying they were make believe. While I now understand your failed attempts to warn me, your actions remain inexcusable."

Billy's eyes became thin slits as the weight of Kate's visit grew heavier on his head. "I assume John has been fine since… well, the last time I saw him."

"Yes, since that time, he has been remarkably fine. He has been since we got married. Like I said before, he changed programs and got his master's degree in education and…" Her voice trailed off. "Fuck it, everything was so normal since you left." She swung her fist before stopping it short of the wall. "I'm sorry, Billy, but I promised myself I would try to forgive you because that's John's way."

"Your anger is well placed, Kate. Nobody is to blame but me. I'm honestly pleased he was doing well since I left."

"Something happened, Billy. Something happened to him. I asked at his school, and nobody sees the change in him. Whatever is torturing him, torments him like before — from inside his head. You remember the last time? How scared he was?"

Billy nodded. The past flashed before his eyes—only it never was the past. For Billy, the present exclusively owned and wore the clothes of the past. He could always remember the fear John wore on his face. He knew Kate had not seen the same fear he had, and this worried him more. "Yeah. It haunts me, Kate."

"Why would he need your help? Why wouldn't he tell me, his wife, of all people?"

"I wouldn't hazard to guess… other than he wants to protect you from whatever scares him."

Kate looked around the room. The drawings from the world of Aeon, the Composer, caught her attention again. "You don't have a hunch?"

"I just need to analyze these recent events. It's a lot to process."

Kate walked back toward the desk. "These drawings are from what? Is this an outlet for your creative passions?"

"Yeah, well part-time. I started a comic book a few years ago. Just to keep my mind off things, I guess."

"Part-time?"

"I also help out at the rehab center nearby. I work with addicts. When I'm not here, that's where I am."

Kate now turned to Billy, and at long last, a slight grin appeared out of the fog time had conjured between them. "Your penance. This is how you're serving your penance, then."

"I can never serve a penance sufficient to erase the stained years."

A hint of grin soon disappeared covered by an emotionless expression as Kate's face grew serious. "I want to believe you and forgive you. I can't, though. Not yet, you understand."

"But, you can't figure out why I'm part of his nightmares?" Billy squeezed his eyes shut, hoping to summon a vision or to string together letters that could dance and put order to the chaos. He could not. "I don't understand it either, Kate. I owe it to him and you to find the answers." He opened his eyes to find she had drifted off—a photo had caught her attention.

"Who is this woman in the picture? I don't mean to be so forward, but it's the only picture in here besides these drawings."

"That's Cass. She runs the clinic where I work. That's where I met her."

Kate shuddered. "I'm arrogant to assume your life has stood still for all these years. I can't ask you to get involved now and turn your back on someone… well, you understand what I'm trying to say."

"Kate, she's just a colleague of mine."

"You haven't changed much. Your mind still plays those games of logic to hide what your soul embraces as reality. That's what caused all this, isn't it?"

"No, Kate. She's a friend who puts patients first. Just like I couldn't refuse your request. There is no decision here."

Kate stood and glanced over at Billy's work area. Her mind appeared to float light-years away. "Um, could you get me another glass of juice, please?"

"Sure." Billy prodded into the kitchen area and began refilling her glass. He glanced over at Kate to find her pulling out what appeared to be her phone. In a flash, she raised the phone in front of one of the drawings pinned to his wall before sliding the phone back into her jogging pants. *She took a picture of one drawing on the wall!* Billy pretended to be oblivious to her actions and, with his head down, delivered the juice to her. Billy began to realize a game was being played, and his role changed from player to pawn. "Please, Kate, you have been pacing around since you got here. Take a seat and tell me everything. Right now, I'm struggling to find a starting point."

Kate pressed her lips tightly, almost as if to trap any words from escaping. She overcame her nervous energy and threw herself onto the one well-worn couch in the room. Billy placed a chair directly facing her and began delicately prying whatever information he could from her.

With her eyes closed and her head tilted up toward the gray water-stained ceiling, she started to inhale. "There is more, Billy. John and I just found out..." She lifted her hoodie over her head and flung it off to the side. Billy's eyes widened, hoping Kate would confirm what he suspected. "Yes, I'm pregnant, Billy. I'm just starting to show."

"Congrats. He must be ecstatic!"

"We had been trying for so long. But he's scared. Scared because he senses something is amiss."

Billy sprung out of the chair and walked to his desk, not wanting Kate to see any expression on his face. "There is someone he can speak to. Someone I trust."

Kate looked up at Billy just as his hand started shaking. "Your intuition frightens you. Your is hand trembling."

"Wild speculation only, which is why you need to go back home and monitor John."

"I believe John would trust you." Kate glanced at the clock. "John will be told I confronted you. I despise secrets." She pulled the hoodie back over herself and move to the front door, taking one last look over Billy's shoulders toward his desk. "Those drawings are yours?"

"No, from fans of mine."

Kate smirked and licked her lips while tilting her head, never taking her eyes off it.

"Everything okay?" Billy followed her line of sight and wondered what it was with the drawings.

"Um… I didn't come here to tell you everything is okay between us. If how you once cared for me is true—I mean, back in the day—then you'll do this for me. I would like to forgive you. So please save the man who was once your friend." She pivoted and, in an instant, opened the door, disappearing into the hallway without waiting for Billy's response.

Billy trailed her to the door and watched her turn the corner, listening to her sneakers squeak as they made their way down the stairwell. He knew everything had changed once again. Or perhaps they never had changed. Kate's return with the news of John's returning ghosts exposed scars of years ago. John and Kate had dispersed from Billy's life like shrapnel from a grenade. Only Billy knew how much of that shrapnel remained buried deep in his gut. He closed the door long after the last echo of her footsteps.

When he turned to face his apartment, it all looked foreign to him. Buried in the core of an eclectic metropolis, the air became dense in his lungs. He wondered how complete was Kate's disclosure about John and the passing years. Indeed, she wondered the same about Billy. The protective coat of lies that shielded them from some truth seemed ill-fitting now. The truth cried out from the wilderness, awaiting discovery.

Billy walked over to his desk and studied the images on the wall. The cartoon pictures captured Kate's attention, *but why?* He walked over to his bookshelf. Reaching back toward the unevenly stacked books, some vertical, some horizontal, he pulled out a notebook, surveying it. Once opened and read, he anticipated breaching the point of no return. That much he knew. The notebook seemed heavy, bearing the weight of dust-covered secrets. Billy had tucked it away for years, protecting it in the best way he could manage while forgetting its existence. In his hand, he held so much of the truth. A truth with the power to destroy or eternally haunt. As he flicked through pages, wave after wave of nausea washed over him. He could easily have shredded these pages or disposed of the words. Instead, he safeguarded them, hoping one day they would make sense.

With the notebook secure in both hands, he moved to the couch and sat precisely where Kate had, her unfinished orange juice on the coffee table. He flipped slowly to the first pages when Amber appeared from under the sofa, scratched the fabric at the base, and then climbed to nestle beside him. Billy smiled. "So that's where you were hiding? You shouldn't have. Kate would love you. I don't doubt that," he said as he gently stroked her behind the ears. He sighed. "Okay, John. Forgive me for not telling Kate everything," Billy stated while staring at the ceiling before turning his attention to the notebook. His fingers lingered over every word on every page. Despite time's passage, every word remained fresh in his mind and painful, like wounds never closed. Memories invaded with each syllable, taunting and teasing Billy with emotions. He closed the book, having filtered each word with logic, hoping to solve the arcane riddle. Almost in a trance, his eyes locked tight to the point of tearing, he flung the notebook towards the couch. He rose to his feet as he held his head between his hands. Amber sat before him, with her head tilted to the left, observing him. Noticing her, he bent down sluggishly to his knees and pulled her close.

He looked at a novel perched on his desk. "This saga has run its course. He must die."

CHAPTER 19

Billy's Light

Two hours later, Billy awoke on his couch, the notebook perched precariously with its pages hanging over the edge. No dream invaded his sleep, nor nightmare. Neither was welcome this evening. For years, a great mystery lurked between each word. Shadows leaped off every page, never taking human form to reveal the face of the unseen evil that Billy sensed. He walked over to his desk, reached for the one book on it, and stared at the cover before flipping through it. He could sense the shadows coalescing in a back alley of his mind into a form. A shadow could conjure a primordial fear, difficult to slay, but a three-dimensional human form can be smothered, he hoped, once and for all, leaving nary a shadow behind.

Not wanting to waste more time, he hurried around his apartment, opening and closing drawers as he went. Angered by the lost time, measured in years, Billy walked to his bedroom closet, pulled out two extra-large duffel bags and began filling them with clothes. Once packed, he settled in on his couch and held his phone in his hand, staring at it before deciding against using it. He looked at his watch, took a deep breath, grabbed his hoodie, and escaped out the apartment door. He needed to do this in person. As he darted through the crowded early evening streets, he wondered what he would tell Cass. Even he had no words to explain it just yet.

Ten minutes later, he arrived at a brownstone and pressed number 404 and waited. A soft voice penetrated through the impersonal static of the intercom. "Yes."

"Cass, it's me. Beam me up, please."

Billy did not wait for the elevator. He jogged up the stairs. She stood in the hallway, awaiting him. "Everything okay? Someone needs help?" Cass's hands rested in the pockets of the faded jeans she wore. Barefooted, she sported a light gray sweater with her brown hair tied at the back and thick black reading glasses balanced upon her nose. Cass was younger than Billy by a year, but despite the stress of her work, she radiated a youth impossible to measure in birth dates.

It was on a spring morning, years ago, when Billy arrived at the Open Door Treatment Center in Brooklyn. Billy, fresh out of university, had come seeking a position there. With no recommendation letter in tow, Billy began performing volunteer work at the treatment center, working in nearby restaurants to afford an apartment. He earned the trust of those around him, and within a year was a regular employee. Within two years, on the strength of recommendation letters from the treatment center, he returned to school to complete his undergraduate degree at night while working there by day. Billy's mom knew nothing of his misadventures or the real reason for his move to Brooklyn. Her pride blinded her from asking questions.

The Open Door Treatment Center was a drop-in center for

anyone suffering addiction issues. Cass had arrived a year before Billy with an undergraduate degree in psychology and a master's degree in social work. Over the years, Cass had developed treatment programs, workshops, and out-patient support programs. Cass never could relish in success as for every life saved, or turnaround achieved, each failure burrowed into her psyche like a parasite. She was serious and hardworking, and Billy offered her an insight into a world outside of her work. Despite her initial misgivings about Billy, including his lack of formal training, his unorthodox style proved a necessary contrast to Cass's rigid, structured approach. As Billy worked diligently to achieve the academic credentials to work at the center, Cass provided emotional support. Billy and Cass built a professional friendship but, considered romance an abstract notion. Cass had dated men over the years, but the late-night calls from patients needing help tested her resolve. Her passion for her work pushed any thoughts of romance aside despite often wanting to reach out her hand to Billy and hold his tightly to feel the vibration of his soul.

Billy proved trustworthy and dedicated to similar causes. She wondered, though, what inspired his boundless creativity. The comic book world he created seemed foreign to her. She did not question it, as she saw the glow in his face when he posted the latest edition. She often wondered what thoughts fluttered through his mind, alone in his apartment with his cat, Amber. More so, she feared that if she dared to soak her dry feet in the ocean, she would be wading in too deep and drown. Like one who feared the water, she stuck to its shores. One day, she thought, high tide would come ashore.

Billy smiled at Cass. He realized how profound his feelings were for her. In the walk to her apartment, his total trust in her comforted him. There were no layers to peel off Cass to arrive at her essence. Her humanity glowed like a bright burning light and would serve Billy as a guiding beacon he could conjure.

"No, nothing's wrong. I didn't have any drop-ins tonight."

"Not even Riley?" she said.

"He came by, but to help me. He's fighting it and so far, so good."

"Shoot, I am acting rude. Come on in. There must be a good reason, right? I mean, for you to be here at this hour." Her voice trailed off, almost sensing the foreboding nature of his visit.

"Yeah, well, I planned to call. But I need the biggest favor."

Cass adjusted her glasses and retreated to the confines of her living area. Without saying a word, she slid off her loafers and eased into the confines of a brown leather recliner. "Have a seat, Billy. This must be a doozy." She smiled.

Billy followed her and propped himself back on the couch facing her. He covered his eyes and sighed, allowing himself to enjoy the comforts of the cushion before being jolted back to reality by a probing voice. "Well?"

"Sorry, um, I lost my train of thought for a second. I'm taking vacation time and will be absent from the clinic this week. Could you just cover my group sessions this week since I don't have one-on-ones scheduled?"

Cass smirked. "Is that it? Sure, no problem. May I boldly ask why?"

Billy leaned forward, his left hand playing with an errant strand of hair above his ear. "I'm going camping this week for a few days. With the snow melted, it's time for me to go back. I've got to finish up my comic book and seem to have hit a dead end."

"My goodness. Are you leaving your cave to complete the latest creation for your alternative following?" Cass laughed, jarring her glasses off her nose. When she saw Billy respond with a faint smile, she changed her tone. "I'm guessing you have a case of writer's block." Cass learned early on Billy retreated to nature whenever he hit a creative wall. Moments alone with nature did wonders for his imagination.

Billy grinned. "You've seen the drill a little too often. Writer's block can be a formidable barrier, and my readers are expecting the next edition of my comic book soon. I trust you still have my extra key in case of an emergency?"

"Yes, from the last time. It was edition twenty-four when you had struggled. What about Riley? How is he coming along?"

"He's been clean for a few months now and dropping by less often. I spoke to him already and gave him an important mission. He has the green light to stay at my place while I'm away. It will keep him busy and preoccupied. Besides, I've given him some chores while I'm gone, including feeding Amber. I kind of also want him to meet someone who may show up while I'm away."

"Meet someone?"

"Let's just say an old friend might drop by while I'm gone. She probably won't, but if she does, I'd like Riley to be introduced to her."

"Who is this person?"

"I shouldn't say because I have doubts she'll show. Put it this way, if she does, I'll make the proper introductions." Billy began shifting his feet impatiently. "It's getting late, and I assume your schedule is full tomorrow."

Cass patted Billy on his shoulder. "Just be careful, Billy. The woods still freeze up after sunset. I remember your brief bout with pneumonia two years ago after one of your March excursions."

"Geez, Cass, the mother hen role suits you better than I imagined. I can handle this road trip and my modest followers. I'm not expecting anyone to trail me into the woods to kidnap me."

"About this next edition, I've meant to ask you something." Cass's batted her eyes playfully.

"Oh, I can tell something is gnawing at you."

"Well, are you ending the story of Aeon?"

"Now, I'm touched. You *do* pay attention! Riley wasn't too sure."

"I am aware of things. Just because I haven't gone to Comic-Con or read every single issue doesn't mean I don't get how much your creation means to you and your readers."

"The last frames remain unfinished. I'm hoping this camping treatment gives me some…" Billy stopped momentarily, his eyes flickered "… closure."

Cass smiled, "Well, I can tell you've been stressing about it. Don't let others influence you. Make sure you end the story the way you want." She lifted her black brows at him and added, "Remember what I told you when we started working together, about when we feel we are in a dark place and can't find a way out?"

"Every light will be an illusion until we seek beyond our senses."

"Good boy." Cass laughed, breaking the tension.

As he opened the door, he turned back to her and grinned. Cass recognized the pure theatrics of his smile. She assumed it was to put her mind at ease so she would not worry about him. Only he knew the true meaning behind the grin. It was merely a distraction that allowed him to stare at her and absorb an image of her, a beam of light to tuck away in his memory in case he would need it. He turned and disappeared down the corridor.

Cass waited for the clang of the stairwell door before retreating to her apartment. She leaned against the door, closed her eyes, and sighed. Her hands clasped together, examining each other. *His hands trembled when he turned the handle.* She wondered what scared him so much. Billy was fearless in a clinical setting. He appeared unfazed by the horrors of the human condition. Today, fear pulsated somewhere in his being. She had detected it. Her mind drifted before returning to her training and what she could control—her patient schedule for the week.

Billy returned to his apartment, adjusting his desk before heading to bed and falling into a sporadic sleep. He awoke at 6:00 a.m. to the soft purr of Amber next to him. He pulled her close and embraced the gentle vibration of her body next to his face. "Don't worry, Riley will take good care of you while I'm away," he whispered to her. "You watch him." Before leaving, he walked back to his desk, surveyed it before taking something off the wall, and into one of his bags. Hours later, as his car weaved its way down the highway, racing farther and farther away from the city sheltering him for years, the future looked hauntingly similar to the past. The lies and half-truths he told followed him. He gripped the wheel tighter and focused on the road ahead, vowing not to succumb to the gnawing fear from the pit of his stomach. His fans wondered what ending awaited the characters of *Time's Musicians* and what was Aeon's destiny?

So, did he.

CHAPTER 20

The Monster Under the Bed

When she rounded the final bend in the road and got the first glimpse of the modest fire-engine-red brick house nestled between a park and a row of townhouses, Kate heaved out a breath that fogged her windshield. In the early evening hours, the spring air carried the frosty reminder of the season just passed. She maneuvered her car into the driveway. As usual, John parked his car at an awkward angle, leaving only the smallest margin of error for Kate. Long ago, she abandoned frustration over John's failings as a driver; he admitted being linearly challenged in matters of both time and space.

She wished they had built the walkway miles longer, anything to avoid the conversation awaiting. Her big-city journey highlighted more questions than answers. She wondered what genie she could summon? Would she be granted at least one wish? Her key penetrated the lock, but she hesitated before turning the handle. With her left hand, she brought her phone close to her eyes, shielding it from the nosy rays of the sun, and scrolled to the images taken near Billy's desk.

When she entered the home, John appeared in her line of

sight, seated with reading glasses on at the kitchen table with what seemed to be a colorful document. He raised his head and smiled at her. Before he could get up to greet her at the door, she motioned for him to remain seated, and in one movement, tossed her hoodie onto the couch.

"How was the meeting? Did you accomplish what you hoped?" Kate could tell by John's face that he knew. It did not help that she was a horrible liar, a weakness John held in high esteem.

Kate gripped the back of the chair and avoided eye contact, finding the hairline crack in the ceiling a convenient distraction. "I didn't attend a conference. Before I fill you in, I needed to satisfy myself if intuition was right. I spent the drive convincing myself I didn't—" She stopped, hating the words that drifted to the surface.

"Lose your mind?" John walked over and hugged her. "I figured you ventured on one of your crusades. I also guessed it was about me."

She stepped back and shook her head. "Why didn't you say anything? Besides, I'm not sure you'll want to listen."

"It has been years since anyone asked me about my dreams or if I had a nightmare and if I had any recollection of it." He smiled and clenched his fingers behind his neck. "I'm not surprised you are wondering."

"You never talk in your sleep. Never. Or at least not that I've ever noticed."

"So, you heard what I said." John's lips began to quiver.

"Yes. I didn't want to say anything and upset you."

"We need to both sit down." John moved back to his chair

as Kate pulled up a seat next to him. "Look, Kate, my insides have been in knots when I wake up, and it's getting worse." Before Kate could interrupt, he held out his hand and swept the air like a conductor. "I could see it in your face, Kate. That look of worry. No one has looked at me that way since I can't remember when."

"I do, John. My mind keeps coming back to ten years ago. Whatever is going on relates to those days because you beckoned to him in your sleep—Billy."

"I said his name?" John's head quivered before closing his eyes, processing the information. "So, you went to find him?"

"Yes. Are you upset that I would do that without telling you?" Kate brought her hands to her mouth, wiping her lips repeatedly. "I so badly tried to convince myself not to go, but I knew I had to."

"Oh, Kate, it's true I would have freaked. Fear hides the righteous path."

"What's changed in the last day? Now it doesn't freak you out?"

"It does—beyond what I can explain. It's just... Well, you tell me first. Did you find him?"

Kate explained how she found Billy's number at the clinic and how she tricked someone into passing on his mobile number. She described his apartment and humble living space, taking considerable time to describe his cramped workspace. John listened intently, refusing to interject and plunging himself into every nuance and inclination in her voice. John knew from Kate's trembling voice that the tale had many twists.

"Billy's work-life extends beyond the rehabilitation center.

He's involved in publishing. I discretely took some pictures."

"Show me, please. I'm guessing it's a good thing I'm sitting down."

Kate's eyes drifted to what John had been reading at the table when she arrived. "Let's just say I may need to strap you down." Her fingers had strayed into her pocket and pulled out her phone, positioning the image she pulled up on her screen. Her hand quaked as John leaned forward to view it.

His eyes twitched intermittently. Never diverting his eyes from the image, he reached for the document before him and slid it to Kate. "This is his!"

Kate glanced down and noticed a printed edition of *Time's Musicians*. "You were reading this when I arrived. Yes, he created all this, John. I had to take a picture because I couldn't believe my own eyes."

"I see it before my eyes, and I still wonder if this is real."

Kate showed John the other photos of Billy's desk area. "He promised me he wasn't behind your nightmares. Shit, I believed him, I convinced myself he was not this monster."

John grabbed her arms. "Kate, I can tell you I didn't get his comic book from Billy."

"This is too coincidental, John. I almost screamed when I saw his workspace. It's covered in these illustrations, and I knew it looked familiar. Then it hit me as I pulled up to the house just now. The images reminded me of what you were reading one night."

"Kate, I got a hold of this through one of my students. One day in class, this kid seemed distracted, and I caught him reading it online. Curiosity got the best of me, and he told me what it was about."

"So you're telling me, you got into comic this because of that kid?"

"Kate, my students browse online non-stop. I keep my antenna up to ensure the content is age-appropriate. The striking colors and title drew me in, so I printed some random episodes to read."

"I haven't seen you with a comic book in ages."

"The story, the images… it's like I *know* them. It feels familiar."

"John, this is Billy telling a story. This is science fiction or possibly—"

"Maybe it's not, Kate." John caressed the cover page. "How did Billy seem? Your visit likely shocked him."

"He seemed heavy in thought. All the emotions of the past, the last time we spoke, and now telling him or almost accusing him of causing your nightmares. It seems absurd to suggest someone could cause the nightmares of another. It's just that I have no one else to blame other than the one person who confessed back then. However, I could sense a sincere concern, but I tend to be an optimist."

"Did you tell him what I said in my sleep?"

"Yes, and he walked away when I told him. He seemed as confused as me. I would have tied him to the chair and ran a lie detector on him, but when I saw the comic book and all the pictures drawn by his fans on the wall, I had to come home and see if I was right."

"Well, you are, my dear." John slid his chair back and wandered to a rectangular window overlooking the kitchen sink.

"Whatever is going on, Kate, I am tired."

"I'm worried, John. You wake up looking so whitish and unrested."

"You don't understand, it's more than that. I'm drained of hiding from myself, fearing whatever manifested itself in my head. The illusion didn't end back then. It wore many disguises to hide what really happened. I just want the damn naked truth."

"So much time has passed. You've never had nightmares or anything like that since we've been together."

"Yet there is a ghost that freed itself from its shackles, and I have this feeling it does not just haunt me."

"What makes you say that?"

"While you were gone, I fell asleep on the couch after school. I was reading one comic book and must have dozed off. When I woke up, I was in our backyard. I've been sleepwalking, Kate, in broad daylight!"

"Back then, we didn't believe him."

"Billy told me I did. I just refused to accept it as true. Today, there I was on my hands and knees digging in our garden."

"The garden remains frozen in spots."

John showed her the scraped skin on his knuckles. "Don't I know it."

"Do you have any idea why you were digging?"

"Kate, I had one thought in my head—to find Billy."

"You are going back to the time you saved him at camp."

"Back at camp, I never feared being able to save him. This time I did."

"John, listen, I will come with you to see someone, a therapist.

I'll be there with you." Kate walked over to him and rubbed his back before hugging him. He turned to face her, his eyes glistening and body shaking.

"I'm worried, Kate. Years ago, I lost a friend, and I'm the one who created the villain. All because of me, Billy became the evil monster hiding under my bed."

"I'm with you, John. Don't be scared."

"I fear turning you into a monster, too."

John could feel the warmth of Kate's body as she pulled him closer to her. She whispered to him, "Seeing Billy made me wonder about the judgment imposed upon him. I guess I've always worried if we judged and convicted him unfairly."

He kissed her on the forehead and cupped his hands behind her ears. "For so long, I feared to enter the abyss, unsure of what I might find. Today, I feel something tricked me into staying in the shadows the whole time. We both realize what I must do."

Kate muttered an inaudible, silent prayer. She worried that John may not recognize the light when he found it or be blinded by its glare.

Little did John understand how the music within him took form in a spectrum of colors splashing across the pages of *Time's Musicians*. A skilled composer using the echoes of past notes to remind John of the music flowing through him. That music would only grow louder now, as would the noise threatening to drown it, again.

CHAPTER 21

To Become the Song

No moat nor drawbridge required crossing. The giant skyscrapers loomed in the rearview mirror. For ten years, Billy lived a chipmunk existence, scurrying amongst the base of the steel and concrete trees in a finite urban forest. Many would find the wide-open highways and farmland ahead as welcome as oxygen to a dying lung. For Billy, the vast metropolis in the background had been a symbolic refuge for his thoughts. The hustle and bustle of daily life kept him grounded in the present. There were souls in the city needing nourishment. His time and energy spent with recovering addicts protected him from his thoughts and the past. But events of recent weeks conspired to expel him from his refuge. Kate's visit was the final sign. He did not understand the meaning behind all the sigils other than that they sought his attention.

The buildings grew less intimidating in size with each mile that passed, and the horizon became an unobstructed, endless sky. Billy clutched the wheel tighter. With each turn of the road, his mind inhaled what lay ahead. He settled his thoughts on the enigma percolating over the previous days. His dreams,

Kate's arrival, and John's increasingly worrisome behavior. *Why now?* He'd placed so much faith in someone he had not seen in years. Even at that, he had spent mere hours with Carrie Woodson years ago. He would understand if she did not get involved now. Though, he realized how alone he would be. The next exit could not come soon enough, and Billy pulled his car into the parking lot of a restaurant. Hungry and needing gas, he required a moment to collect his thoughts. Carrie was privy to the puzzle pieces Billy chose to share. He suspected Kate had struggled through the years with pieces of the puzzle as well, resolving perhaps that it was not hers to solve. His hands trembled. Surprised by his inability to control his worry, he clasped his fingers, and the memory of Cass's concerned look flowed through him.

The shaking stopped like a chill subdued by a warm blanket. Would Cass' opinion of him change? His eyes opened, a new world of emotion erupted within him. He *cared* what Cass would think. She, too, would read the notebook one day and perhaps even meet Carrie. He wondered if he was prepared for Cass to fill in the paint-by-numbers image of himself he had left behind. What would she see? He knew he kept the truth at a distance from her but with good reason. A pang of hunger interrupted his thoughts just as he entered the fast-food restaurant. An unavoidable future awaited ahead. The past would carve the trail.

Rather than eat in the car, he settled into a corner booth with the burger, fries, and soft drink he'd ordered. He placed his phone before him on the table. Emails loaded onto his screen, one after another. He scrolled through them, looking for any ones relevant to his journey. As he dipped his French fries into the pool of ketchup spread on a wrapper, he sought comfort in a text from Cass: "All good. Riley has moved into your apartment. Promise to read the finale." Billy smiled, taking far greater comfort in the text than the greasy fries. For sure Carrie had not arrived yet. Perhaps she never would.

Out of the corner of his eye, Billy spotted a group of young teens settling into an adjacent booth. He assumed they were grabbing lunch before heading back to school. He had no intention of eavesdropping in on their conversation. Besides, their voices overlapped, making any specific words inaudible. They were loud and engaged in a full-blown debate. But it was not about just anything. Just as Billy thought he had filtered the noise out, unmistakable words broke through the chaos, "I am telling you—Aeon will die at the end!"

A handful of ketchup-drenched fries slipped from Billy's fingers, staining his light blue jean shirt before landing on the floor. Billy discretely sidled to edge of the bench to listen further. He avoided the chatter of social media related to his comic. An online comic book was not just a job for him—he'd never planned or expected to profit from its creation. The moment when he first released his creation into cyberspace represented a leap of faith. An outlet for his nomadic thoughts and ideas, the world of Aeon was more central to Billy's identity than he ever cared to admit. All he asked for in return was whatever contribution the reader considered fair. For those who wanted a printed copy, he requested a modest fee to cover the print and mailing costs. He never imagined it spawning a separate reality. Everyone would soon find out how much he wove the fabric of this fictional world from complex veracities.

He wondered whether he should interject in the conversation. His innate shyness would never allow it. Fan interaction seemed so odd on social media. He also disdained the coldness of typing a well-thought-out response and then waiting for a rebuttal. Sometimes, there were no responses. Some feedback could be brutal, hurtful, and repulsive. Later an email or post would arrive offering sincere gratitude for the creation of a welcoming universe light-years from their inner chaos. The feeling was mutual.

"Are you saying Aeon will die? Fuck off, dude. What a shitty way to end it."

"C'mon, of course, he will. They got into his head, man. He can't hear the music anymore."

"What a sucky ending. We'll see."

Billy could tell the boys were shifting in their seats, agitated. They began speaking over one another, and he could no longer discern what they were saying. The third boy who had remained quiet throughout rose from his seat, slung his backpack over his shoulder and spoke. "Guys, I'm heading back to school. You're freaking me out arguing over a comic book fantasy like a bunch of kiddies."

The other two boys shook their heads dismissively and slid out from the booth to join him. They emptied their trays into the garbage bin near Billy's table. One boy looked over at Billy and met his probing gaze. "Sorry, sir, do I know you?"

"No. I overheard you guys talking about Aeon."

"Why? You into that, too?" The teenager took two steps toward Billy.

"For fuck's sake," interjected the boy who was already moving toward the door, "just like I said, children and geezers into nursery rhymes, too."

"Give it a rest, Hugh. Just because it's over your dumbass head."

Billy smiled. "By the way, no offense taken. I.... well, my nephew is into it. Is it ending? He'll be pretty pissed."

"Yeah. We were just talking about that. What is your guess, sir? I mean, what does your nephew think?"

"Oh, I haven't asked him about it in any detail. I would just suggest that things don't always appear to be what they seem." Billy grinned and looked down at his shoes.

"So, Aeon can bring the music back? I mean, hear it again?" The boy's voice rose, and his friend advanced closer to him, while the third shrugged and continued toward the door.

"My nephew guessed that Aeon can hear still the music, he just doesn't recognize it as music because it's different and blended with the noise."

The two boys laughed and nodded more out of respect for Billy's words than in actual agreement. "That's a bit out there." Seeing Billy shift in his seat, he continued, "No disrespect, sir. I suppose anything is possible." The boy next to him smiled and tugged at his sleeve. Without waiting for a response from Billy, both turned to leave, gesturing a goodbye with a wave of their hands.

"Boys." Billy's head lifted from facing his shoes to the teens. "Anything is possible. Maybe the story isn't meant to conclude. Kind of like a song. Once sung and absorbed, it only ends until it's sung again, and each singer creates a new version of it." He assumed they heard him as they broke stride when he spoke. He continued watching them until they left the restaurant, and long after they left, he stared in the direction they'd departed. Billy smirked. "You become the song. That's the trick."

Aside from the staff, and with the distractions now gone, an eerie quiet scared Billy. The boys would not be returning to save him from his thoughts. Even his phone showed no signs of life. Not even a blink of light to announce a message, email, or missed call. If only Kate would text him, she had been mistaken about John's nightmares. It would still be too late once the journal he kept was read, and the veil lifted to expose the reality. The last fry hung seductively from his plate. Once eaten, any excuse for procrastinating would become irrelevant.

Left alone in a small-town restaurant, with no road to concentrate on or teens to eavesdrop on, his simmering thoughts started to percolate. In mere days, a giant web had lured the people of Billy's past and present into its silky grip. Billy wondered how each pawn would be perceived and how everyone would react once drawn in. He sighed, resigning himself to the task at hand. Nourished, yet feeling empty, he marched to his car. His eyes drifted to the sky and the distant mountains. The purr of the engine was the only audible sound to the naked ear, but Billy knew better and tapped his fingers on the steering wheel to a beat. To become the song, one must first learn to listen, tune to the rhythm, and then add your own sound. A lesson long ago absorbed but never forgotten.

While uncertain he could help anyone, at his core, he knew he must throw himself into the path of the evil lurking behind the shade. Billy pushed the car forward toward the screams. The source must be muted.

CHAPTER 22

The Thoth Institute

Miles of forest towered over him, watching him. The trees stood along the very highway carved through them years ago, tolerantly waiting for the day when the last car would pass, and they could swallow the road whole. Billy realized that his past now stood over him like these trees. The farther he drove, the denser the trees became until lone pine and birch trees became indecipherable. He glanced over at his phone to see another signal strength bar disappear. Within an hour, he surmised, nobody would be able to reach him. Nor would he be able to reach them. On the horizon, he could see the aura of the sun in various shades of orange, blinding to the eye but soon to surrender to the blackness.

Billy checked the clock on his dashboard and nodded to himself. He would arrive before natural light had faded. It had been an hour of driving down gravel roads off the main highway. *I should see some sign soon*, he thought. Then, as if on cue, he noticed a faded sign off to his far-right that read Camp Ehnita. The car slowed, searching for a path in the thickening bush that lay ahead. Billy sighed loudly, wondering what existed of Camp

Ehnita besides the sign. He slowed the car and stopped in what remained of the old parking lot at the camp's entrance. Under the diminishing light, he noted no other vehicle.

Once parked, he stared at his phone. He had a dying signal now. He reached for it and thumbed through his text message history, scrolling back and forth with his thumb through the parade of messages from Kate. With each read of Kate's texts, Billy modulated the tone of her voice in his imagination, hoping to get it right. For years, he could only recall the angry tone of Kate's voice punctuating each syllable like a sharp knife into his stomach. Now Kate's voice seemed drowned by the melancholy and worry of her visit.

In recent days, the strange dream and thoughts of his last days at Hobart had so consumed Billy's mind that he now feared they had destroyed any logic. He wondered if this was all pure madness. Billy leaned against his car. He had retreated to a solitary life in a city of strangers years ago. Here in the woods, surrounded by the silence and night waiting to conquer, an uncanny feeling of the inevitable formed in his gut. What if the truth would remain as elusive to him as it was to everyone around him?

A distant howl of a coyote startled Billy and focused him on the here and now. To him, it was no more sinister than the discord of sirens and screeching tires that filled his apartment at all hours. The coyote wail reminded him, he was not alone. With an hour of travel down unpaved roads and his last bottled water now pushing the capacity of his bladder, Billy walked toward a nearby bush to relieve himself. As he turned to return his car, the sun reappeared in its final descent as the clouds that had curtained it scurried through the sky. The bright rays drifted in between the outstretched limbs of the trees and lit up the abandoned parking lot. In the fading light, Billy could see a broad outline of the lot and noticed how chaotically he parked.

He walked briskly toward his car as passing clouds filtered the light and spat out darkness. His duffle bag emptied, he grabbed his flashlight. The light created a path for Billy to follow. He reached into the car, took his sleeping bag and blue plaid jacket. He tucked two granola bars into the side interior pocket and checked his flashlight. His phone flashed a bright red light on and off. The last hurrah of a dying battery.

The woods stood against a background of black, waiting for him. As he took small steps into the woods, the cool moisture of the green grass was a sign of snow that had covered these woods just weeks earlier and the muddy ground that was ahead. Billy often camped to relax over the years, but he'd never returned to the place where he'd met John until this evening.

By the time he reached the main campground area, his hiking boots became caked in thick mud. With the sun below the horizon, Billy tightened the grip on his flashlight and buttoned his plaid jacket over his hoodie. His last memory of the log cabins arranged in a large semi-circle was from the backseat as they drove away. Now the cabins were almost invisible, hidden by the branches hanging just above. Billy imagined how, by midsummer, the trees in full bloom would render only a hint of a human presence. At the far left side of the camp, Billy found a faded number eight carved on the wood plaque of a door, leaning unevenly to one side. The door was unlocked, and aside from the faint creak it made, opened quickly. The light switch no longer worked, and Billy relied on his flashlight to illuminate the interior. Bunk beds remained where Billy remembered them, only without bedding and covered with cobwebs. A massive bunk bed occupied the opposite side. Billy's light searched the cabin for any signs of recent activity. He found none.

The lunch at the greasy spoon hours earlier contributed to nausea overwhelming him. He trailed his flashlight along the floor, searching for any marks from boots or shoes. He lowered his head, resting it on the palms of his hands as he swayed forward, shaking. There was little he could do tonight. He could feel the sting of dropping temperatures and decipher the howls of more coyotes off in the distance. Armed with a faltering flashlight, venturing outside in the dead of night was imprudent. Experience had taught him to be cautious. A cellular signal was unobtainable this far into the woods and the trek to the car pointless with a roof over his head. From the bowels of his bag, he tore off the wrapper of one granola bar and then another before washing them down with water. John was not here for him to follow out to the clearing, so he settled down in his old bunk, imagining John in the one above, pensive and eager to explore. Death was delayed once, thanks to John.

Nestled alone within the woods in a closed-down campsite, serenaded by the sound of hungry coyotes, and with very little light could weaken even the bravest souls. But Billy slept. Tomorrow would come soon enough.

He awoke then next morning to the first rays of sunlight and, by 9:00 a.m., had driven for hours until his car pulled up to the main archway of a campus. Rather than a series of stately

Victorian buildings, hidden here in the woods amongst oaks and pines were modern buildings bearing a strong resemblance to low rise, urban office buildings. Billy shivered at the contrast with Hobart College. He got directions from the campus security guard and drove down asphalt paths until he found a parking area near a three-story, square-shaped structure. Students walked about here in a methodical and robot-like manner, heads down, most with earphones. Everyone immersed in their own worlds.

Billy parked the car but kept the engine running for a time, enjoying its mechanical calm. Minutes earlier he had passed the exit that leads to Hobart. This was a different world, with few non-essential signs either on buildings or roads. The students seemed not to interact, and it lacked the buzz of activity of most campuses. He assumed minds came here to hide, or souls came to perish in silence.

Invigorated by a deep breath, Billy shut off the car engine before marching to the nearest entrance. The only sign he found read "The Thoth Institute" in bold, death-black print. Unable to see any other symbols, Billy entered the main door only to be greeted by two security guards. Billy slinked back, noting that the guards were both older, more muscular, and imposing.

"Your business today, sir?" barked the first guard in a baritone voice. Many people speak in low tones to sound imposing. These guards did not have to.

"I'm here to see someone." Billy's mind went blank. "Yeah, um, a Mr. Laughnon."

The guard's eyebrows twitched. "You mean Dr. Laughnon."

"Yeah, that sounds right."

Billy reached into his wallet and produced the identification they required. Within seconds, a phone call occurred, and Billy received directions leading to an imposing staircase.

"Second floor. Corner office to your right."

Billy nodded and brushed by the guards. He slowed his gait enough to observe his surroundings. The walls were a grayish tone and almost devoid of any pictures or works of art, with a very sterile vibe to everything. Billy passed by a doorway to his left and noticed an extremely thick-looking steel door with a complicated keypad perched on the side. A small, rectangular sign above the door stated Research: Pass holders Only. Curious, Billy veered toward the door only to be startled by the booming voice of the guard. "End of the hall, sir."

Unnerved, Billy drifted back to his original path and headed for the stairwell at the far back of the corridor. The freshly mopped marble stairwell glistened as Billy trotted up before tumbling forward, the top step slamming his shin. The pain ripped through his leg and up his spine. He clenched his hands before lifting himself off to continue. At the end of the hallway, he spotted a woman seated at a large desk. He approached the counter, making a game out of avoiding the rays of lights that stretched out from narrow slats. The silence puzzled him. On a regular day, a university campus would be abuzz with activity, even on the second floor. Billy noticed that none of the office doors here had nameplates, just a three-digit number, and each entry was closed. A student sat on a metal chair outside one of the offices. Billy smiled at him but received no reciprocal acknowledgment.

An older woman wearing a plain white blouse and beige

pants greeted Billy at his final destination. "Dr. Laughnon will see you right away. Would like water or coffee, perhaps?"

"No, thanks. He's a busy genius, so I assume his time is invaluable."

"Yes, he had to squeeze you in. He has a lot to do before his book tour and various speaking engagements."

"No rest for the wicked, right?" Billy smirked.

She did not react. Instead, she knocked on the door and opened it.

A balding man with black-rimmed glasses sat behind an empty mahogany desk. The man seemed insignificant compared to the sheer girth of the desk. He motioned for Billy to speak. It was only when Billy reached the front of his desk that the man rose, extending his hand ceremoniously before settling back in a leather chair with an extra high back. The bureau was barren except for a brown leather notebook and a novel Billy recognized. The man wore a white overcoat, covering a navy pin-striped suit, white silk shirt, and a dull gray tie with a symbol at the bottom of a snake curled around a staff. Billy zeroed in on the man's face, noting the green eyes, charcoal-colored hair with hints of gray, and thin reptilian lips. The man's hands were broad with knuckles that protruded.

"Thanks for seeing me. This meeting was frustratingly difficult to arrange."

"Young man, you can imagine how busy I am. Especially since just returning to this country."

"Yes, sir. A novelist, a researcher, and I assume you teach, too."

"Oh, I don't teach. My research keeps me occupied enough. I mentor. Yes, that is what I do. I work with knowledge-thirsty students and advise them. My passion lives on through my research."

"I found your book fascinating, so that's kind of why I am here."

"Yes, you mentioned in your correspondence that my book piqued your interest, specifically as it relates to some research you're doing. You didn't state where you were conducting the research. When we arranged the meeting, you were to disclose which university you're associated with."

"The reason I couldn't say anything is I work for an organization that requires confidentiality."

Dr. Laughnon flipped his pen. "Good lord, I hope you are not wasting my time."

"Sir, I'm sure you of all people understand what it's like to perform research on behalf of someone who requires confidentiality. Such confidentiality comes with a price." Billy's voice grew low as he stared at Dr. Laughnon.

"It goes without saying."

"To put your mind at ease, you can do whatever due diligence is necessary. I assume you read the document I sent you."

"I skimmed through it. My understanding is you are seeking someone to carry on the research and partner with you and whoever you represent." Dr. Laughnon leaned back on his chair as his left hand took off his glasses to clean them.

"Yes. Sort of," Billy replied. "Let me explain."

"Very well. I have what you sent right here." Dr. Laughnon yanked open a drawer and pulled out a stapled document. "So, you're interested in the powers of the human mind?"

Billy grinned as he glanced at the document. It took him

hours to put it together in a manner necessary to entice Dr. Laughnon. "I had no interest until I saw it myself, first hand."

"Please, I've read your paper, but I want the story to accompany your voice. Particularly, this person and the place where this power manifested itself."

"A year ago, I made acquaintances with this interesting fellow my age. A colleague referred him to me. This subject was plagued with addiction problems while demonstrating unusual mental abilities. Naturally, I was skeptical."

"Yes, including the ability to not only enter someone else's mind but reflect thought using someone else's mind as a conduit. At least from a layman's perspective."

"I'm a layman, so I appreciate keeping it simple. This man seemed capable of manipulating brain waves emanating from one's mind. He claimed the capacity to synchronize his brain waves and merge them with another person's brain waves." Billy paused for dramatic effect. "The kicker is he could overtake someone else's mind with this combined wave. Kind of like a ventriloquist throwing his voice, only, in this case, his mind could hijack that of another person."

"Well, while my book is fiction," — the man grinned — "much is based on my extensive research. This ability for an ordinary person to have such powers sounds a little ludicrous. The advantage of fiction is you don't have to include footnotes explaining your research."

"When I read your book, I could see the expertize you had in this field and thought I needed to see you right away."

"Well, I am certainly interested in learning more. In particular, please describe this place or location that appears to amplify this power." Dr. Laughnon leaned forward with his eyebrows twitching in unison.

"Yes, I've seen it myself. Within this place, this person can apply his power to individuals miles away. The natural layout creates a natural frequency that amplifies and distorts brain waves."

"You've seen this done?"

"Not done to me, but I've witnessed his quite impressive demonstration."

"My naïve friend, I hate to tell you, but you have been duped. You never let the subject control the experiment. An old magician's trick. I hope you haven't been fleeced."

"Sorry, sir. Are you insinuating I've fallen prey to a hoax?"

"Exactly. I trust you're not out of pocket your life's savings. My career has been spent researching this field, yet I could not come close to replicating what you suggest. As a matter of fact, I'm convinced this person read my novel and used it as a basis to perpetuate this fraud upon you."

"Sir, with all due respect, you do not understand. I'm not trying to get you to give me any money. I'm offering you this subject to examine so you can judge for yourself."

"Ah, so you want me to debunk this myth and waste my time."

"It's not a waste of time. Let me explain it further." Billy squirmed in his chair for effect and stuttered to convey a sense of nervousness. "The person who has these powers is interestingly connected with your novel."

"No wonder I could not find any information about you." Dr. Laughnon picked up a Mont Blanc pen from a stand and tossed it to the floor, ignoring Billy's last words.

Billy chuckled. "I'm a comic book creator. You never heard of *Time's Musicians*? I have quite a following."

"Oh, good gracious. A damn comic book. I am a renowned scientist, and I wasted my time with this. Let me ask you, who wrote this letter you sent me and this paper?" Dr. Laughnon's faced turned beet red as he flung the document at the adjacent wall.

"That was a limp toss. No offense to you." Billy walked over and nearly caught the document before it settled on the industrial carpeted floor. "Truth is, sir, I admit those are not my ideas. No, I supposed they could not have come from a comic book creator. I put this document together from memory based on one I had read about ten years ago."

"No kidding. It came from that hoaxer who made you waste my time, I bet."

"Yes, sir, you're right. But I mean, you thought it had some merit, or else I wouldn't be here."

"I expected to find the supporting research attached." Dr. Laughnon looked at the back of his wrist. "Enough time on this. Please leave. If you want a copy of my novel, get one from my assistant. Goodbye."

"Don't you care about my friend's identity? He is familiar with your past work, Dr. Laughnon. I tried to tell you, this is related to your novel and life's research."

"He is a fraudster, young man, get it through your head."

"I understand, but he seemed to be familiar with this Institute. Or rather, about this school back when it had a different name."

The older man's face seemed devoid of any color other than a hint of rouge around his cheeks. "Who is this individual?" he bellowed.

"I don't feel comfortable saying because I don't have his name." Billy's eyes squinted. "He told me it was 5871."

"What was 5871?" Dr. Laughnon's body aggressively lurched forward.

"5871 was his number here." Billy lowered his voice. "He mentioned a tragedy, a horrific event that happened, and that's when he left the Institute. For the longest time, he avoided discussion about it." Billy hesitated again. "He might talk to you."

Dr. Laughnon seemed locked in stone. Billy could detect the faint twitch under his nose. He could almost overhear the words trying to assemble themselves in his mind.

Billy continued. "I suppose you are not interested, and perhaps my acquaintance is a brilliant magician who tricked me, but he seemed to possess a lot of information about this place and about *you*. He says his powers result from the brilliance of what they did here. He figured they halted everything because of the suicide, or perhaps I misunderstood."

The man swung around his chair and retreated to the far window. "Suicide? Just vicious rumors from jealous colleagues," he said. "Look, I feel sorry for this man's obvious mental issues, so I suppose I can placate him and put to rest this nonsense."

"Well, you are likely right. I should just send him off to make a fool of someone else or another school."

"No, no. Alright." He made his way around his desk and reached into his pocket for a business card. "Have him contact me. I will make arrangements to test his hypothesis myself for the sake of his sanity."

Billy held the card in his palm before inserting it into his wallet. "If you don't mind, I will call you once I speak to him. He may not be comfortable to meet you once I tell him how dismissive you are of his theory."

"Young man, don't mistrust his theory. It's his experiment that's dubious—and his whole preposterous story."

"I'll just mention you are prepared to meet him without noting your skepticism."

"Yes, that would suffice. I head out for various engagements and won't have much availability. Where is this place where he showed you this experiment?"

"Oh, you would like to see his magic trick?" Billy declared sarcastically.

"Well, he claims there's a place that has some acoustic and even an electromagnetic field that affects brain waves and the deflection of those waves."

"Like distortion and feedback. Those are the words he used. This place causes distortion and feedback like to a guitar except, in this case, it's to the mind."

"I am capable of staging an experiment to debunk the theory diplomatically. Is it far from here?"

"Not really, it's about a two-hour drive. Though there are issues, sir, given your age and health."

"Frankly, I don't understand. I'm in good health for my sixty years. Where is this place?"

"It's in a cave, an ancient opening on the side of a mountain, kind of like a black hole on Earth," Billy smirked at the face the doctor made, agreeing to call him once he had gotten the green light to arrange a demonstration. "Dr. Laughnon, one last thing. Could I perhaps tour the facilities? They are impressive."

"Very well. This is a private graduate school, with much of the research carried out funded by private benefactors. You will require an escort. Wait in the hallway. My righthand man, Dr. Backsaw, will give you a quick tour."

A tall, muscular male in his late thirties met Billy in the hallway, looking more like an MMA fighter than a doctor. His version of a tour was a series of hand gestures and grunts. Billy did not expect much conversation, and after the first exchange of words, Dr. Backsaw brought him to the dorm area, housing the students. Each room had minimal furnishings, with natural lighting coming through thin slats that could only charitably be considered windows. As Billy stalked through the classroom area, a thick door at the far end of one corridor caught his attention. It had a keypad instead of a door handle. By chance, the door swung open, and a woman wearing a lab coat emerged. The door swung closed again. Billy caught a glimpse of the bright white corridor, with oval-shaped walls and a ceiling that appeared to slope downward and go on forever behind the door. Billy, by instinct, moved with pace toward the door before the mighty hands of Dr. Backsaw, grabbed him at the wrist, swing him around. Dr. Backsaw rocked his head, waved his finger at Billy, and grunted. Billy realized the error of his ways. The tour ended, and Dr. Backsaw walked Billy briskly out to the door. Dr. Backsaw appeared thrilled to have finished his interaction with Billy as he smiled before turning his back and leaving. Billy retreated to the parking area.

Far behind him, he sensed an older and more anxious man

staring at him from some unseen window.

Billy paused at his car and looked back on the building he just left. He could not shake the sinister feeling of having roamed its corridors before. That possibility made no sense. Then, as he positioned his car key into the lock, he pictured a younger version of himself in that building. The revelation overtook him, and he slumped forward before composing himself. He had been here before. That much, he was sure. As one truth exposed itself, the burden of its meaning and significance made things clear to Billy—no matter what, he could not turn back.

CHAPTER 23

Dr. Woodson, I presume

Carrie Woodson's eyes looked back and forth from the apartment number to the sliver of paper she held. The address matched. While she fought hard not to formulate any expectations of what she would find, she nevertheless detected an emptiness. This is where Billy had landed. Did Billy choose this location to serve his exile? Almost forgetting her role in this tale, Carrie closed her eyes, overwhelmed by the one emotion she sensed: loneliness.

Carrie knocked on the door ignoring the doorbell. Almost immediately, she could make out the telltale noise of chaotic movement. Through the thin walls, the sound of footsteps making their way to the door filled the hallway. The person on the opposite side struggled with the lock. A male voice begged her patience and voiced frustration about unchaining the door. The door swung open, and a familiar man appeared before her.

"Dr. Woodson, it's actually you. You are at last here." The man's eyes threatened to exit their sockets.

"You seem surprised."

"Billy only left early this morning. He was doubtful you

would make the journey. I was worried anyone would even show." The man's voice seemed to struggle for air amidst his excitement.

"Well, I'm here." Carrie frowned. "Please take a deep breath before you suffocate, young man. When you find some air, explain to me what you mean by *he left*. Is Billy not here?" Carrie ignored her host and walked past the entrance into the apartment, leaving a bewildered Riley in her wake.

"Please come in. I am so sorry for my behavior." Riley soon realized he was addressing an empty corridor. As he turned, Riley observed Carrie surveying the room, her head darting like a hyper pigeon. "Excuse me, Dr. Woodson, my name is Riley."

Carrie turned around toward Riley, smiling meekly as he stood helplessly to the side of a tattered couch. "Riley, you live with Billy, I guess? I was not expecting anyone other than Billy."

"No." Riley blushed. "I don't live with Billy. I'm a patient—not his, mind you—and a friend." Riley's voice trailed off as he replayed her question. "He asked me to stay here until you or someone came. I'm relieved it's you. Very relieved."

"What's going on? Where is he?"

"He went camping, but I don't know where. You see—"

"He left to go camping after contacting me?" Carrie paced the apartment.

Riley frowned. "He hasn't gone camping in a while, and the urge just seemed to strike him. He likes to go when he's working on his comic book and needs some inspiration."

Carrie looked over the fidgeting man. "I recognize you. You're the guy who helped Billy with his computer."

The man's hands shook as he reached out and grabbed

Carrie's right hand, which dangled at her side. "Riley, ma'am. I'm Billy's friend. You're here to help him, right?"

Carrie pulled her hand away from the man's grip when her eyes settled upon the marks on his forearms. Her hands reached back and clutched his hand with her palm and pulled him toward her. "Riley, it's nice to meet you. Do you know why Billy needed me?"

"No, but I plead that you help him with whatever is driving him."

"And why is that?" Carrie smiled.

Riley moved toward her. "Because it's Billy."

"Because it's Billy!" Carrie's eyes widened. "Rather than go around in circles, perhaps you can indulge me with meaningful information."

"Dr. Woodson, you're here, too, because it's Billy. That's why you trekked into the city. The great Dr. Woodson would not leave the comfort of country life or retirement for just anyone. Right?"

"Please call me Carrie. But, the *great* Dr. Woodson sounds authentic. Look, I drove what seemed like ages, leaving a spouse and teenage son behind."

"Carrie, please have a seat. I can get you something to drink. Anything you would like?"

"Water is fine."

Carrie could sense Riley's anxiety. Her professional instincts overcame her initial frustration over Billy's absence. Furthermore, it had been her first foray away from home since her retirement. "Riley, why don't you have a seat and tell me about yourself and then explain to me why I'm here."

"I need to first disclose I'm a recovering addict. But, you guessed that already what with the scars from where my arm was marked up. This is not about me, though." Riley paused. "Whatever you need, I am here to help you. I mean, you coming all this way to help Billy. It's the least I can do."

"That's the plan. Tell me your story first. You have my attention."

Riley hesitated for a moment, uncomfortable in taking up Carrie's time, but Carrie had leaned forward, showing visible interest in his story. Over the next few minutes, Riley told the tale of how he was a young computer programmer working tirelessly, yet enjoying each minute. One day, a fellow employee showed up to work and opened fire. Riley arrived late, having overslept after multiple late nights. He soon learned of the murder of three of his colleagues and friends. For months, he could not perform essential functions or express a clear thought. Soon enough, anti-anxiety meds were prescribed, and before he realized it, he became addicted and was living a zombie-like existence. Before he awoke from his stupor, he lost his job, his girlfriend, and was homeless. In a lucid moment, while visiting a local animal shelter, he met Billy, who, by chance, was there to get a rescue cat. Billy took an interest and brought him to the clinic where he worked, and within days he was in a treatment program.

"Billy helped you through all this?"

"Carrie, I am alive, thanks to him. I mean, I'm nowhere near fine yet, but, well, I'm here." Riley stared at the window. "I hope you're not surprised. Billy is one of a kind."

Carrie bit her lip. "I guess I shouldn't be. I trust the recovery is going well?" Carrie paused but continued when Riley returned her smile. "Does Billy also suffer from an addiction? Is that why I'm here?"

"No, Billy does social work with Cass. He works at the rehab clinic where I first checked in." Riley's hand began scratching the edges of his short black hair just above the ear. "Sorry, Carrie, it's a nervous habit."

"Tell me more about yourself besides what brought you into Billy's world."

"As Billy likes to say, I'm just like a wounded bird with a damaged wing requiring healing, so he can fly again. That's me. Billy made me his personal cause. I can't explain it too well, but when Billy met me and listened to my story, he became obsessed with my well being. He referred me to Cass, who is like the best person in the world. Well, second only to Billy." Riley became silent, observing the change in Carrie's demeanor. "Something I said about Billy just struck a chord with you, didn't it? I see it in your face."

"Goodness, young man, you are analyzing me of all people." Carrie feigned anger. "Who is this Cass?"

"She is the head counselor. I started sessions with her after I came back from the detox center. Intense stuff. I survived. Been clean for months." Riley grinned. "I got a job programming again and even have my own apartment. Even more minimalistic than this one."

"And Billy and Cass are?"

Riley laughed. "Carrie, I wished Billy called you to talk about relationships because he is clueless." He continued to laugh, clearly enjoying discussing someone other than himself. "Their relationship is professional. That's what happens with two introverted people devoted to their work. So, yeah, I hope Billy called you for advice, but I doubt it."

"Did Billy tell you about me and what happened years ago?" Carrie began to try to peel away a layer of the mystery.

"Look, Carrie, Billy never speaks about his past. Never. I have tried, and when I do, he pushes me away and keeps me at a distance. At one point, I stopped asking. He helps so many people I didn't want to jeopardize that. His comic book work is his muse and outlet. That's my opinion, Cass's too."

"He's told you nothing at all? Nothing about why he contacted me?"

"He was your patient, wasn't he?"

Carrie sighed. "Riley, he never was *my* patient, not in the traditional sense. Our paths crossed very briefly."

"It clearly left an impression, or else you wouldn't be here."

Carrie drifted from room to room. Her eyes searching and probing as if pondering her words. "As a child, nothing frustrated me more than a missing puzzle piece. Four hundred and ninety-nine pieces assembled, with even one missing piece, the picture—for me anyway—was never completed. It drove me nuts as a child. Put it this way, Billy is that puzzle piece."

Riley's head slumped forward into his hands. His shoulders sagged from an unseen burden. "Oh, I wish I had the piece you are missing."

"I am getting the notion Billy was acting strangely." Carrie moved into interrogation mode, her eyes laser-like.

"He's gone camping before, always by himself and usually to work on his comic book. A few times he's gone to visit his mom down south, and even once to a Comic-Con. His mom's health has been shaky for a while, so she rarely travels. This time he seemed frazzled and pensive. I just thought it might be misgivings about ending his comic book series."

"Did he divulge why he needs me?"

Riley's eyes drifted above as if looking for answers hidden under the dull, grayish-toned ceiling. "For some reason, I'm uncertain he wanted you to help *him*. It might become clearer once I give you the journal he kept."

Carrie slouched back into the couch. "Give me a journal! He said nothing about giving me anything."

Riley dashed to a bookshelf. He leaned book after book to the side until Riley reached far behind and pulled out a spiral-bound notebook. Like a nervous witch searching for a spell, he flipped page after page. He then stopped to stare at the well-worn, royal blue cover,

Carrie leaped to her feet. "He kept a diary?"

"Not that I am aware," Riley stammered. "Honestly, I peeked. I assume it was okay if I did. It's not a diary."

"You haven't read it yet? Did he ask you not to?"

"No, he told me I could. I just..."

She finished his thought. "You feared your feelings would change."

Riley nodded affirmatively. "I've known Billy for what seems forever. He saves so many people, and so many kids love his comic book. I just couldn't because of what I may learn."

"Oh, young man, every day for me is about finding that unique insight. It may be a positive revelation," Carrie said with a smirk as she began to survey the apartment again. "And he evidently trusted you to be here and trusted you alone to give me this. That says a lot about the high esteem he has for you."

"He would have left it for Cass, I suppose, but she's a workaholic, and he didn't want to burden her."

Carrie smiled. "If anything, before I leave, I'll take a stab at that Cass relationship or lack thereof."

"We should focus on this," Riley replied, his voice taking on a lower tone as he dangled the notebook in Carrie's direction.

"Sorry, I understand you're worried about him."

"I thought I would be less worried when you arrived. Now I'm freaking out that you knew him back then."

"Like I said, he was not my patient in a technical sense."

"But, curiosity is only part of the reason you made the journey."

Billy's desk captured Carrie's attention. Riley's words fluttered about the room like flies, with Carrie aware of their presence but ignoring them. Riley scratched his cheek and followed Carrie, tossing the notebook onto the desk.

"I'm tremendously curious. Billy never spoke of why he left university?"

"Not in any detail. He changed programs and enrolled at a smaller school to get a degree in social work."

"He was exiled, Riley."

"Expelled. You mean expelled."

"Expelled is so punitive. It conveys the notion of punishment for a crime or bad act. No, I consider it exiled. The college wanted him as far away as possible."

Riley stared at Carrie, his dark eyes opened wide, his hands clenching and unclenching to the tune of his heart. "I'm not following. What happened, and..."

"What was my role? That is what you want to ask, isn't it? You have that accusatory look. Don't worry, I'm not offended."

"He was one of your students, perhaps? I'm guessing since you didn't say patient."

"No. He was in a New Age program involving the merging of the arts and sciences. Not only that, he excelled in it."

"Now I'm buzzing. What happened?"

Carrie was now back on the couch, scooping up the notebook and motioning for Riley to sit on a nearby chair.

"Billy authored an email accusing the college of conducting experiments on campus."

"What kind of experiments?"

"The stuff of nightmares." Carrie frowned.

"That's horrible. And they expelled Billy for that?"

"No, they punished him because it wasn't true." Carrie raised her right eyebrow to emphasize her point. "They punished him for playing a vile joke."

"A prank. That is a crazy accusation to make. Billy wouldn't be so cruel."

"That is the thing. Billy told them he did it to get even with someone." Carrie hopped up again and paced, drawing out the drama. In fact, she remained distracted by Billy's work area.

"Get even?" Riley's eyebrows arched.

"Yep. Peer jealousy with a smidgen of personal jealousy. At least, that's what Billy told them."

"Who was he jealous of?"

"His roommate."

"Well, I've known my share of college roommates who

despised each other, but I can't imagine something this extreme."

"Riley, he wasn't any roommate, this was his friend. Someone he knew back in his teens." Carrie waited for comment, but the weight of her words seemed to have smothered Riley. "They handed me a thin folder, less than a week, and just three meetings with him."

"That's an impossible task. I mean, why did they—?"

"They wondered if Billy was dangerous."

"I can't believe you would get involved. I mean, you let Billy get expelled."

"They considered a far worse punishment. If it wasn't me evaluating him, I fear some wretched soul would perform the task. Besides, they never let me finish, anyway."

"So, years later, he sought you of all people."

Carrie shrugged her shoulders. "Until now, I've had no contact with him since that last meeting about ten years ago."

"Sorry if I seem…"

"Shocked. I would expect no less. When he tried reaching out to me the other day, my reaction was a lot like yours now."

"Let me ask you, Carrie, and please be honest. Would Billy be so vindictive?"

By now, Carrie hovered over Billy's desk, her hands shuffling papers and rearranging those strewn over it. "Your gut instinct would be as valid as mine."

"You're not going to tell me, are you?"

"Well, I'm still trying to figure out why I'm here. More importantly, why he isn't."

Riley walked back to the couch to retrieve the notebook.

"Dr. Woodson, this is the one thing he was obsessed with you getting."

"I will get to it. This comic book world he's created fascinates me in many ways. My connection is personal." Carrie recognized many of the comic books littered around the apartment from ones she'd seen in Maris's room.

"I sneaked a peek at the inside cover of the notebook," Riley admitted. "There's a date. Does November 2007 mean anything?"

"2007!" Carrie's mouth dropped. "Let me see that." Her full attention now turned to the notebook and the inscription on the inside cover.

"Let me show off my investigative instincts, Dr. Woodson. That was around the time you met Billy, isn't it?"

"Smartass amateur. Yes, I handled Billy's case in the spring of 2008. I would have to check my notes to be exact." Carrie flipped through the pages, ignoring the presence of another human in the room. "Um, Riley, it's been a long trip for me, and I would like to call my wife and son."

"You want to dissect that notebook now, don't you? Listen, Billy sought your support, so rather than go back to your hotel, you can stay here and, at worst, watch his cat."

"That works. I sense a hefty reading waits for me. I also wouldn't mind snooping around."

"You don't want me hindering you with questions. I get that, and I'm not offended."

"Come back in the morning, Riley. I'll need you to help fill in the blanks as I'm overwhelmed with questions." Carrie stopped and shook her head. "I'm so sorry. Billy asked you to house sit.

You can stay here if…"

"No worries, Carrie. Like I said, I have a place to stay, and frankly, it would be best for you to stay here. This is Billy's sanctuary, and no one understands him better than his cat, Amber."

Riley gave Carrie a brief apartment tour before making his way to the front door. The fridge filled with a supply of food and the cupboard full of cookies were the highlights. After noting Amber's food requirements, Carrie reassured Riley she would be fine alone. Just as she was about to close the door on him, she reached out her hand and grabbed his. The sudden display of tenderness surprised Riley. Up until that point, his interaction with Carrie had been almost clinical. Carrie smiled and tucked her lips inward before speaking, her eyes seeking his until she could see her own image in them. "Riley, you're putting on a brave front and are worried about Billy. I'm here now, okay?"

"I suppose so," Riley said hesitantly. "Billy doesn't trust too many people. I mean, to get close to him. You're here because he has faith in you."

"His home says so much about him. All around this apartment, I see pictures of comic books, but not one picture of Billy. The only picture he has of a real person in this whole place is the one with this woman holding his cat."

"Oh, yes, Christmas last year. Cass brought him a cake and a gift for Amber, this scratching post thing."

"Riley, I hope to achieve closure. A picture tells a thousand words." Carrie released a stunned Riley from her grasp. "One favor, until I sort this out, please say nothing to Cass about my presence. She might impede my progress, asking too many questions lacking answers."

"Sure thing," Riley said. "I'm sure Billy would prefer that."

The door closed as Carrie gave Riley one last smirk.

"Wow. That Cass girl needs some good advice," she said aloud, glancing over at Amber, who stood perched on the couch's arm studying her. "Oh, you are a cute cat. You know full well what I'm referring to. Nothing but those comic books and the one picture he has is of you and Cass. Like I needed thirty years of professional practice to figure this out."

Amber meowed in response before turning on her back, inviting a neck rub.

"Oh, great. I went from Marie and Maris to a dingy apartment in Brooklyn with a spoiled cat." Carrie began rubbing the underside of Amber's neck. "Now, I'm talking to a cat, too!" She laughed aloud.

Carrie settled into the couch and phoned Marie and Maris, answering Maris's queries concerning the creator of Aeon with imprecise explanations. In fact, Carrie was silent regarding her accommodations and the frustratingly little knowledge she garnered. Her guilt in not following up with Billy through the years and reluctantly accepting his fate were her motivation. Satisfied to discover an ample supply of milk in the fridge and a mug to her liking, she returned to the couch and placed the journal on her lap. She dismissed the notion it was not a diary and opened it to the front page to find written in bold blue ink, "November 2007."

Carrie's eyes did not wander off any word in the notebook. Not the digital clock that flashed with the change of every minute, not Amber leaving the couch on and off to go to her food bowl, nor the wail of the outside city traffic could conspire to steal Carrie's attention. Even her breath seemed suffocated by the sheer power of each word flowing through her brain like a raging flood. "Oh my God!" she muttered to herself, shaking her head.

Upon completing her first read through the notebook, she rose, paced the apartment, refilled her cup, and then settled back on the couch. Satisfied she had convinced herself that the notebook could not be documenting factual events, she reconsidered her analysis of it. An hour or so later, her energy waned as she succumbed to her thoughts. Every so often, she dozed off. Images emerged in her sleep and just as swiftly disappeared. The imageries remained vague, but the feelings in the pit of her stomach were genuine. A sense of foreboding caressed her intestines before tying and tightening them together in tight knots. No, she would not leave or quit without finding the truth.

In the early hours of the morning, Carrie dozed off on the couch, exhausted by her thoughts. In her sleep, she could not escape the world she had now entered—her mind reassembled what she had just read into vibrant pictures. Carrie began to mumble, "I will find you. I will find you," as Amber crouched Sphinx-like, balancing at the couch's edge, a vigilant guardian.

CHAPTER 24

The Destroyer of Music

Just before 9:00 a.m. Carrie awoke to a gentle rap on the apartment door. She gathered her bearings and made her way over. "Who is it?" she asked.

"Doctor, it's me, Riley. I thought I should check up on you."

Carrie fumbled with the chain on the door and opened it. Riley stood before her with a concerned and very different look. Gone was the heavy burden of hair on his face, and his black hair sported hints of auburn in it. While still gaunt and frail in appearance, he appeared younger looking. "Hi, Riley, please come in."

Riley smiled at Carrie, handing her a small nondescript paper bag. "Bagels. New York bagels. There's a container of cream cheese, too. I thought you could use a bite."

Carrie smirked. "An offering to a god, right? Well, thanks. I guess I obviously enjoy a good meal."

Riley smiled. "I kind of thought you don't get good bagels where you live. I see you were up early." Riley gestured to her attire.

"I sort of fell asleep in my clothes. I'm glad you're here. Has anyone heard from Billy yet?"

"No, Cass hasn't, and neither have I." Riley paused. "When Billy goes camping, he stays offline, so we don't hear from him for days and then, poof, another edition of *Time's Musicians* gets posted. Then he returns."

Before Carrie could make her way to the kitchen, Riley had sped past her and in minutes had coffee brewing. Carrie retreated to the bedroom, changed, and emerged to find a steaming cup of coffee and a bagel plated on the oval kitchen table.

"Wow, this is better than any hotel!" Carrie laughed.

Riley smiled. "I've spent a thousand hours here. It's a special place with magical healing powers. I went through a tough time and Billy took me in when I feared to be alone. That couch over there saved me." He pointed and began chuckling. "H.R. Pufnstuf. Good ol' H.R. Pufnstuf."

"Excuse me. Did you just evoke a memory from the days of my innocent youth? Nobody watched H.R. Pufnstuf except me."

"Well, Billy did. Told me, he discovered the show by chance, and he watched reruns wherever he could find them. Told me it got him through a lot. A tale about an outcast who finds a magic flute and gets taken away to this wonderful, colorful world."

"A mean old witch wants the flute."

"The boy's name was Jimmy."

Carrie slid to the edge of her seat. "I guess he saw a lot of himself in that boy."

Riley laughed. "No, he saw himself more like good ole H.R. Pufnstuf, the dragon who protected the boy. Remember that line—oh, Billy says it all the time."

"I am forgetful now at my age. You must remind me."

"He can't do a little 'cuz he can't do enough. Or something like that." Riley stopped as Carrie seemed preoccupied, glancing over at the notebook with regularity. "Did the notebook tell you anything?"

Carrie seemed startled that Riley had noticed. "I'm not sure." She shivered. "Fill me in about his activities and behavior before he disappeared. Anything out of the ordinary for him?"

Riley reached over to add milk to his cup. "Before we set up the call with you, I noticed nothing except that he looked drained, like exhausted."

"Like he had sleepless nights?"

"I just thought it was about the comic book."

"But it wasn't that?"

"One morning at the clinic, he was staring into space, and he told me it been a while since he had nightmares. I get them all the time, so it surprised me he never had them."

"Did he describe the content?"

"No, he just thought because I had my share, he didn't want to trouble me."

"He works on his comic book over at that desk?" Carrie pointed a small desk dwarfed by drawings pinned to the wall above it.

"Those drawings are from his cult followers. He loves getting them and posting them. Yeah, that's where he does his magic.

With all the trouble he sees at the clinic,"— Riley pointed to himself— "that is his fortress of solitude." Riley's eyes opened wide.

Carrie put her coffee down. "A eureka moment, Riley?"

"When I was here days ago, his phone kept going off. Like someone kept messaging him."

"I imagine it frequently occurs at a clinic."

"No, his reaction was strange. He looked at the text and would just freeze and kind of bite his lips. Then another text followed, then another, until he shut it off."

"Did he tell you who it was?"

"I should have asked. He just pretended like I hadn't noticed or anything. I figured it wasn't my business. Then, the next day, he had me line up this call with you." Riley pointed to the notebook. "Did this notebook offer any useful insight?"

"Riley, give me some time to collect my thoughts."

"No worries. I have to leave anyway to start my shift."

Carrie laughed. "Please come by later, and we can work together to fill in the blanks." With those words, Riley dutifully departed.

Loneliness. It was the only word Carrie could use to describe her impressions when she approached the apartment door the previous evening. She now became overcome with a strange comfort. Or perhaps Amber's cooing presence nearby gave her that feeling. Seated on the hard burgundy-stained desk chair, Carrie rotated the coffee mug in her hand, swirling its contents. She wondered how many drops from leaking souls had slipped over the cusp on her watch. With her handwritten notes resting next to the notebook, her eyes traced a path along the surface of Billy's desk. Besides the usual keyboard, mouse, and monitor, the desk, like everything else, seemed ordinary. On the corner of the desk was a stack of comic books. Amber leaped off the couch over to Billy's office space, knocking Carrie's pen to the floor. "I'll give you some attention later," Carrie shouted in mock anger to her. *Oh, great, talking to the cat again.* Carrie reached the side of the desk to retrieve her pen. As she reached down, she fingered something thicker and more substantial than a comic book on the floor. It was a book. By its awkward position, she surmised it had accidentally fallen off the desk.

Without paying much attention to it, Carrie placed it on the left-hand side of the desk. Then nosiness got the better of her, and she brought it closer.

The Magicians of the Mind, a novel by Dr. Arthur Laughnon.

Intrigued by the title, let alone the fact that a doctor wrote a novel, Carrie turned to the back cover. "A psychological thriller about a boy whose supernatural abilities allow him to enter the mind of others and the brilliant scientist who must stop him to save the world."

I guess this isn't a comedy. The author's bio section aroused her interest.

"After years spent researching the powers of the human mind and thought, Dr. Laughnon's first major novel draws upon his experience on the front lines of innovative, experimental science." The bio mentioned some university in Germany that Carrie couldn't recall, plus vague research projects at unnamed North American institutions. The photo of the author, nor his name jogged anything in Carrie's memory banks. Then again, she never cared much for remembering the names of academics, or obscure

researchers, let alone their faces. She leafed through the novel and found a reference to Dr. Laughnon's current employer, The Thoth Institute. The esoteric sounding name tweaked her curiosity. Frustrated, Carrie tossed the book back on the desk, choosing to distract herself with a second cup of coffee. The thought of sitting and waiting for the phone to ring or Billy to return irritated her. Ten years ago, she stopped looking for answers against her instincts. This time she committed herself to unearthing them.

Coffee mug in hand, Carrie stared out the window at the busy street below, her thoughts strung out like a clothesline across a deserted alley. For months, Carrie longed for a mystery or a sense of purpose—now, amid one, she grew restless and frustrated. Energized by an elongated sip of her coffee, she glimpsed at her phone to find a text from Maris wishing her a good morning. She smiled and reminded herself of her promise to him. She had to help the creator of this adored comic book. Amber arrived at her feet and weaved in and out of her legs with each stride she took, purring as she slinked around. "Maris. Yes, Maris!"

The book's details were inputted into a text to Maris. He promised Carrie to scrutinize the novel and research The Thoth Institute. Pressing Send, she slumped back into the welcoming cushion of the couch and closed her eyes. They popped open, and she began composing a second text. "Maris, please don't forget." She knew Maris could find whatever information existed on the internet much quicker than she. With Maris's recruitment for this mission completed, Carrie made herself at home in Billy's apartment, soaking in its vibe. In between feeding and playing with Amber and taking a walk outside, she settled into the couch with Dr. Laughnon's book in hand. She expected Riley to return in the evening, hopeful he could shed light on Billy's journal.

Before she knew it, Maris had arrived home from school and responded to her request with a confident, "I'm on it."

The novel occupied her mind causing her to shiver. Only a few pages into it, something familiar about the story nibbled at her. Each page became a burden for her to read and more troubling than the last. Her instincts were roused. Since Riley visited in the morning, an unnerving quiet had settled into the apartment. Convinced she had missed something, she returned to Billy's desk and began to study the various drawings hanging over the desk. Carrie stared at the brightly decorated wall. A world of superheroes created by one young man.

She remembered the words of Oscar Wilde in *The Picture of Dorian Gray*: "It is not he who is revealed by the painter; it is rather the painter who, on the colored canvas, reveals himself."

While the size and shape of each image were unique, the vibrancy of the colors struck a universal chord. It reminded her of the power of paintings she had seen in the stained glass windows of medieval European churches. Each offering from an adoring fan impressed her. One image, in particular, got her attention, it was not amateur work. Instead, it appeared to be an original, ripped out comic book page. The discoloration along its edges and weathered look gave it a vintage appearance.

Carrie's eyes squinted, and her head tilted slightly. She wondered if all along, she'd been asking the wrong question. It was not about whether Billy was a hero or a victim—perhaps the more significant question was what Billy aspired to be?

Carrie's phone broke the silence with the distinctive ringtone reserved only for Maris.

"Maris. I am so glad to hear from you."

"Mom, you will never believe this. Like, this is so messed up."

"What are you talking about, sweetie?"

"This novel, Mom. This novel. It's *Time's Musicians*! I mean a rip-off. Only the plot is so warped."

"Warped?"

"It's, like, written by the villain, the destroyer of music."

Carrie shielded the phone microphone with her palm. "Shit." *Was Billy in danger?* Carrie now wondered how big a lie she'd told Riley when she told him not to worry. *Or was someone else in more danger?*

CHAPTER 25

The Sleepwalker

Not twenty-four hours into her mission, as she now thought of it, Carrie had grown fond of the couch's soft embrace and a purring cat next to her. She reclined back, placing her feet up on a tan ottoman, as Maris reported back to her.

"Okay, Maris. I am sitting down now. You couldn't have read the entire book already."

"You must be kidding, mom. I just started flipping random pages and read the back cover. Mostly, I looked up some comments on the internet."

"What is the novel's premise?"

"It's about a boy with supernatural power. He can communicate with everything around him using music. His mind plays music."

"And he isn't the hero?"

"No. So there's this dude, a scientist. The government hires him to save the world from this boy."

"Why?"

"It's because his power is so strong that when he gets angry, his music drives everyone around him insane." Maris's voice grew excited.

"The main character is not the boy?"

"It's this scientist instead. No one understands why everyone goes mad except him. He's been researching this power for years, and everyone laughed at him."

Carrie reached for a notepad on the nearby end table and began scribbling.

"Listen, Maris. Did you perform a search for the name of the school I sent you?"

"Not yet, but I will."

Carrie thanked Maris and asked him to text her anything else he found out. Maris' surrender of the phone to Marie was an even more difficult negotiation, especially when he learned Carrie was staying at Billy's apartment. After explaining to Marie the twists and turns of her undertaking, she told her she would likely remain at least two more days.

Marie stated in complete seriousness, "You sure you're not making this up? I mean, just to make your retirement a little more interesting."

"Oh, Marie. I've become sympathetic to mice running through a maze. I'm not sure I smell cheese up ahead or a mousetrap or both. Every turn is a wall I keep bumping into."

"Well, I'll send your cape to the cleaners when you return. Just don't occupy Maris too much with non-school work. Studying comics won't keep his grades up during the exam period."

"Marie, this is his world I'm in now. The world of Aeon. When this is resolved, I might get a personal comic book."

"Good lord, Carrie. You never stop." Marie laughed. "Okay,

please take care of yourself. You find trouble wherever you go."

"Nothing I couldn't handle. Oh, someone's at the door." Carrie turned to see the handle twist. "I'll keep you posted."

Riley entered carrying two large, stained brown bags. "I thought you would be hungry, and perhaps, I could join you for supper. If you didn't mind?" Riley said.

"Not at all. This mystery requires collective brainpower."

"I also had to lie to Cass. I know she would be here in seconds if she suspected Billy's plight." Riley said.

"I promise once I figure this all out, she will be debriefed." Carrie grinned. "Put it this way, she couldn't be objective if my senses are correct." She winked at Riley, who nodded back in agreement.

Riley took the bags and began pulling out cutlery and plates from the kitchen. "Szechuan food, Carrie. Got it from a place Billy and I discovered. It's an ex-junkie go-to place. I'll just have a bite and make it an early evening."

"Your insight may be invaluable. Honestly, you know Billy better than anyone."

Riley scratched his ear. "I kind of hoped you were way ahead of me by now. You dissected Billy's journal again, right?"

"Oh, boy, did I ever." Carrie's head swayed, her chestnut-tinged bangs swinging along her forehead.

The duo ate rapidly. Riley wondered what Carrie had learned and when she planned to share it. He grew impatient. "So what's in that notebook? I am dying to find out."

Carrie did not respond. She bounced out of her seat and walked to the end table before plopping into her favorite spot with the journal in her lap. She motioned for him to be seated.

"Well, it's a diary of sorts. Let me put it this way—when you first walked into the clinic as a patient, they observed you and recorded those observations."

"That's how Billy and Cass describe the process."

"Billy's journal is a log of detailed observations he recorded over a few months."

"Observations about who?"

"His roommate."

"Why would he be observing his roommate?" Riley seemed surprised.

Carrie turned to the first page and began reading to him.

November 2007

I cannot remember the exact date it started. It might have been four nights ago, likely five. Who knows when you're sleeping? Sometimes I remember dreams or nightmares days later. They seem like a frame from a film, except the frames are out of sequence. I supposed they are just random projections of my imagination.

I guess I didn't make much of it at first. He likely sought a snack from the common area. Lots of us guys are always sneaking around the dorms at all hours. It kind of reminded me of the days back at camp. I was hoping it was like that. Well, except perhaps the part about me almost dying.

Last night though, I learned John's erratic behavior was far more complicated. John was not awake. I am sure of it. He was sleepwalking. I know because I asked to accompany him. Shit, I had the munchies, so I thought I would join him. He just shushed me. That isn't what spooked me. No, it was the look. His eyes rolled back. The hazel color in his eyes shined in the darkness, but I could only see a glimmer. Clearly, he existed in a different world and place. He kind of nodded at me. No smile. None. I figured he wanted to be alone, so I stayed behind and drifted off back to sleep.

Hours later, he returned to our room. Our beds are about six feet apart, so privacy was a luxury. Well, I listened to this strange sound, a high-pitch wail, like a cat in pain. I approached his bed to find his head buried face down in his pillow. The noise stopped. I put my hand on him to check his breathing. His pajamas were drenched in sweat, and he twitched a little, like a shiver. I pulled the cover up higher and let him sleep. The next morning, nothing. He didn't remember a damn thing and looked at me funny for asking about it.

The more I thought about it, I recall John wandering earlier that week. I suppose it's stupid, or I'm just paranoid, but that is why I'm writing it down now—just in case it happens again. I mean, John has been through some shit, like a lot of kids I knew when I was young. So I'll keep track. Hopefully, this was an isolated occurrence.

Like a skilled narrator, Carrie allowed for her now spellbound audience to catch his breath and let it all sink in. She broke the silence she created. "There's more."

Riley's brown eyes seemed hypnotized. He shook in disbelief.

"I don't understand. There's a whole notebook of this. How many times did it occur?"

Carrie did not answer, extending her hand and flipping through all the pages. Each page danced like a marionette before him. She replied, "About forty pages of documenting his roommate's behavior."

"Isn't John the reason they expelled Billy? I don't understand why he kept this hidden."

"No, but when you read the rest of it, it will explain a lot, even too much."

"Too much?" Riley stammered. "What exactly was going on?"

"Beware as the subject matter is intense, Riley. John remembered nothing about his own sleepwalking. Billy attempted to tell him at various moments until, out of frustration, he just documented it."

"Many people sleepwalk, dream, or have nightmares. Often, they're fantasies," Riley said, struggling to articulate his thoughts. "I feel you're suggesting there was a deeper meaning to this that only Billy understood."

Carrie looked at Riley. "Billy trusted you with this. Take it and read it, please. You might help connect this story from the past to the present." Carrie moved toward the door. "While you read, I need to take a walk and get some polluted air into my lungs." She laughed. "I want to give Marie and Maris a call and need some privacy. I'll bring back cookies."

Riley grinned. "Sure. If it helps Billy."

Riley's slender fingers swept aside the imaginary dust from the cover of the journal. His actions were mere procrastination. When his hand first touched the journal, just where Billy described it would be, he hesitated before retrieving it from its hiding spot. Even with Billy's blessing, he chose not to read it when he first held it. As he flipped through the pages, the handwriting and blue ink overwhelmed his senses. He could feel the intimacy and intensity of the thoughts woven together with each word. Entering Billy's mind, he reasoned, would confirm or deny his perceptions of him once and for all, and he feared his gut was wrong. So he'd set it aside to wait and hope for Carrie Woodson's arrival. Now, his instincts told him that Billy needed him.

The front page flipped open and then another, and then another, his fingers pressed the edges of each page tighter and tighter as if clinging to the edge of a cliff. With each word, Billy's voice took over from his, and before long, the world of Billy ten years earlier swallowed his attention.

Nothing happened, or I assumed nothing happened for a few nights. I was too damn exhausted to remember. Exams are coming, and my workload is draining me. So, yes, perhaps I had noticed nothing unusual at night. But something is going on with John. It's not just him sleep-walking at night or talking in his sleep. It's his behavior today, and I guess, if I think about it, it has been going on for a while.

We were walking across campus to the commons area to meet Kate for lunch. A hundred feet away, he stopped dead in his tracks and looked around in circles. He held this position for a minute, eyes squinting. Then he just dropped his backpack and started running. Stunned, I just stood still. He came walking back toward me and seemed to shake. I asked him what was wrong, and he kind of just gave me this blank stare and said he thought he saw someone he recognized. He was pensive the entire day, more than the last few days. He hardly said a word to Kate. A sentence or two at most. Kate was too much into her studying to notice, I suppose. It would all be irrelevant if John's bizarre meanderings did not escalate.

I crashed around midnight or so. Last I remember, John was eating crackers on his bed. Around 4:00 a.m. and I wake up because I have got to pee. I tried to get up real quiet not to wake John. Only when I look, he's gone. His blankets were all over the place, so he definitely was asleep at one point. He was nowhere to be found. A faint light from the hallway cast a shadow on the wall, and that's when I knew our door was partially open. John had truly vanished.

The halls exuded a Halloween vibe, creepy and hushed. With it being an exam period, the silence did not totally surprise me. If John had the munchies, the caf would be his destination. The vending machines were well stocked. I didn't see him right away, nor did I try calling his name, either. As I stood at the entrance and looked around, nobody was visible, so I decided to leave. Then, I could hear breathing. Even if I were to try, I could never forget it. No, it was not normal breathing. It sounded like someone gasping for air after holding their breath for too long. Then the breathing stopped—totally stopped—but not before I determined the source. Under an elongated cafeteria table, the outline of a foot, not a foot in a running shoe, but a barefoot, was visible. When I crouched down, I found John on all fours, like a petrified kitten. I had seen that look before. Too often, mind you. Like a child hiding from a parent, an angry parent.

"John, peekaboo. You can eat chips in our room. I don't mind the crumbs." I tried to laugh, I did, but when he turned his face to me, I did all I could to not scream. In the dark, his eyes opened so vastly, it seemed like an ocean of white around this tiny island. He put his finger to his mouth to quiet me and then returned to his crouch, just staring out into space. I crawled right next to him and got my mouth close to his ears. I could see his body trembling. Not shivering cold but scared-shitless trembling.

"John, is everything okay?" I slid my hand along the laminate floor and grabbed his wrist.

"Quiet, I don't want to miss him. Not tonight. He's here. Somewhere."

"Who, John? Campus security?"

He responded, but in a way, which made me wonder if he processed what I said. "No. I'm sure I saw him today. That means he's still here."

"On campus, the person you thought you saw is here?"

"They have to be. I promised to save him."

When I woke up this morning. I looked at my hand, finding the words "Save him" inscribed on my arm. I wrote it there so I wouldn't forget. How could I?

We spent over an hour crouched together, waiting for him. He may have wanted to chant like we used to. I started humming, and that is when he started freaking out and grabbed both my wrists. "Stop, do you understand what'll happen if they catch us?"

I tried to ask him one of the millions of questions I had. He just grabbed my wrist tighter and begged me to be quiet. I prayed he would snap out of this state. No longer was I certain if he also recognized me. After about an hour of waiting—or rather, John waiting and me just staying quiet—he crawled out before wandering off as if nothing happened. Not once did he glance over.

His first class was at 9:00 a.m., and even though mine was later, I made sure I was up. Hell, how could I sleep? When I told him what happened, he listened and was silent for a long time, like he was processing something. Then he just looked at me and told me I must be imagining it or had a bad dream. How could I even say to him I had been observing him? Alone in the room, after he left, I convinced myself that I was tripping out. I also thought perhaps it had been exam stress. Amazing what the mind can do. That scares me.

Riley analyzed each word as he tried to squeeze any insight out of Billy's detailed accounts. Page after page contained a painstakingly vivid record of Billy's surveillance of John. Some pages were dated. Some were not. There were gaps between the dates, which Riley assumed were for Christmas break or vacations. He tried to stitch together the information into a cohesive tale. In doing so, and with each page, he found himself right with Billy as if he could solve this mystery with him.

The narrative grew darker as time passed. John's daytime behavior became more erratic and paranoid to the point where Billy noted a distance developing between them. Riley reread the following passages repeatedly.

> *I could sense John's frustration with me growing to where I have seen his fists clench when I bring up things he cannot seem to remember. Today it was expressly sad. He saw me having lunch with Kate as I always have done on Mondays. He became upset because we were alone this time and not with other classmates.*
>
> *Well, when we returned to the dorm, he asked if I was jealous. He said that I was having these hallucinations of him because of my unresolved feelings for Kate. I grinned at his outburst, and later, he apologized, pretending not to take them seriously. It hurt me, which he's never done before. Later, I noticed him outside. Some snow blanketed the ground, and he only wore his runners. His elbows were on his knees while his palms smothered his face. The sun has a way of highlighting things, and I swear I could see tears accumulating in his eyes. Whatever the hell was going on, I was making it worse by questioning him. I once thought of showing him the journal. No longer do I consider it such a great idea.*

Riley a deep breath and sipped on the tea he had made. "Don't give up, Billy. He needs you," he said to himself before moving on to the next page and the next page after that. The pattern had a sinister clockwork precision to it. In the pre-dawn hours, John stalked through the dorm, taking random paths but always searching. With each episode, Billy tried harder to converse with John, only to be dismissed. Each episode ended with John abandoning his hunt and returning to bed, never speaking of his prowl the next day, let alone acknowledging Billy's presence. At times, Billy's handwriting grew erratic, with words scarcely discernible, no doubt desperate to document the previous night's adventure.

Riley placed the notebook to his side and stared straight ahead. Billy had recorded the return to campus, the snowfalls of the winter, and the first thaw. As the end of the school year approached, a sense of impending doom dominated the tone of Billy's entries. The unexpected change in John's behavior from the fall to the spring was evident, but for Billy at ground zero, doubt began to show.

> *Last night, I did not follow John. Nor did I follow him some nights last week. Not out of fatigue (I'm not a big sleeper), and it's not like he takes off every night. I just wonder if it's me who is imagining all this. My recording it all is a clever illusion of my mind. If I write it, it happened, and therefore my sanity exists intact. What if I am wrong, and this is some perverse mind game, a clever nightmare haunting me day and night?*
>
> *When I ask John if he had a dream or nightmare, he just laughs at me, telling me he has not dreamed in years. Kate is getting annoyed with me, too. I have stopped even mentioning John's wanderings. Kate and John*

started dating last month. Whether I'm happy for my friends is irrelevant. John's accusations stalk my thoughts and stain my motivations—or rather, my perception of them. Do I imagine all this because I feared the blossoming of their relationship? I wonder if John is right. I fear being smothered by feelings I cannot digest and choked by words trapped in my throat. So I choose to be happy for them and sleep, not with peace of mind but with noble intentions.

It all changed tonight. Out of the blackness, I was awakened by two strong hands shaking me. John's quest required a sidekick.

Amber leaped off the couch and onto an end table before disappearing into the kitchen area, causing Riley's heart to skip a beat. He stared at the front door, wondering when Carrie would return. His fingers followed the edges of the notebook, measuring the thickness of unread pages. He wondered what lay ahead. Content with her meal, Amber returned and nestled next to Riley's feet, purring as if on cue.

CHAPTER 26

Follow the Screams

Riley returned to the journal, so absorbed with the tale, he had not even noticed Carrie's arrival. She settled in on the far end of the couch, nibbling on a cookie.

> *I could not see his eyes, but I could hear the raspy whisper of his voice. He told me to follow him with nervous intensity. His voice grew agitated with each second that passed. For a moment, I thought he was wide awake and not sleepwalking. By the time I exited the dorm room, led by John's hand, I knew I was wrong. He pulled me along down corridor after corridor, up and downstairs, running faster with each second. Down a long hallway leading to the library, he stopped and let go of me.*
>
> *He tugged on the locked library door and then turned and leaned against it and slid down the door until he'd curled himself tight like a ball. And then he began to sob. I tried to make him tell me what upset him. He kept*

shaking his head, saying he lost him. I then asked him about who he lost. He reached out and pulled hard on my pajama top, tearing the collar, and told me, "They took him. It's all true."

He kept looking at me with this frightened look. After asking John if he recognized me, he just grinned for a second and said, "I trust you because you followed me tonight."

I promised him I would help him find whoever he was looking for. He got up and told me we had to find the corridor with a sign on it labeled "Research Area - Prohibited". The door had a tiny rectangular window, through which this blindingly lit corridor was visible. We would be sure when we saw the linoleum-tiled floor sloping downward to another door where the passage ended.

He stood up and led me back to the cafeteria. We sat facing each other. He seemed distracted by the clock on the wall and kept telling me we had to find him by sunrise. Once we found him, I was assured, I would understand.

John began telling me how one night he awoke with a headache. For a few nights, preceding the headache, this horrible murmur invaded his brain. Not a buzzing sound, but a stifled voice. One night he awoke, the murmur having morphed into a clear human voice. The voice kept repeating a number and telling him to come to join his new friends and to save them. Sleep was futile, and soon he heard footsteps from an upper floor.

He left his room and followed the sound of the footsteps

until he met with what he assumed to be another student. Only this student wore a top like a hospital gown tucked into baggy jogging pants. He also seemed younger than John. The young man's hair was long and black, and he looked like he had not slept in days. John asked him where he was going. He told John he awoke in a hospital ward. There were five or six beds in a row, each with a young male lying on their backs wearing a hospital gown like him. A light with a reddish tint to it silhouetted the walls of the room.

The stranger could not recall how he got there but, when he awoke, this voice in his head continued talking to him nonstop. Scanning the room for a radio or television, he found none. There were no headphones in his ear, and none were visible on the others. When he started to get up, two men wearing gray lab coats barged through the door. Each wore these hospital masks that covered their faces. Both stood over him for a second, ignoring his pleas and questions. Then one of the two men shook his head and became agitated. He had a headset with a microphone and was whispering to someone through it. The other man nodded in acknowledgment, producing a syringe and needle.

The young man could not process everything and barely had time to move before one man was on top, holding him down. Within seconds he could feel the sting of the needle. It was then that a blood-curdling scream emanated from one of the nearby beds. He looked over to see a patient frantically pulling at his ears as though in excruciating pain. Blood started trickling down.

The two men who entered remained stationary. They seemed confused. Suddenly, another man sprinted through the door. He had no mask on and was wearing a white lab coat. These old school black glasses and a receding hairline highlighted his head. In a monotone voice, he started yelling at the two men, and one rolled off the young man and joined the other at the screaming patient's bed. All three hovered over this screaming patient and tried to subdue him. With all the chaos taking place, the young man noticed an open door and fled.

Throughout his escape, a murmur continued in his head. When he stopped running long enough to focus, he realized the murmur was, in fact, the sound of faint screams, the coming together of multiple voices.

The young man told John how a primordial instinct begged him to flee. He zigzagged through a maze of long, sterile, bright-white corridors until he came to a door with a keypad. He typed in a three-digit code, a code that kept repeating itself in his mind since he woke up, one that he'd overheard one of the men in lab coats say aloud. The door opened, and he found himself in an area that looked like a regular office building with classrooms. Before long, he had come upon John in this corridor.

The young man then started to shake and mentioned the injection and became dizzy. Before John could react, they heard footsteps coming down the hall. John attempted to calm him and promised he would be okay.

The young man freaked and said assistance was not heading their way. They were coming to get him. He then started running down the hall, his footsteps staggered more and more with each step. The last John saw of him, he'd turned back once more to yell, "Don't let them catch you. Get the fuck out!" John scrambled in the opposite direction, back toward his dorm room, never looking back. John remembered a numbered patch on the young man's gown: 5871.

John hesitated when telling me this—his lips quivered—and then he said, "You have to help me find him." So we spent the better part of the night wandering down the corridors of our dorm. Now and then, we ran by fellow students, often in various stages of undress, doing what university students do. I made sure I spoke when a nosy one dared to confront us. John's eyes bore a faraway look that spooked them. A look I recognized from my past. The look of soul searching for a nest high above the wreckage of their existence. That type of look.

Fatigue won out, and John retreated to our dorm and crashed on his bed. I pulled up the uneven metal chair we had for guests and sat close to his bed, listening for any hint of words from his sleep. I knew I could take those words and piece them together. While he made not even a peep other than his heavy breath as he slept, I tried to write everything down that happened tonight. I also walked into the bathroom and just analyzed my own reflection. I needed to commit to memory every detail of my appearance just to convince myself I was real.

The next morning John awoke and left for class without making a noise. I found myself in my bed, my pajamas on, and collar sporting a two-inch tear. When I next encountered John, it was in the hallway, while heading toward classes. His hair always made him seem paler than his pasty complexion actually was, but today he looked dead, his white skin marked by a ghoulish gray tint. I could tell he was swimming in thought as I spoke to him. From the corner of my eye, I could see the rectangular envelope sticking out from one of his books. He proceeded to show me a letter from the Graduate Institute of Human Scientific Advancement, which was further down the highway from Hobart. They had accepted him into one of their master's programs. I was unaware he had applied.

I had applied to a graduate program at another nearby university and was awaiting my acceptance letter. For years we planned to attend the same graduate school. When he showed me the letter, I realized how much had changed. Any sadness lasted for an instant only, no match for my sense of dread. He laughed at me when I asked if he recalled sleepwalking and changed the subject. Before I could say a word, he told me I need not "watch" him anymore because once he graduated, he planned to get his own private dorm room. He did not even wait for me to react before walking off. The semester ends this week. Exams are next week. I have no choice but to figure this out fast.

Riley's reading stopped. The next entry was dated April 2 and was unexpectedly brief. He flipped forward in the notebook, finding no additional entries before returning to the April 2 date.

> *A horror haunts my friend John. The memory lurks within him and consumes his sleep and feasts on his being by day. Whatever I do, please do not judge me, my friends. His is a soul worth saving. I cannot allow his light to be dimmed or his song muffled.*

CHAPTER 27

Superheroes

Riley turned to find Carrie seated at the kitchen table, arms folded. He was startled to see her there staring at him, and the notebook fell from his lap. He spoke in a soft voice, his lips pressed together so tight that the words seemed to gasp for air as they escaped his mouth. "Carrie, we need to go find this John guy. I'm concerned now."

"I see you have been reading at a quick pace." Carrie did not look at Riley as she moved toward Billy's work area. "If you have a clue about what's going on, then you can enlighten me."

"I can't even guess what Billy described. This was ten years ago, Carrie. Did Billy discuss John?"

"He never conferred any details about John other than concern. I'm still not sure why he didn't, but the tale is more complex than I imagined."

"The sacrifice he writes about at the end. His expulsion occurred soon after."

Carrie stopped at the desk and turned to face him. "Yes. It seems that way. We need to locate the sleepwalking main character from Billy's journal."

"I never met John or have any information about his whereabouts." Riley could see a twitch in Carrie's eyes.

"I didn't understand why he wasn't here at first." Carrie nodded her head, affirming her own suspicion. "Now, it's making sense, especially leaving the notebook behind for me to read."

"He wants you to help John! But why now? Why not ten years ago?"

"My theory is a foe who had no name has emerged from the shadows."

"Goodness, Carrie, you sound like a narrator from like—"

"A cartoon, possibly a comic book?"

Riley's mouth dropped. "Please don't make fun of Billy's work."

"Far from it. There is a connection. The Dr. Distortion character of *Time's Musicians* is trying to corrupt the minds of the youth with his music. To distort their music, he will gain power over them."

The journal caught Riley's glare. He reached for it and scrolled through multiple pages before finding the section he sought and staring at a page. "John claimed to hear a noise in his head. The young man, patient 5871, he saw these boys subjected to a strange noise that made one go literally into a psychotic state." Riley slid the notebook to her as if it were a virus-laden tissue. "Oh, my God, Carrie."

"You're wondering if it all could be true. John's sleepwalking was an awakening of an experience."

"Could something so traumatic be repressed—could his mind bury it?" Riley's voice grew breathless as its pitch elevated.

"Only for it to rise to the surface at night in his sleep, months later. Billy assumed the events documented occurred at Hobart."

"Perhaps John shared a revelation with Billy," Riley spoke in whispered tones.

Carrie walked over the sink, silent and selecting the words to present to Riley. "You forget the villain. There always is a villain."

"You're scaring me now. Besides what you've read in *Time's Musicians,* what makes you so confident?"

Carrie pointed to Billy's desk, and the novel placed ominously there.

"What does this novel have to do with it?" Riley walked over, shaking his head, and began examining the cover before flipping it in his hands to read the back cover. "Hmm, it's kind of similar to Billy's comic book. So someone is ripping off Billy's idea?"

"My young padawan read the author's description."

Riley flipped to the bio section and read each line. "Did you ever meet him or read any of his works?"

"Never. Right now, he is an enigmatic character, author, and researcher. Fortunately, I have a talented investigator at my disposal." Carrie said, keenly aware of Maris's internet abilities.

"Well, at least Billy will have help when he returns." Riley offered.

"I am tired of having that feeling for the last ten years. From the day Billy left my office, my gut told me to expect a day like today."

"Well, while Billy is away, we need to find John, wherever he is now," Riley mused. "Conceivably, something in here will give us a clue." Riley pointed to Billy's work area.

Carrie grinned. "The trail of bread crumbs Billy left for us may have always been in plain sight. I should get an update soon. Riley, would you mind getting me a sandwich? I assume you're hungry, too?"

"I take it you want to be left alone for a bit?" Riley asked rhetorically. "No worries. You can slip on your superhero costume while I'm gone." Carrie smirked at the joke, and Riley disappeared out the door.

As she awaited Maris' update, she scrounged the apartment and selected a random edition of *Time's Musicians*. By chance, it was the episode where Dr. Distortion originally appeared in Aeon's universe. Amber sidled up to Carrie's right calf and rubbed against it. She reached down and picked up the purring cat, holding it to her chest. "Oh, Amber, Dr. Distortion is no match for us old-school superheroes." She laughed defiantly, never wondering how ludicrous she sounded. Marie would enjoy witnessing Carrie with her guard down. Power spawned responsibility, Carrie supposed, but also the ability to not give a damn about other people's opinions.

CHAPTER 28

The Graduate Institute of Human Scientific Advancement

Almost on cue, Carrie's phone buzzed. Over the years, she'd convinced herself that a hard stare at it, if done long enough, would elicit a ring. Maris may not be the most punctual of teens—not that any teen could be—but when tasked with a mission that interested him, no one could match his tenacity. Maris's voice filled Carrie's ears in bursts of jumbled words and frenetic energy.

"Slow down, Maris. I could only catch a few words. You say you read most of the novel?"

"Yep. It's pretty *effed up*."

"Is it that similar to the comic?"

"Yes and no, Mom. The main character in the novel spends the story trying to track down this boy who has special mind powers."

"I kind of got that last time we spoke. Did you get to the ending?"

"It ends with the doctor finding the boy and being able to access his mind and erase his powers."

"How does he do it?"

"He discovers what he calls the 'sound of the universe' and synthesizes it into the background of a video game."

"And he gets the boy to play this game?"

"Yeah, and when he does, it takes over his mind, and he can no longer use his powers."

"What happens to the boy after he loses his power?"

"Oh, he becomes like everyone else, and in the epilogue, the doctor visits him and offers to take him under his wing to rehabilitate him."

Carrie became quiet, replaying Maris's synopsis over and over in her head.

"Mom, you still there? I found Dr. Laughnon… or rather, not much."

"What did you discover?"

"Um, I needed Mom's help. She asked if she could help. She can Google better than you can."

"High praise, I'm sure. What's the story with this author, the so-called doctor?"

"He did scientific research at various universities. Mom looked into these academic databases, where they publish research and stuff."

"So, he has published research out there?"

"That's just it. She found like no trace."

"No trace," Carrie smirked. A supposed scientist, a doctor, without a trail of published work seemed ridiculous. Unless…

"She says there is an explanation. She said you would without difficulty guess who performs research that's under the radar. Her words, Mom, not mine. *Under the radar*."

Carrie clenched her fist. The realization tore through her, almost paralyzing her. Clandestine, government, or private research. That would leave no trace if the sponsor wanted to keep it a secret. "Oh, dear." She sighed, hoping Maris would not hear.

"That was her reaction. She did not look happy and said she hoped she was wrong."

"Tell Marie when she gets home that she has her moments of brilliance, too."

Maris laughed. "I will."

Carrie switched the subject and reviewed the highlights of Maris's activities in her absence, hoping to avoid any more discussion about Billy. He seemed frustrated that Carrie had yet to connect with his icon. Just as Carrie started to say goodbye, Maris piped up, "You forgot about the university, where Dr. Laughnon teaches."

"The Thoth Institute. Maris, by chance, did it used to have a different name?"

"Yep. It changed names almost ten years ago from The Graduate Institute of Human Scientific Advancement." Maris struggled to even hear his mother's breath. "Mom, you there?"

"Yes, I'm here. I'm just finding this place on a map."

"It's not very far from where you worked for Dr. Edelman."

"Geez, Maris, you have quite the memory."

"I listen to your stories. Even the boring ones." Maris laughed.

"Before I hang up, I was wondering if you've seen anything posted about *Time's Musicians*?"

"That's why I keep asking you about Billy, Mom. The last episode should be available online within days."

"Days!"

"Yeah. There was a post today from one of my more reliable sources."

"Thanks, Maris. That is very helpful."

"Mom, just find Billy. When you do, convince him to continue, please."

"Sure thing. I will do my best."

"You never fail, Mom, that's why you're you."

Carrie grinned as she hung up the phone. Her lips began to quiver, and her right hand twitched. She tried to contain her nerves and reclined back in her chair, heavy in thought. "Why can't my instincts ever be wrong?" she asked, almost expecting an answer from Amber.

CHAPTER 29

The Sounds of the Ocean

Somewhere in LaJolla, California, Charles Edelman's phone rang. It rang and rang and rang. Long since retired with his wife, he rose early each day to enjoy the sound of waves rolling in and out beneath the constant Southern Californian sun. Weak knees meant golf became a curse to him. As he was sipping coffee from his balcony, the ringing seemed persistent, irritating. His wife appeared to have disappeared to her morning yoga ritual. He dared not call it a class. Ritual seemed to capture her addiction to the "exercise art," which was her term for it.

Once he answered, it startled him to discover Carrie Woodson's voice invading his phone and ears. "Carrie, it has been a while. How is retirement treating you?"

"Charles, I can only assume retirement is treating you well. I could never totally be retired." Carrie paused, not feeling any need for small talk. "I require more information about that Thoth Institute in New Hampshire."

"What?"

"Or you remember it as the Graduate Institute of Human

Scientific Advancement." Carrie's tone became sarcastic and intentionally so. The pause before the response confirmed her suspicions.

"Oh, Carrie, you're not digging in the ancient ruins, are you?"

"You didn't believe I would let it go so easily, did you?"

"Carrie, let sleeping dogs lie. I've always been on your side."

"I appreciate it, but the mummy you thought you buried came to life."

"Shit." Charles sighed, and he began to tap his fingers fretfully.

"Be honest with me, Charles, were you aware of any odd research carried out at the Institute?"

"No, but of course, I had suspicions. I never spoke to anyone from there."

"But, surely, you've heard?"

"Rumors, Carrie. A multi-million dollar, state-of-the-art, scientific campus built in the heart of an industrial area, carved out in the backwoods."

"Government research?"

"Worse—the unholy alliance of governments and private funds is far more terrifying."

"Governments, plural? As in, not just ours?"

"Money does not recognize nations. That is not news to you."

"Why didn't you advise me? I could have done something more."

"That's why I didn't tell you. I had my suspicions, so I took a specific course of action. However, that was then, Carrie. Something has come up now?"

"It was all true. My instincts, my gut, are yet to be wrong.

Now I am almost certain."

"This is a minefield. So, they rebranded the place?"

"Diabolical branding. A soul cannot be rebranded, just suffocated."

"A new patient has come to you?"

"More like evil from the shadows, I suspect."

"You've always been in the art of soul-saving, Carrie. I know you. It qualifies as a dark art, and you practice it better than any sorceress."

"You make me sound like I perform witchcraft."

"I meant it as a sincere compliment. I wish I had it in me to go to the lengths you do for your patients. So, what is this evil?"

"Did you ever meet Dr. Laughnon?"

"Never, the name does not even faintly ring a bell."

"Well, he was connected with the Institute years ago and just returned."

"What makes you think something ominous is afoot?" Charles said as he placed his coffee down.

"I'm not sure. I thought you might have valuable information."

"Carrie, my advice is for you to start enjoying your retirement." He stared at the breakers crashing toward the shores. "The waters may seem calm and still one moment, but the riptide will pull you in and drown you in a second."

"Geez, Charles, now I can go sit on a porch and sing songs from *Margaret Poppins*."

"I'm serious, Carrie. You and I come from the pristine academic world of politics, budgets, and professional jealousy. The playground of Dr. Laughnon reeks of danger."

"You underestimate the depth of my magic bag, Charles. You always have. Enjoy your retirement." Carrie did not even wait for a response, she tossed her phone on the couch contemptuously and made her way to the kitchen. Feeling caged in this Brooklyn apartment, Carrie paced the floors, returning to Billy's desk often, with a nagging dread of dealing with a puzzle with ill-fitting pieces. Then her phone rang. She frowned at the number. "Yes, Charles. Bored with watching waves?"

"I take your sarcasm with the respect intended, Carrie, so no need to apologize for hanging up. Let me reveal what I learned through my former colleagues. Just rumors, but undeniably relevant."

"I won't hang up now. You've got my attention."

"There were rumors of deaths on campus at that Institute. Accidental deaths. My sources witnessed nothing first-hand, so it hearsay, but they supposed some risky research was being carried out, and accidents occurred."

"Risky research? For Christ's sake, Charles, I got the impression it was a think-tank type of place for geniuses, not some weapons plant built next to a nuclear power plant on a flood plain in an earthquake zone."

"I cannot say more because they are all just rumors. I just called you because, if they're true, you are dealing with life and death, Carrie."

"Charles, battles for souls are historically life and death."

"You never showed me that philosophy degree you seem to have. Never appeared on your resume when we first met." Charles laughed.

"You don't remember, do you? That is your quote from your

formative years," Carrie retorted. "If someone had asked me to give your retirement speech, or if they had even invited me to your retirement party, I would have reminded you of that quote."

Charles grew silent, rubbing his hands together. Yes, the constant and predictable sun. He chose this place to retire because it was devoid of surprises. Rare were the thunderstorms. "Carrie, promise you will tread with utmost caution in all of this. Don't hang up until you promise."

"I can never do that. By the way, my home is located in the woods next to a mountain. We get severe storms, sometimes thirty or more feet of snow. My bones ache in the winter, and I get frostbite when I'm not careful. Then the spring comes, and I can watch the Canadian geese fly by in March. There's a robin, I'm sure it's the same one, that builds her nest in our tree, and I forget about the hardness of the previous winter and have hope and appreciation for the coming months. So I can promise nothing because helping someone find that hope is what I live for."

Carrie hung up, and Charles fell asleep with the sun warming his face to the steady beat of waves massaging the shore. Only Charles never woke up again.

CHAPTER 30

John

The thin layer of dust accumulating along the windowsill drew Carrie's ire. She swiped at it from left to right and back again with equal vigor, creating a whirlwind of cat hair. She'd waited too long and relied on too many others to get results. Perhaps age and complacency had defeated her.

Carrie returned to the workstation after cleaning her hands. Desk drawers opened and closed multiple times. Comic book drafts lay scattered about, as Carrie no longer worried about their order. She reached for the novel, committing to memory the image of Dr. Laughnon on the back cover. She had tried calling to speak to Dr. Laughnon, but to no avail, reaching a voice mail each time—a sign of a very busy man or a man who wished privacy. The voice message noted his unavailability for weeks.

Sensing Carrie's frustration and moodiness, Riley returned to see if any progress had been made before excusing himself to return to the clinic and his part-time work there. Preoccupied, he did not notice the man brushing by him at a frantic pace as he descended the stairwell. He wore a blue windbreaker, well-worn jeans, and brown shoes. The man stood at the apartment's entrance, his eyes shifting to his phone and the number on the door. Satisfied, he rang the bell.

Carrie ambled toward the door assuming Riley had forgotten his wallet or keys or phone. She unlocked it and turned away, not noticing that the visitor was not Riley.

"Excuse me. I thought this was Billy's apartment."

Carrie froze. A man stood before her eyes with short brown, wavy hair, a pale face, and a small nose. He was marginally taller than her. His eyes were round, with barely visible wrinkles, as he smiled at her. Carrie was at ease in his presence, and intuition electrified her heart. "This is Billy's place. Are you...?" Convincing herself that her instincts betrayed her, she paused, now uncertain.

"My name is John." He extended his hand and reached out to her. His gazed wafted beyond her, surveying the background. "Excuse me, but I came to see Billy."

Carrie grabbed John's hand, almost yanking him off his feet, pulling him into the apartment. "This is Billy's place, though he's not here. I suppose you have no clue where he is?"

"No. Sorry if this seems rude, but who are you?"

"My name is Carrie Woodson. Doctor Carrie Woodson."

John's eyes closed heavy in thought. "A doctor. Is Billy all right? Kate described him as spooked when she visited."

"*The* Kate?"

"Yes, my wife Kate. She drove here the other day. It's a complicated story, and I don't want to burden you."

"John, I am the psychologist who evaluated Billy before they expelled him from Hobart."

John slumped backward and leaned against the door. His body trembled, and he put his head down. "Are you visiting because something happened?"

"He reached out to me. Before I arrived, he went camping, telling everyone he would be back in a few days. Apparently, to clear his head and finish his comic book."

"He must have left shortly after Kate," John's tone grew uneven.

"Why did Kate see him, John?"

"It's all because of me. She was worried and thought Billy might be causing my strange behavior."

Carrie escorted John to the couch and made him a cup of tea as he explained to her the purpose of Kate's visit. He recounted how calling out Billy's name in his sleep and the nightmares he could not explain.

Carrie listened intently, not saying a word. "Kate didn't travel with you, or is she waiting at a hotel?"

"No, I needed to do this alone. Kate wanted to come, but I refused. She does so much work with rescue animals, and they need her. Besides, she is expecting, and this is my problem." John became distracted by Billy's work area and the drawings on the wall. Carrie watched him rise from the couch with his hands reaching for the illustrations, never touching them, as if feeling an unseen force. "He always viewed the world in a uniquely beautiful way." John reminded himself of Carrie's presence. "His creation is amazing."

"You don't sound like someone who harbors much of a grudge against him." Carrie realized the sharpness of her words. "I mean, you speak of him admirably. I'm confused."

"Doctor, that happened years ago. I still don't understand, which is why it terrifies me now. I imagine how fearful I was then. Billy faced fear like no one else I ever knew." John turned to face Carrie. "When we met in camp, I saved him from this sinkhole he fell in. I was lucky to find him in the blackness. The thing is he never showed fear, even when I dragged him to safety. Instead, he looked… serene, just one with the earth. That look remains etched in my mind." John sighed. "I'm sorry. Kate thinks I came here to help myself. My reason is more complicated."

Carrie leaned forward. "First, call me Carrie. I'm all ears, John. I came here for the truth."

"When Kate visited, she took photos of this work area, his desk and drawings and all that. A few weeks earlier, I caught one of my students reading an issue of this comic book. It called to me, Carrie. It called to me for some reason. When Kate showed me who was behind it, well, I took it as Billy's way of communicating to me. It's absurd, right? But I'm here to help him fight whatever lurks in anonymity."

"John, you first must heal yourself first and suture your own festering wound."

"One morning, a month ago, I woke up and turned to Kate. She looked like she was studying me. It reminded me of Billy's awkward behavior. He tried to explain, and I attacked him. Not in a physical sense. I attacked him with the only weapons I had, ugly ones—jealousy and Kate."

"Billy assumed you were sleepwalking because of a trauma in your past. Your mind shut off the part causing you great pain and fear."

John's eyebrows raised. "You either are the greatest psychologist of your generation or…"

Carrie smiled. "Oh, I got a cheat sheet. I'll explain, but please tell me what triggered you this time."

"I can't do this to Kate anymore. Billy tried to help and, well, look at what happened. My nightmares and fears cannot hide in obscurity forever. I am ready to face them." John paused and looked at Carrie. "Yet none of this seems to surprise you. What did Billy tell you?"

Carrie grinned and walked to the kitchen table and came back with the notebook. "I doubt you are aware Billy documented your nighttime journeys."

John's eyes widened. "We were students. He was always scribbling, doodling, and taking notes. I just assumed that was his diary."

"Not quite. Billy watched over you and tucked what he witnessed away, never even showing it to me back then."

"And now?"

"He made sure I got a hold of it."

"Let me understand, he reached out to you, disappeared, and then left this for you." John began to tremble.

"This will be difficult, John. Please, read this journal." She paused. "I am warning you because it may trigger things. However, I will be here with you."

"I trust you. If Billy called for you, I must trust you." John glanced up at drawings. "Aeon deserves an appropriate finale."

Carrie handed the notebook over to John, and he opened it with anticipation of a child. With his attention absorbed by the words, she moved to the desk and swept up the novel sitting at its far corner. She assessed he would not be ready to see that yet and retreated to the kitchen area. A villain, at worst, was expected. She instead encountered a frightened man-child. Trained to see gaping wounds hidden beneath the shield of an emotional barrier, old wounds not healed reeked of the foulest stench to her. John's emotions appeared frozen within him except for his eyes, which glistened with traces of moisture.

Discretely, she thumbed through the novel, reading and rereading passages, glancing at John intermittently. Finally, she heard a heavy breath from John and slid the novel into a kitchen drawer. The notebook lay open at John's side as he stared into space.

"John, is everything okay?"

He ignored her at first. His head drooped and, while responding to Carrie, his eyes appeared to blink at a rapid pace. "He tried to help me, and I treated him like the enemy. I was so insecure."

"It scared you, John. Whatever happened to you—I'm just hypothesizing—was too traumatic to consider real."

"Billy was… *is*, I mean, a brilliant person. I knew about his feelings for Kate and how shy he was. I used it to combat my fear of him. Billy's closeness to Kate petrified me."

Carrie did not leave her seat, and her tone became somber. "No, John. That is the easy way out. You feared what you knew had happened." She hesitated, trying to gauge how much he had read. "Do you remember a patient, number 5871? Are you there yet?"

"No. I have no clue."

"If you feel comfortable, read on. At some point, you brought

Billy into your nightmare."

He reached over to the notebook and continued reading.

Amber sidled into view and rubbed against Carrie's leg, reminding her of the empty water and food bowl. Carrie smiled, thankful for the distraction, ever mindful of John's comportment. In between preparing sandwiches and sending texts to Maris and Marie, time passed at a sluggish pace—except for John. Past and present were bonding through Billy's words.

The dead-eye stare of John into some unseen abyss was an indication John had reached the final words. Carrie walked over to John and sat next to him.

"Carrie, you've read this?" She nodded affirmatively. "My nightmares, the patient 5871, and all of that, what's your professional opinion?"

"Your painful subconscious thoughts were released. I can tell you I suspect you were privy to a horrible event. You noticed when the journal ends?" Carrie didn't let John respond. "The last entry is likely right before when my role in this started and tersely ended."

"Oh, my God." John leaped to his feet with nervous energy and began pacing around the room. He circled and circled the room at a dizzying pace, his thoughts motoring him. He stopped at the window overlooking the living area. "I wrote and sent the email, Carrie. It was never Billy—it was me." He began a slow whimper followed by bottomless gasps, the truth choking him.

Carrie rushed over as he began panting. "Listen to me, John. I doubted Billy sent that email. What are you aware of now? Tell me."

John caught his breath. "I woke up one morning and had all these messages popping up from all the people who'd received the email. I didn't know what was going on until I read the original email. It was from me, accusing the school of conducting experiments on students. I freaked because I knew no one would believe me and would just label me as crazy. Everything in my memory banks went blank, including writing an email."

"You accused Billy, I assume?"

"No, I told him what happened, and he could see how scared I was."

"Scared you would get expelled because you had no recollection of what happened?"

"Carrie, it terrified me they were going to..." John gripped the arms of the chair. "Commit me, Carrie. Send me to a fucking institution."

"I don't understand, John. They wouldn't institutionalize you over this."

"They would if my erratic behavior wasn't an isolated incident. Carrie, I've been a patient before."

CHAPTER 31

Patient John

John wiped his eyes and observed Carrie's reaction, which lacked any indication of surprise. "As a child, they sent me to an institution for almost two months. I can't describe how scared I was to even consider the possibility of being sent back. You already knew of this, I'm guessing."

Carrie grimaced. "I didn't. Now I comprehend why they wouldn't give me information beyond name, rank, and serial number."

"Billy didn't tell you?"

"No, he never told me. If he did, we wouldn't be here right now." Carrie continued, "I suspected Billy never wrote that email."

"Carrie, he was protecting me. That morning, I became hysterical with anxiety. I told him I didn't remember sending the email, and the accusations I'd made were so serious they would think I lost touch with reality. The irony is, I had, Carrie. I questioned my reality to the point of fearing my next thought. Shit, I even had Billy spinning in circles." John reached over and grabbed the notebook, waving it in front of Carrie to prove a point.

"So, you never thought Billy tried to embarrass you and set you up?"

"There's one thing you need to understand. I *believed* Billy when he told me he did it. I swear I did. Because I needed to."

"John, the primordial survival instinct kicked in. You needed it to be him and not you."

"I can't even make it up to him. I ruined his friendship with Kate—the things she said to him when she heard about it…"

"In the brief time I spent with Billy, I learned how strong a character he could be. This great need drove him to protect you from your nightmares. For him to document everything he witnessed, it's clear he feared for you." Carrie grabbed John's shoulders. "He saved you, and for several years, it worked. It's only recently that the ghost has returned again."

"I convinced myself that Billy concocted all of this, so I moved in with Kate. She never noticed anything unusual after I changed schools. The mirage was wonderful until it ended."

"Since Billy was compelled to stay away and since you were fine during all these years, you logically assumed he was to blame."

John could no longer face Carrie. "I had my doubts over the years." His lips twitched. "Carrie, if that nightmare was my memory replaying a trauma, the reality is dreadful."

"I would call it wicked, if true." Carrie squeezed John's shoulders. "Sadly, it appears to be the case."

"Billy was not part of it, and during our Hobart days, we were roommates since our first year. We attended the same school." John paused, his voice almost inaudible. "Except that summer."

"What summer?"

"Right before our last year. Billy and I were invited to spend the summer studying at a nearby graduate school that had opened, with other young university students looking to study advanced research of the human mind."

"My understanding is Billy stayed behind."

"No, his dad had taken ill in the spring and moved with his wife to Arizona. He only had a few months to live, and Billy wanted to spend one last summer with him, so only I went."

"Tell me more about this program."

"Well, it was a summer retreat, and they had you stay on the campus. During the day, there were lectures from these very innovative thought leaders in consciousness, cosmology, spirituality, and other very diverse fields. The enjoyable part was being with all these young, like-minded thinkers."

"What about at night?"

"We stayed in these common dorm rooms. When I close my eyes and visualize them, I keep imagining these private hospital rooms, very white and sterile."

"Was there anything else unusual?"

"Headaches were pounding my skull into submission. My eardrum throbbed for days." John paused and looked for the notebook and flipped pages agitatedly. "Shit." He brought the journal close to Carrie's face. "In my nightmare, I complained about these headaches." John's face shriveled up, and he moved around the room. "I find it strange that when you asked me about that summer, I can only piece together this vague outline of what I did there. Like many details are escaping me. Nameless faces parade through my mind then disappear. I refer to them as familiar strangers."

"Your memory's been blocked, even erased to a degree."

"Blocked. Funny you should use that word."

"I'm not in the funny business."

"It may explain the freeze frames, Carrie. For a long time, I've had these moments when a visual splashes into my memory, followed by another and another, and then I'd stop them. A voice would play in my head, halting them. I never recognized the voice, assuming it was mine."

"It may not have been yours. Let's discuss those freeze frames."

"They were nothing I could place or associate myself with. Images of people I can't identify. Before I could string the frames together to get a story, I would hear this voice."

"Part of your memories were jammed by a prompt."

John walked over to Billy's desk. Carrie could sense a groundswell of emotion percolating within him. John appeared to be fitting pieces together before her eyes. "Billy's actions spared me from the Institute."

"What?"

"Before Christmas, I received a letter from the grad school, offering me a full load scholarship to study there."

"You never went there because they became disinterested in you."

"I suppose so. I received a letter about a month after the email episode, which politely stated that the program envisioned had been terminated."

Carrie smirked. "Perhaps a coincidence."

"Nothing is coincidental or as it appears. I suppose I escaped and moved on. Kate and I just had this quiet period together, and one day, I went into teaching."

"You abandoned your study of the mind and all that search for universal wisdom." Carrie grimaced. "I'm sorry that sounded sarcastic. It wasn't meant to be."

"I have this feeling I was saved by what happened."

"No, you saved others by sending that email whether you have any recollection of whether you did or didn't. When I told Billy that you were graduating and moving away with Kate, he smiled and then caught himself. I suspect he knew you would be safe with Kate."

"Until lately. I erased everything that happened that summer from my mind. The more I set my mind to it, the more frustrated I become. If I didn't read it in this notebook, these would all be wild delusions of a damaged mind."

"Your subconscious is awakening from a deep slumber, John. When you rest your mind at night, whatever you hid is growing in the dark and beginning to expand. Your nightmares will get more intense, I'm afraid."

"For ten years, I have been fine."

"Or you thought so. The burial of memories, painful ones, burdens more than your mind."

"I'm not worried about me. I need to find Billy."

"You're connected in this in a way neither of us understands right now." Carrie stopped from saying more and telling him how Billy had likely untied all the knots or was close to it.

"Does it make sense to you? Why all this is happening?" John stared at Carrie.

"I'm still searching in the forest. I've been in this apartment, staring at Billy's work area, the drawings, and studying his notes. We are both drawn back into it in different ways."

"The present is both past and future," John replied. "We were part of this song years ago, and it seems like some conductor has returned to the stanza last played long ago."

"An eloquent way to say your past has returned to haunt you." Carrie laughed. "The operative word is *haunting*. If what we've talked about is true, you witnessed experiments being done on students, and you were part of them."

"You mean the headaches and the voice? The fact I can't remember details of that summer?"

"Yes. Billy noted a change in your behavior once you returned to Hobart in the fall of 2007. You were repressing memories, and the process became more difficult and took a toll on you."

"The night of the email, I likely had a flashback—a brief memory that was vivid enough to compel me to send the email."

"However, whatever trigger prevented your memory from replaying the events you witnessed came back online by the time you woke the next day."

"Mind control. They messed with my fricken mind. But who? There were just lecturers and speakers representing various areas of science."

"I've read Billy's journal a dozen times. The subject ripping his ears off because of a sound in his head." One of Carrie's texts had been to Marie, an expert in neurosciences. "One of the controversial sciences is the study of sound waves and their effect on brain functions."

"Controversial science is a polite expression. Try military

research."

Carrie nodded. "It explains a lot of the secrecy. Regular programs don't get shut down so rapidly—only those with private funding do. Investors would be vilified if these experiments were exposed."

John became motionless, the whites of his eyes smothered by the lids pressed tight over them. Anger tore through him. His mind. *Someone had played with his mind.* "The only things we have that are our own are our thoughts, our ideas. To contemplate that even there we're not safe..." He opened his eyes and jostled open a nearby window, inviting in the foul city area and a cornucopia of sounds. "When I was a kid, they thought I was different and tried to understand my mind at the institution. They send me there because I had these ideas that a group of people at my school thought were not normal for a child. They weren't violent or sexual ideas or anything like that. Ideas about the universe and our part of its soul. A child must be mentally ill to possess such notions, so they evaluated me, trying to understand the inner workings of my psyche. All because I had ideas."

"No one protected you?"

"I grew up in a foster home. Unlike Billy, no one ever adopted me. We met at a camp for underprivileged children. I got lucky when a psychiatrist took over my case by some fluke. He told me I didn't belong in an institution, vouched for me, and got me into a public school with a program for similar kids who like to color outside the lines." John smiled. "At the time, he was nearing retirement, a Dr. Edelman from what I recall."

Carrie shook her head and chuckled. "Now it's making sense."

"You've worked with Dr. Edelman?"

"He assigned Billy to me after the email incident and was my mentor during my formative years. I just never knew he played a superhero, too."

John could not hide the smile that broke through. "We are in the right apartment to talk about superheroes." The smile dissipated, and his tone grew low. "There is an evil out there, Carrie. You wouldn't need superheroes without them."

"John, I imagine a great cleansing wave is building and will crash the shore soon. Or maybe it's a pissed psychologist with anger issues." Carrie winked at John, enjoying her moment of levity.

John walked away and moved toward the art decorating Billy's wall. He stood and studied the images. "What are you trying to tell me, old friend?"

CHAPTER 32

The Sound of Time

Beneath John's calm outward appearance, Carrie sensed emotions swirling. She could only guess at what memories scrolled through John's mind. Many, she knew, were like jagged edges of crushed glass spread over the delicate, pristine surface of his mind. Whatever happened, he had not fully processed it, and as the waves of memories rolled in, they were nothing like the storm brewing behind. John seemed almost childlike in his demeanor.

As the springtime sun began its descent, and the shadows invaded the apartment, John began to fidget. "Any news about Billy? Has anyone heard anything at all?"

"Afraid not. Billy told his friends that he would return soon enough. We must just sit back and wait."

"Do you mind if I stay here? I can crash on the couch if the cat doesn't mind." John chuckled.

"I would recommend you settle in. Billy wanted us to meet at some point, whether he expected it to happen so soon, I can only hypothesize." She hoped to keep a close eye on John overnight. Whatever secrets he stashed away by day, appear to be released at night. "Your wife, Kate, must be worried about you."

"Worried enough to travel here alone. That's Kate. I'll call her and explain that Billy will be back and that I'm in good hands now. The other revelations can wait until I return home. A pregnant wife has enough worries." John picked up his phone and excused himself to place a call to Kate and update her.

Carrie left John alone and phoned Marie from the lobby, well out of John's earshot. Frustrated that Billy remained true to his word—offline—it did not surprise her. Clearly, they were all pawns in a well-orchestrated plan devised by Billy. Carrie explained the progress made by John.

"Carrie, are you sure you're fine being alone with John at night?" Marie said in a nervous tone.

"I have been alone with patients before. Besides, at this moment, he seems to feel safe with me. That's more important."

"Does he have information about this Dr. Laughnon you had me researching? Have you mentioned him to John?"

"I'm not there yet, and John may not be ready for that revelation."

"What if Billy went to visit Dr. Laughnon?"

"That thought crossed my mind, but when I tried to get ahold of Dr. Laughnon, they told me he would be out of the office for the rest of the week. Besides, Billy is on a camping sojourn."

After finishing her call with Marie, Carrie returned to the apartment and found John at the kitchen table, holding a novel in his hand and staring at the back cover. *Shit, he found it.*

"You were hiding this from me. I was searching for a yogurt spoon and found this novel in the dishtowel drawer."

"It was on Billy's desk. It's a novel that's uncannily similar to his comic book, with one big exception.

John flipped through the novel. "You mean someone ripped off his idea?"

"The novel's villain is a boy with special mind powers."

"The villain?"

"Yes, and the hero... let's just say he seeks to control this boy's mind to save the world."

John dropped the book and looked at Carrie in disbelief.

"Let me ask you, John, does a Dr. Laughnon trigger any memory? Look at the back cover, specifically the author's description. Was there a Dr. Laughnon where you studied that summer?"

"I would recall such a distinctive name."

"What about the picture under the bio?"

John picked up the book, examined the small thumbnail image before shaking his head in the negative. Carrie could see the faintest twitch of his right eye.

"You were hiding the book. I doubt Billy kept this in a kitchen drawer." John smirked as Carrie blushed.

"As I said, it had been sitting on Billy's desk, or at least on the floor next to his desk."

"I understand. My reaction could be unpredictable, I suppose." John's lips quivered. "Billy had all these clues around him."

Carrie's eyes became narrow slits as if someone had inserted a fine filter in between her lids, and every minute facial gesture of John's was squeezed through it for processing. "I've been in this bloody apartment two whole days and have a million questions. Your presence is providing responses to a couple of them."

"Imagine how I feel. Billy's been in the middle of my whole mess. This is all my mess. Now you're thinking like I am, that someone messed with or has tried to mess with my mind."

"You were vulnerable. My instincts tell me Billy had some epiphany. Your wife's surprise visit likely motivated him to contact me."

The knock on the door sounded purposeful. Not only loud, but it came via bursts of two knocks followed with three more. Carrie recognized it as Riley's knock. She had forgotten to warn Riley to stay away. Alone with John, she could make progress much quicker in a short period and avoid any belligerent behavior toward him.

The spicy aroma of Mexican food and Riley's exuberance dispelled any plans to speak to Riley discretely through the door. Before she could react, Riley had already cupped John's hands in his and shook them enthusiastically. "It's great to meet you. And you are?"

"I'm John. The one you were looking for."

Riley's jaw fell. He gripped the bag he carried tightly. "I can't believe it's you. My name is Riley. I guess you can consider me to be Carrie's sidekick. While that isn't true, it just seems that way."

"It's nice to meet you. I guess you're a friend of Billy's?"

Riley grinned and delighted in describing his initial encounter with Billy and how Billy had helped him through the most challenging period in his life. From her vantage point, Carrie could see John's demeanor change, his eyelids closing, and lips tightening. Riley, too, could sense John's distress. "I hope I'm not upsetting you."

"No, Riley, it's just that I'm the reason for all this drama. For so many years, your friend Billy shielded me from a lot of pain."

Riley reached out and grabbed John's shoulder. "It's funny, but I said the same thing to him once. I was messed up, and he got all caught up in my drama, and I'll tell you what he told me. 'I choose to help you, Riley, because you are worth it.'"

"My drama is just starting, I fear," John stated.

"Billy has a reason for everything. When he comes back, it will all make sense."

Carrie motioned the two to the kitchen, her appetite taking control of the situation. Any apprehension over Riley's unannounced arrival became irrelevant. As Riley entertained John with tales of Billy's exploits, Carrie witnessed an aura emanating from John. His soft hazel eyes twinkled, and the corners of his mouth pressed upward, revealing a dimple on the left side. John's appearance transformed, bearing a resemblance to the young college student of his youth—before his world and mind were hijacked. Anger began to boil at the pit of Carrie's gut. Nothing brought the full fury of her being to the surface more than a precious mind and soul damaged. Her partner in life could dare to repair the physical wounds, those that she could see. Carrie's plight was to find the unseen wounds, to close them up, but also to destroy the proverbial knife that created them.

With dinner over, John listened attentively to Riley's detailed accounts of Billy's behavior in the preceding days. Then one phrase caught John and Carrie's attention. "The only time I recall Billy acting unusual was the day he found an envelope shoved under the door."

"When did this occur, and what were the contents?" Carrie leaned forward like a skilled prosecutor.

"Well, I could show you what was in it. Hanging there on the board, dead center." Riley got up and marched across the room and tapped his finger at one picture, almost hidden behind the others. "This particular page was in the envelope."

John burst between the two and reached out to it. "I could not put my finger on it. The color is so faded and vintage quality. I thought it looked out of place. Mind if I examine it?"

Riley nodded as Carrie studied John and could see the sudden bolt of assertiveness in him as he maneuvered under the surrounding pinned pictures and pulled out the tacks holding up the page.

John pulled it toward him and flipped the page to study the backside. "Holy fuck. Excuse me, but holy fuck." John's voice ascended to a high pitch. "Where did he get it? You said an envelope. Did someone give it to him?"

Riley shrugged. "He woke up one morning, a Saturday, and there was this knock on the door. Footsteps scampered down the corridor, so by the time he opened the door, the hallway was empty. Billy almost slipped on this beige envelope."

"Based on your reaction, this page has some significance to Billy and to you?"

John smiled from ear to ear. "I'll be damned. The boy who found the black hole."

"Wow," Carrie's eyebrows raised in unison with Riley's. "You're speaking in many tongues now that I don't understand."

John took the page and meandered to the sofa and plopped down on it, testing the rigidity of its back support. He brought the page up to the light, laughing. Realizing a captive audience awaited his oratory, he turned to them. "This is the missing page from the comic book, the first comic book Billy ever read."

Carrie's mind raced. "You're not serious? I didn't understand the black hole comment, it's been so long, but is this about the boy who went missing?"

John nodded his head. "Sorry, I got so excited that I forgot who knew about it." He glanced at Riley, who stood silently, bearing the look of a three-day-old glazed donut. "I take it he didn't tell you what it was."

"No, I wasn't here when he got it. I came by, and he was so hyper and kept asking if I ran into anyone in the corridor on my way here. He just told me it had sentimental value. It was the first thing he hung over that desk. Two weeks later, he started working on his comic book. It was his inspiration, he said. He said it was from the first comic book he ever read."

"Did he ever tell you the story about the missing boy?" John asked.

"I don't think so. My state of mind was muddled, and if he had, I'm not sure I would have understood." Riley's head shifted downward.

John leaned forward and patted Riley on the head. "Oh, my new friend Riley, there may be a lot we have in common—more than you think. When Billy was young, he met this boy in school who gave him a comic book, only one page was missing. The last page."

"You're kidding me. That's an unusual gift."

"This was before the boy vanished."

"Vanished!" Riley's eyes began to blink as he processed the

information.

Carrie put her arm on Riley's shoulder. "Billy saw him last before he disappeared."

"What? Did they suspect Billy hurt him? No way. He would never..." Riley grew agitated as Carrie squeezed his arm tightly.

"They never found a body," Carrie spoke in a low, somber tone to calm Riley down.

John looked glum. "Billy was in grade five. He thought he was about to visit this black hole within this mysterious cave and then time travel."

"The kid disappeared, leaving Billy with this comic book without the last page," Carrie continued.

Riley's mouth dropped open. "Then this envelope arrives, out of the blue, years later."

"Billy got his ending—closure, I suppose." Carrie's voice seemed to tail off like a song fading out.

"It didn't ever end for Billy." John pushed the page toward Carrie and pointed at the description. "Now check out the back page, across the bottom, in blue ink. It's signed."

"'Escape is for the believers. — Dieter.'" Carrie whispered the words as she read.

"Dieter, Carrie. That was his name, Dieter." John pointed to the page.

Carrie's nose shriveled up. "When I met with Billy, years ago, he only told this story to one other person since he was a child." She looked over at John. "I assume he told you."

"At camp that year, when we first met." John lowered his eyes. His voice trailed off as he shut his eyes in thought, remembering his own anxiety that led Billy to share the story.

Riley got up and began pacing. "No, you don't understand. I had rarely seen him so happy. He just stared at it all day with this goofy smile. A guy in his mid-twenties, grinning about a page from a comic book."

"To believe Dieter survived and was alive would validate everything for Billy," John stated.

"Well, even if he was the messenger, he avoided a reunion. That's quite the magic trick, I suppose, returning years later." Carrie turned to Riley. "So, Billy created this comic book right after he received this?"

"The first edition came out soon weeks later," Riley said and paused. "But, where's the funky map?"

John flipped the page, front to back, and back to front. "What map? This is all I see."

Riley appeared confused. "My memory is slipping, but I could have sworn there was this hand-drawn map on a separate page that came with it." Riley started searching the cork bulletin board overlooking the desk. "These drawings are undoubtedly covering it." He slid his hand behind the drawings, checking each one. "It's not here."

Carrie followed Riley. "You said funky. I'm not sure what a funky map is."

"It came in the envelope, behind the comic page. I remember it had all these symbols written in pencil and a dotted line that ran through it like a maze. I didn't ask Billy about it. It just stuck in my mind because he stared at it, laughing, and then tucked it away back here."

At the center of the room, John stood frowning. *He took the map*. "They never searched the cave for a body."

Riley's eyebrows arched. "What did they speculate?"

"Billy made up the story for attention."

"And Dieter just vanished?" Riley stammered.

"I assume they thought he ran away from home," Carrie replied.

"No one believed Billy. They refused to look into those caves because they were frightened of what they might discover. Most adults don't explore what challenges their sanities. It scares them," John declared.

Carrie looked around the apartment. "Riley, is anything else missing from this apartment? Like, do you notice anything else that Billy took with him?"

"I already checked, Carrie. His closet is missing his sleeping bag and a pop-up tent. He has gone away before, to camp. He took his laptop, too."

John leaned back on his feet, his head tilted back, hands deep in his pockets. "The black hole represents a portal to escape into alternative worlds and realities. Camping likely is where he finds peace, or at least now finds peace."

Riley looked at him and grinned. "Carrie, John is on to something. Ghosts, demons, and fears are not foreign to me. Damn, if I had this peaceful place of refuge, I would head there, too—regularly."

With the sun closing in on the horizon, the evening shadows overtook the room, blending into the backdrop of the dimly lit apartment. The story of Billy's mysterious visitor had taken everyone's mind off the current riddle. The distraction proved temporary, though, as the night reminded everyone of the present. John's hands began to tremble as he poured milk into a glass, and Amber scurried to lick up the errant drops.

Carrie needn't see the outward signs of anxiety. The revelations of the day, she imagined, were like an ancient river methodically carving through the stone facade of John. Over time they would erode whatever protection he had erected, and a wide canyon would open, leaving him to face the ugly trauma of the past. "John, I'll be just down the hall tonight."

"Thanks, Carrie. It's just not the nightmares I fear so much as what I don't remember." John walked over and scooped up some blank papers off the printer tray and, along with a pen, handed them to Carrie. "Please. If I do anything tonight, write it all down."

"Don't worry. My son showed me how to record off my smartphone." She fumbled with her phone and grew frustrated before grabbing the pen and paper from John. "I still like the old technology." She laughed, declared her goodnights, and retired to her makeshift bedroom, planning to call Maris and Marie while expecting a sleepless night.

"John, I'm in no rush to leave," Riley said. "I can keep you company. At least until you tire of me yapping and doze off. I've spent more than a few nights in this apartment, so I have some experience with what it's like to fear your thoughts."

"Riley, I'm not the most fabulous sleeper, anyway. I would like to listen to more stories about Billy and would appreciate your company."

For the next few hours, Riley sipped on Ovaltine while entertaining John with Billy's exploits. John alternated between sipping on his milk, nibbling on a cookie, or texting Kate to reassure her, never giving her enough information to cause her to worry.

With his back leaning on the sofa, John placed his milk down before gazing at the shadows on the ceiling. "Riley, I doubted Billy's story, too, about the black hole. I fucking doubted it, too."

"You mean, you thought he made it up?"

"I used to be like Billy. I believed someone could be absorbed by one universe and be reborn in another."

"Hey, man, I watched Star Trek reruns, too."

"You don't understand. I believed in magic until one day... I became cynical and became a true magician, albeit bumbling. When you are a magician, nothing ever is real anymore."

Riley smirked, stirring his cup of brown-colored milk. "You only forgot. Time creates many illusions. The magic is so incredible, you convince yourself you are the only one capable of creating it."

John closed his eyes and gestured with outstretched hands to the images on Billy's wall. "He never stopped believing. And for fuck's sake, he paid the price because of my fear. You and Carrie must hate me. Like, despise me for all this."

"I would not be here—I might not be *alive*—if it weren't for meeting Billy. Who would open their apartment in Brooklyn at 3:00 a.m. for a scared, recovering addict? Don't underestimate my ability as an illusionist during my addiction. Billy could always see through my act and find the budding magician."

John smiled. "I'm still fearful about what's out there, about what I can't remember. I used to have dreams and nightmares and then spent my waking hours bathing in them and their meaning, or rather, whatever meaning I gave them." He started to giggle. "Then one day, I awoke in the morning and realized

I couldn't remember any dream, not even my nightmares. That scared me—that there ceased to exist places to visit in my sleep. Nowhere for my mind to go. Just darkness, pure blackness. The kind that suffocates you from the inside out. When the music stops, and it's only silence."

"I'm pretty sure Billy has his fears. No doubt, he has seen his share of darkness, too." Riley leaned forward and patted John on the shoulder.

"But he never feared the dark. He learned how to make music from it with his comic books. Billy is the musician placed here for that purpose, I suppose—to keep the song playing. When I first opened his comic book and read it, it seemed spookily familiar." John smiled.

Riley grinned. "Oh, it's his pride and joy."

"Why isn't he continuing it then?" John's eyes narrowed.

"We're hoping that's just an internet rumor. He doesn't talk much about it. Once, he said that a story never ends, like a song that's played by different musicians."

Riley yawned and, as if connected, John's eyelids sputtered then shut, and his legs spread out on the couch. With John fast asleep, Riley made his way across the room, giving Amber a gentle scratch behind her ears before she scurried off and took a curled position at John's feet. Riley departed, reminding himself tomorrow would be busy. Billy would return, the great mystery solved, and life would readjust. Riley thought of John on the couch and recalled Billy's theme that all musicians were welcome. Riley imagined a new musician would join the song. He hoped he could dance to it, too. Overlooked and forgotten, the final edition of *Time's Musicians* was about to be posted.

CHAPTER 33

He Remembers Everything

Billy turned on his phone and checked his signal. There was one phone call he was expecting. Almost on cue, his phone buzzed. As expected, the incoming number was blocked.

The voice of Dr. Arthur Laughnon sent a shrill shiver down Billy's spine. There would be no small talk.

"Listen, young man, I can only suppose what game you're playing with me. I've been doing my homework and decided not to meet with you tomorrow. My book tour schedule is demanding, and I am presenting my research to various interested colleges. I am traveling for the next few weeks and too busy to chase fairy tales."

"This is no game, Doctor. My friend was one of your patients years ago. He remembers you. Let me be clearer. He claims to remember *everything*."

The man grunted, growing impatient. "As I stated, I have a book tour coming up and various speaking engagements."

"But don't you want to see the results of your research? It

worked, Doctor. All the time, effort, and testing on those patients reaped dividends. This one man, he has enormous powers of the mind now, thanks to your work."

"Bring him to my office, then."

"He's scared. Too scared."

"Why should he be?"

"The deaths, Doctor, the deaths that occurred at your school. To be exact, in the research area." Billy pulled each word like an elastic across his tongue before releasing them. *Deaths.* He could hear Dr. Laughnon's breath tremble beneath his lips. A long pause ensued, and Billy shoveled more words into the silent abyss. "Yes, Doctor, there were deaths. The funny thing is the living perceive death as their destiny and reality. To the dead, is their reality, life?"

"Look, I am tired of this game you're playing. I am not aware of any deaths."

"Patient 5871 knows everything. What of the other boy, whose ears bled as he tried to dig out the sound taking root in his brain? Shall I go on?"

Dr. Laughnon's voice grew lower in tone. "What do you want, young man?"

"I seek the same thing as you. Reset his memory like only you can, like in your novel."

"I thought this was your friend."

"I want his power, Doctor. Show me how to get in people's minds. Once you see what he can do, you will understand why I want that power."

"And what about your friend?"

"I crave to obtain his power and return him to an original

state, his mind an empty vacuum within my control. I fear, Doctor, that if you don't help me, his memory will destroy you."

Dr. Laughnon's tone changed from agitated to calm and low. "Very well. Where is this place your friend would like me to validate his power?"

"The caves on the outside of the town of Galt. It's only thirty minutes from your school. Can you please be there at around 7:00 p.m.? I will text you the coordinates."

"Yes, I'll be there. I trust you will be alone with your friend."

"Do you think anyone would believe me except you? He is, after all, your creation, and after all these years, you'll be pleasantly surprised. He fears demonstrating his ability to anyone but you because others would consider him—" Billy's voice stopped as the doctor's chimed in.

"Weird. They would consider him weird. Yes, many of my patients were once considered weird or outcasts. All they needed was me to program their minds in a certain way—my way, with all of my knowledge."

"Like a software algorithm in need of a programming genius."

"Perhaps I have misunderstood you. I am looking forward to seeing you again, young man."

"You can invade the mind of my friend, again, right? We can harness his power?"

"I have devoted my career to it, and my research will never end. It would shock you to discover the extent to which there is a demand for my research. Your friend could be a wonderful addition to my current research endeavors."

Billy gasped. *Current research?* "Well, you can add me to your staff, so you can mentor me then."

"We'll determine if you can be a good apprentice." Dr. Laughnon laughed with phlegm-filled hoarseness. "Just bring me this subject of yours, or should I say, return me my old subject. At 5:00 p.m. tomorrow, not 7:00 p.m., while there's still some light, so you can witness the fruits of my research first hand."

Billy swiped his phone closed. His chest filled with heaviness. His eyes watered as he stared at the mountains lined unevenly at the horizon. The voice of Dr. Laughnon replayed itself over and over in his mind, and Billy couldn't help but worry about his friend. *What did they do to you, John? What did they do to you?*

Minutes later, he ventured into the nearby coffee shop and connected to the free Wi-fi, pulled out his laptop, and, within minutes, the latest edition of *Time's Musician* was available for download or viewing. He shut down his phone before returning to the campground.

The light of billions of stars gathered before Billy. Outside of his tent, he imagined each star as a musical note, twinkling on and off like a string plucked by some unseen hand. Years ago, he had almost died here, running through the night before being pulled into the earth as though it wanted to suck him into its eternal embrace. He wondered, as he had through the years, what was his purpose?

He liked to be alone when the world around him would click into the universe he created and revel in the kaleidoscope of colors and characters of his imagination. Cass and Riley grew accustomed to Billy's disappearances for a few days here and there. Both wondered about his instinctive need for isolation. They struggled to understand that out here, with an endless charcoal sky above him, Billy was alive and connected to a world he could never hope to see or even describe. Billy stared hypnotically at the moon before closing his eyes tight, as if in prayer, and returned to the confines of his tent. Tomorrow the past, present, and future would assemble.

CHAPTER 34

A Gift

It began with a barely audible high-pitched note, a sound that seemed unsure of itself. As John's frustration grew, he tightened the pillow around his head, covering his two ears. The wail continued, muffled but persistent. The sound echoed, bound only by his skull. He awoke, finding himself in one bed amongst many lined up with military precision, in a space decorated with the comforts of a college dorm. He recognized his surroundings as the dorm where he'd spent the summer on an educational retreat. Unchanged by his awakening, the sound continued, louder and steadier, not a single note but multiple pitches. They poked at his eardrum, unlike any song, bearing no hint of rhythm or melody. No other student appeared to be affected.

He threw himself back on the thin cushion that poorly imitated a pillow, pressing his eyes shut. Then he heard it, distinct and blood-curdling. *"Please find me. Help me. Make him stop. Make him stop. Help us!"* The voice paused to John's relief, replaced by a parade of screeching yowls trampling through his petrified ears. His mind raced to thread together the noise into a logical procession of sound. Soon he'd translated the sounds into words—consistent cries and pleas for help. Out of the first voice grew different voices, consistent in their horror.

John froze on his bed, his feet unable to move. Images began to form before him. No longer confident whether his eyes were open or closed, he felt helpless as each image formed and leaped into his psyche only to disappear and be replaced by another and another. Frame after frame of some movie gaining speed and lucidity, as if projected by a mad genius, flashed before his eyes. Time stood still, allowing the film to unwind before continuing, John's heart beating faster with each frame. A story emerged, assembled and packaged by John himself. A final image flashed and then disappeared with none to replace it. The movie had ended. John's eyes squeezed tight before exploding open in panic. His mouth widened, gasping for any air. Like a newborn unsure of how to breathe, John shivered as his body convulsed. Then a voice, one awaiting a tranquil moment, wormed its way through John's mind.

"None of this is real. When you awake, it will all be dark and calm. Your mind will be clear. It is not real. Nothing is."

The mantra replayed itself repeatedly like a torturous chant. John tried to visualize the images that had flashed before him, but with each image, the words repeated. "None of this is real."

The soothing hum coming from a distant horizon seduced John's ears, growing more intense and overpowering the voice that kept trying to plant the same message. A vision passed before John of an endless sky filled with millions of stars, whose lights turned on and off before him, as if at the mercy of some hyperactive conductor. The hum became human-sounding as it merged with a voice familiar and young. John smiled. "Fuck. He's humming a Tool song!"

John sprang up from the couch, his eyes alert and wide open. Amber rested comfortably on his lap, purring contently. From a nearby chair, Carrie's shimmering eyes studied him intently.

She pulled up her chair closer to him and reached out, squeezing his arm. "You're safe, John. It's me, Carrie. You're safe."

"Carrie, where am I? I mean, I thought I was..."

"You had a nightmare, John. I thought you might, so I came in here less than an hour ago to monitor you."

John rubbed his eyes as his head rotated around the room, examining his surroundings. He looked down at Amber and scratched her ears before leaning forward to whisper to her. "It was you, Amber. Thank you."

Carrie looked at him, puzzled. "I've been here with her, John. Her specialty is sleeping. She's mastered that art."

"Her purring, that sound, that amazingly soothing sound, it stopped the voice. It stopped that motherfucking voice." John's hands clenched.

"What voice?"

"The voice kept telling me to forget, telling me it wasn't real. It has been cleansing my memory all this time." John paused as Carrie's eyes widened. "Carrie, I remember what happened. Everything. It came back to me, bit by bit, piece by piece." John's voice drifted off.

"You recall what happened to you? The horrible things? Is that it?"

"The voices of these boys filled my head. Not one boy, more

than one. They were all calling for help, they wanted me to find them to get them out."

Carrie leaned back in her chair. "So, no one did experiments on you? Or you cannot remember?"

John's lips twitched. "I would hear the voices in my head, and I thought I was going crazy. Instead of telling anyone, I searched for them on my own. No one would listen to me, let alone understand. One night, I found this passageway that led to a separate part of the Institute. It was this creepy research facility." John paused, and through the moonlight could see Carrie's face, thoughtful, processing each word. He stopped talking as the intensity of the memories pressed hard on his heart, and tears began to trickle down his cheek. "They were torturing these boys with some experiment to play with their minds. I stumbled across Patient 5871, and then he disappeared. I must have told Billy in my sleep." He paused again. "Maybe this is all just a nightmare. Maybe I imagined it all. It's too…"

"Sinister," Carrie finished. "John, this happened, I have no doubts. Those nights months later, back at your dorm with Billy, a trigger raised all these submerged memories, and your sleep-walking brought back your search for these boys."

"And that voice, it would erase my memory. Whose voice is it, and what the fuck is it doing in my mind?"

Carrie got up from her chair and cleared a spot on the sofa next to John. "Dr. Laughnon's book is about the hijacking, for lack of a more scientific term, of someone's brain waves, and replacing them with his own. Like a puppet having its thoughts and actions played out by another person, a ventriloquist."

"But, Carrie, I wasn't part of that research. I'm now sure of it.

I was in a different area of the Institute."

"You were, but your mind could absorb and process the waves of those in the research facility. Don't ask me how—I struggle to turn on a smartphone, so this is out of my league. However, that's what your story suggests."

"Oh, Carrie, it would be easier to say I'm just plain nuts. I couldn't be in tune with someone's thoughts. I'm a freak, but not that type of freak."

Carrie put her hand upon the back of John's head. "You have a gift, and I am grateful it belongs to you. The boys who were being experimented on were likely going through intense trauma, powerful enough to amplify their thoughts to the one person receptive to them, however far away. That was you, John."

John began to shiver. "I didn't help them. They called for me, and I could not save them. What's the point of this gift when you cannot save those who call for you?"

"Yours is a journey. It hasn't ended yet."

"Billy saved my life. He sacrificed to protect me, Carrie. They accepted me at that school. I could have been one of those test patients or, worse, the one performing the experiments."

"Trust me. The battle is just starting.."

"Will you help me, Carrie? I must stop it from happening again. What if the research continued?"

Or it's about to start again, thought Carrie. "I hope not but suspect otherwise." She wondered how naïve she had been, had always been. Covert and unethical research had long existed, often in the darkness, accepting necessary evils to benefit mankind.

"What if I'm wrong, and this isn't real? If none of it was. My mind could be playing games with me."

"My spouse is an expert in the neurosciences. Years of study and experience, top of her class, and guess what she tells me all the time? The brain and the human mind are a mystery to her, even more now than when she started her studies. And what I tell her—and this drives her nuts—I have known this all along. Everything is real, John, just as nothing is real." Carrie smiled, her teeth shining through the night.

"Now, I see why Billy called you. You dabble in philosophy, too." He laughed.

"I'm thinking something triggered your nightmares again. When did your wife notice them?"

"About six weeks ago, give or take. That's when Kate first mentioned my sleepwalking."

"And the first time you saw Billy's comic book?"

John's eyebrows twitched erratically. "I just learned it was Billy's creation."

Carrie yawned, realizing she did not want to share her intuition with John just yet. Soon John joined her, his body reclining back on the sofa, mental fatigue befriending physical fatigue. "We can talk more in the morning. The great comic book creator should be back sometime tomorrow and can shed more light on this. Unless you want to talk some more? I'm a night owl, so I doubt you can outdo me."

"No, I expect Riley will be back, and I'd like to call Kate early tomorrow. A good sleep would do me wonders." John then rubbed his eyes and stopped, leaving his palms covering his eyes.

"Your worst memories have been exposed. Does sleeping

frighten you?"

"No, I'm not worried about sleeping. I'm more worried about forgetting again."

Carrie leaned forward and pulled John's hands from his head and held them tight. "I doubt you will forget because you don't want to anymore. Besides, I'm here now. One thing is clear—your friend called me to help you. We've met, and we'll figure this out together."

John smiled. "I hope Billy can forgive Kate and me."

"We all owe Billy an apology. Ever since he left my office after our last meeting, there were moments over the years when I thought my instincts were wrong. I wondered if I had been fooled by a sociopath or not done enough for a martyr." Carrie rose and made her way back to her temporary habitat. She turned to wish John a goodnight. "If you need me, I'm a shout away."

"Goodnight, Carrie. When the sun comes up, the world will be different, I promise." John raised his hand in a Vulcan salutation. "Sleep tight and prosper."

"Oh, great, a Trekkie, too. Goodnight. Bagels are on me in the morning." Carrie laughed aloud and closed her door.

John awoke to an empty apartment. It was almost 9:00 a.m. He assumed Carrie had left for a stroll or to hunt down more bagels. Just then, he noticed the blue light of his smartphone, notifying him of a message. By habit, he ignored such notifications, but this time he felt compelled to check it. He reached over to the phone and scrolled through the unread messages. He got to the most recent one. It was from Kate.

"I suppose U R asleep. *Time's Musicians* posted. PLEASE

CALL."

He crawled to the side of the couch and leaned over to Billy's desktop computer. With a few keystrokes, he located the site. The final edition of *Time's Musician* was, indeed, available online. John's heart raced as he examined it page by page, his fingers caressing the words on the screen with reverence. By the time he got to the last page, John had his phone in hand and began calling Kate. When he got to the last page, he gasped as his phone tumbled through his grasp.

He retrieved the phone just as Kate answered with raspy hoarseness to her voice.

"Oh, John, thank goodness you called. You've seen it?"

"Yes, Kate. There is so much to tell you."

"What does it mean, John? Did you learn anything?"

"Kate, I know what happened to me back then, but…"

"I don't understand." Kate paused, trying to stitch together the little details she knew. "What connects this with the comic book?"

"Everything, Kate, everything. One thing is certain. Billy is in grave danger, and he cannot imagine the depths of the evil he is up against."

Kate's voice grew shrill. "Does that mean you're in danger?"

John paused. "Not anymore, Kate. My next steps are clear. You can help me. I just hope it's not too late. Please pay a visit to Hobart College. They need to have the full story about their neighbors down the highway at the Thoth Institute."

CHAPTER 35

The Last Edition

Carrie's early morning bagel trip included a detour. She asked Riley to meet her and introduce her to Cass. Now that she understood the circumstances of her initial meeting with Billy years ago, meeting Cass was a necessary step—the girl in the one photograph Billy had in his apartment. When she arrived at the clinic's door, she felt woefully unworthy. These were the battlefields of the war Carrie fought on a different front. Like a modern general, she had been far removed from the front lines. With each step past homeless men and women, some younger than Billy, when she'd first met him, she could feel her ego melt the fake plastic aura coating her for so long.

Cass eagerly opened the door for Carrie. "Dr. Woodson, I recognized you immediately. Please come into our little world." She took Carrie's hand and led her inside. "Forgive me, I have so many emotions going through me right now."

Carrie smiled. "Please, it's Carrie. I asked Riley to fill you in. My apologies for keeping my visit a secret. Meeting you without at least a few answers wouldn't be fair." Carrie followed Cass to a small office.

"Riley filled in so many of the blanks about Billy very early this morning." Cass paused. "Except, we know him to be a special soul, so if you had said otherwise, we would have had a problem." Cass adjusted her glasses.

"I needed to be sure, Cass." Carrie smiled. "Now, I need your help."

"Sure, Carrie. Anything for you." Cass blushed. "You're the reason I do what I do. I've read all your articles."

Carrie smiled. "Wow, it took a pilgrimage into the city to find someone who read them. I'm the one honored to meet you and am humbled by the work you do."

"This is my calling. It's as simple as that. Please, tell me what I can do."

Riley jumped in at this point. "We need to find Billy," he said. "A text coming from you would get his attention."

Cass's voice trembled. "Are you worried about him? Is he in danger?"

"He needs to learn that John came to see us and remembers everything," Carrie said. "I'm worried that Billy has figured things out and may try to take on something greater than he can handle. Or hopefully, he just went camping."

"In a crisis situation, Billy would make the first sacrifice. He can be very strong-willed. When he goes away, he's out of range or shuts off his phone."

Carrie said, "What about his mom?"

Cass shook her head. "Since his dad passed away back when he was at Hobart, he tries not to worry her."

Carrie looked at Riley. "Well, let's get breakfast and hurry to Billy's apartment."

"Let me clear up my calendar and come back with you. I want to meet John. It's important to me."

"Sure, we'll wait, but hurry. John was in a deep slumber when I left. I pray it's been a peaceful one. I just can't predict how all these discovered memories will affect him. More importantly, I want him around when Billy returns."

Cass reviewed her schedule for the day and found the staff to fill in. She wiped her glasses and raced ahead of Carrie and Riley towards Billy's apartment. "I'm going ahead. Get the food and meet me there."

Riley and Carrie arrived, bagels in tow, to find the door to Billy's apartment door ajar. Inside, they found Cass wandering from room to room, her head swiveling systematically.

"Cass, what's wrong?" Riley yelled.

"John's disappeared. He's nowhere to be found." Cass stood over the couch and pointed at the blanket strewn aside.

"Crap!" shouted Carrie. "Did you turn that on, Cass?"

Cass turned to Billy's desktop monitor, where Carrie was pointing. "No, it was already on."

Riley raced across the room, slid the keyboard out from its compartment, and began typing. "Someone was definitely on this within the last hour according to the web history log. Billy doesn't password protect this bugger, so it's not too hard for anyone to access it."

Riley settled into the chair and within seconds, had the computer humming with activity. Carrie balanced on the arm of the couch, impressed by the speed of Riley's keystrokes.

"You're like a fish in water with this stuff, aren't you?" Carrie marveled. As if on cue, Carrie's phone buzzed with a message notification. "It's my son, Maris." Her initial displeasure upon realizing the text came during school hours was surpassed by her surprise at the content: "Mom, *Time's Musician*, the last edition posted. Luv you."

Carrie shoved the phone in Riley's face. "Billy's posted the last edition."

Riley looked at her. "I know. That's what John searched for on this machine." Carrie's eyebrows raised in astonishment. Riley laughed. "It's what I do. I guess it's what I was born to do. It comes easy to me."

Riley flipped back to the front page, and colorful images filled the screen. Carrie's eyes burst open wide, the brown color glowing, hinting at shades of chestnut with gold intertwined as she scanned the screen. Riley clicked on one page after another, checking that Carrie was ready to move on.

"Almost on the last pages, ladies."

"Hang on a second, let me take a closer look." Carrie leaned so far forward the bangs of her hair blocked the screen. She examined the on-screen image with forensic precision. The penultimate page contained three frames, two side by side, with one rectangular box across the bottom. The main character was depicted in a cavern within the earth. Lost inside, music emanated from him only to be absorbed by the sterile white walls created by Dr. Distortion. As the doctor enters the chamber with the hero, a violent vibration shakes Aeon, who drops to his knees. Instead of hearing his music, a distorted version played, torturing him. Before long, there is silence. The first frame depicts Dr. Distortion standing over a fallen Aeon, announcing that he has gone beyond distorting the sound and has mastered the power to muffle it and kill Aeon once and for all. The second frame depicts Dr. Distortion shocked to discover that Aeon has morphed into the cave itself. New sounds emerge from the walls as infinite notes combine, representing all the musicians assembled by Aeon. Dr. Distortion holds his head in panic as a thought bubble reads, "I have become part of you and will unleash your song." The last frame on the page portrays a cavern empty of beings but, bursting with colors and musical notes converging.

"Ready for the last page?"

"I guess so, Riley," Cass replied as Carrie moved even closer to the monitor.

With a click, a caption in black letters scrolled against a white background: "Ten Years Later." Below the caption were two frames. In the first, a young teenage boy stands at the mouth of the gaping cave emanating a strange light and sound. The boy is reaching out with a trembling hand toward the cave with a thought bubble over his head: "Welcome back, John" In the last frame, the boy is smiling as he enters and disappears into the cave.

Carrie stared speechlessly at the screen. Never one for a loss of words, she fought a losing battle against the tears forming along the base of her eyes.

Riley swiveled his seat to face her and tilted his head. "John! There was no John character in *Time's Musician* before today."

Carrie reached out and grabbed Riley's hand. "This is John's story, Riley. It always has been. Now, John and Billy's whereabouts concern me. It's about creating a world safe for John to explore."

Cass moved away from the desktop and focused in on Billy's wall. "That old comic book page hasn't gone anywhere." She began removing the pins that held the other drawings. "And that map is missing, right?"

Riley pushed back his chair and leaned forward. "Like I told you, it's been missing since, well, Billy left."

She rose from the couch and leaned over Billy's desk and began studying the drawings again, almost toppling over Riley, who stared at her, puzzled. "There is only one cave from Billy's past. The map's creator discovered an escape." Carrie spoke as if only to herself.

Cass ran to the kitchen and began filling Amber's bowls with food and water. "We need to move fast. That cave is in Billy's hometown. I'm sure we can find it."

Riley stood in stunned silence at the frantic pace of the two women as they made one final sweep of the apartment looking for clues before meeting at the door. Carrie spoke to Riley. "The posse is assembled, but we need a sidekick, you coming?"

"For sure I am." Riley leaned over to pet Amber, who purred contently. "Amber, your master needs whatever cat magic you can conjure."

As they piled into Carrie's car, they could hear a faint hum coming from her. "H.R. Pufnstuf—is that what you are whistling?" Cass asked.

"Yes, sorry. I hope I'm not bothering you."

"Oh, no. A boy, an outcast, finds a place where he's accepted only to be hunted for the one gift he has. No, Billy would have liked that as his posse's theme." Cass said.

Carrie's smartphone flashed with a message from Marie.

Before opening her car door, she snuck a peek at it. "Carrie, Charles Edelman passed away." Carrie paused and opened the car door to get in. She gripped the wheel tight.

Based on Cass's estimation, a five-hour drive awaited them—longer with traffic in the city. The image of the fallen hero weighed profoundly on all three.

CHAPTER 36

A Song is Heard

Late afternoon clouds cast an ominous shade over the trees, masking the entrance to the cave. Everything seemed different from the moment when, as a child, Billy excitedly followed Dieter through the foliage in hopes of entering a black hole and traveling through time. Now, in his early thirties, the weight of the years began to press heavy on his shoulders. The sky even seemed to have texture as each breeze scratched his face as if the wind carried pigments of fine sand. Everything became surreal to him as though he were an actor dropped into the middle of a movie set, some hidden camera observing his every step. Except everything around him appeared real and three dimensional, while he felt like one of his drawings, lines, and color, contained by the page that anchored them. Billy sighed, wondering if this was how the world looks before death. That thought seemed to leap out at him, causing him to step back in panic. For so long, he'd convinced himself that his chosen course of action was the right one, and he'd never considered the consequences or how he was woefully unprepared. He inhaled, hoping to once again find the inspiration that brought him here and the intuition to act as circumstances required. The sun peeked through a cloud and exploded in a bright orange aura so brief, yet so intense. A cloud soon blotted out the light, and Billy shivered as a pointed finger press on his shoulders.

"We meet again, comic bookman," said the voice behind him.

The voice was steady, each monotone syllable wormed through Billy's eardrum. Billy knew who it was. He hadn't heard footsteps and surmised the doctor had parked a distance away. The touch of Dr. Laughnon caused Billy to shudder. Billy lurched forward and pivoted to confront him. The man appeared younger than at their meeting days earlier. Sporting a black shirt with gray slacks, the man also wore a thin trench coat down to his knees. His glasses were round with a thick black frame. His nose appeared to be an afterthought to his face, with a tiny bony tip and two thin slits for nostrils. When he opened his mouth, Billy could see his symmetrical white teeth, which appeared trapped by oversize lips that were a strange shade of violet. Dr. Laughnon's hands retreated to his pockets as he scrutinized Billy. "Where is this friend of yours?" he asked, taking a step toward him. Dr. Laughnon appeared confident, even aggressive, in his body language.

Billy reassured himself that he held the upper hand since he'd chosen this location. "He's up at the caves, Doctor." He forced a smile. "Please, follow me."

Billy's pace grew quicker as they made their way through the overgrown bush. Despite it being hours before sunset, the denseness of the trees gave a nighttime feeling to the woods. Billy grinned. He'd hoped to entice Dr. Laughnon to a later meeting under the cloak of darkness, a further advantage. Dr.

Laughnon's insistence on the earlier time made Billy apprehensive. While he carried a flashlight, Billy kept it hidden until he arrived at what appeared to be a wall, decorated by the thick vines clinging to it. Billy had reached the base of the mountain and began running his hands below knee level in search of an opening. In his peripheral line of sight, he could see Dr. Laughnon calmly standing over him with both knees bent, not saying a word. After several minutes of probing, Billy stumbled upon an area devoid of any plant life and could now see the gaping wound in the earth. He did not recall it being so easy to find in his youth. He remembered even Dieter struggling to find it, despite having visited it many times previously. Perhaps the wind had played games, moving the leaves that covered it like blinds.

"This is it, Dr. Laughnon." Billy paused and looked back upon the man almost twice his age. He searched his eyes for a clue, for a hint of what lay beyond the tunnel linking his eyes to his soul. A piercing light blinded him—Dr. Laughnon had drawn his flashlight like a gunfighter.

"Oh, this is it," Dr. Laughnon growled. "It's quite a discovery to have found some mystical place that enhances one's powers. Perhaps you should lead the way inside, where we can have a talk." He licked his lips. "Or we'll have a talk after your demonstration."

Billy put his head down and followed Dr. Laughnon's light, crawling ahead through the opening and stumbling into the pure absence of illumination inside. Billy turned on his pocket light and positioned himself to monitor the man's entrance. The intense light from the flashlight preceded the doctor, crawling forward aggressively until he was inches from Billy. Frightened, Billy tried to slide back, but he soon bumped against the stone side of the cave wall. Dr. Laughnon pressed forward and positioned his face close to Billy's.

"So, mister cartoon man, please introduce me to your friend and let us see what powers he possesses." He leaned back on his legs and began to chuckle. "Tell me the truth about this game you are trying to play with me."

"Oh, my friend knows much about you, Doctor. Much. That's why he's hiding deeper in the caves. Follow me if you want to witness real power."

"Follow you?" Dr. Laughnon's voice grew louder. "Can your friend not invade my mind with his thoughts? Even your mind? Is this not what you promised? Why would I go farther into this cave with you?"

"Because, Doctor, he was a patient of yours, number 5871. And whatever you did to him gave him this special—"

Doctor Laughnon lunged forward and grabbed Billy's arm, squeezing it securely at the wrist, forcing his light to fall out of his grasp. "Patient 5871!" Doctor Laughnon squeezed harder. "There is no patient numbered 5871. At least not anymore."

Billy struggled to resist the doctor's grip. Without only the erratic flicker of natural light, Billy did not notice a third man entering the cave shrouded in the shadows behind Dr. Laughnon. A set of strong hands soon reached past the older man and pinned Billy to the wall.

"Hold him still!" Dr. Laughnon commanded. "Let me get my needle."

The stale breath of the second man flowed through Billy's

nostrils as he lunged on all fours at Billy, landing with both knees pinning down Billy's outstretched legs, two pointy knee-caps pushing down hard on his thighs. The pain receded when the prick of a needle entered his arm. Dr. Laughnon counted with metronomic precision to ten and then ordered the other man to release Billy. For an instant, he thought his circumstances had improved, but the temporary relief from no longer being constrained disappeared once he realized, to his horror, that the pain ended, too. He had no sensations in his legs.

"The feeling must be sickening, young man, to believe you are in control of your destiny, to believe you'd hatched a plan to lure me here. I outsmarted you, Mr. William Daintree of Hobart fame. This moment is long overdue."

Billy grimaced and gritted his teeth. "My legs..."

"That's nothing. My associate, Dr. Backsaw, has just injected a nerve agent to keep you still until we decide your fate." Dr. Laughnon flashed his light in Billy's eyes, blinding them. "Patient 5871 is dead, young man. An unfortunate statistic in a great research project..."

"A sick project." Billy interrupted, trying to avoid the glare of the light.

Dr. Laughnon leaned back on his legs and shook the flashlight haphazardly on the cave walls. "So symbolic. This cave is like a barren mind, and I am the bearer of the light cutting through the empty darkness!"

Billy lowered his eyelids and held his breath for a few seconds. *He called me William Daintree of Hobart. He discovered my identity and email.* "Doctor, I put an end to your work. It was me who sent the email shutting you down."

Dr. Laughnon's hands clenched. "Until you contacted me, I was never certain why the Institute suspended my research. Deaths happened, but nobody cared." Dr. Laughnon explained to Billy how he'd been warned it was in his best interests to leave the country until an appropriate moment to continue his research. Years later, he'd found out through someone at Hobart about the email and how a call for a formal investigation sparked fears at the Institute of an investigation leading them to the "controversial" experiments. "For ten years, I waited for an opportunity to continue my great gift, the study of the human mind. I waited and wrote a novel based on my research. Recently, a fellow researcher beckoned me to return and continue my endeavors." Dr. Laughnon chuckled and nudged Dr. Backsaw, who was sitting stone-like next to him. "Never did I imagine that I could also enjoy the gift of revenge." He now moved toward Billy and whispered in his ear. "When you mentioned meeting patient 5871, I knew you were lying, and so I did some digging. So, the young comic guru is a Hobart alumnus. Imagine my surprise to discover data concerning your old roommate. I must track him down, too…"

Billy shivered, and a tear rolled down his cheek. He struggled to find any feeling in his legs and had minimal movement in his hands.

"Tell me, what was your plan today? To lure me into the cave and do me harm?" Dr. Laughnon motioned to Backsaw, who moved to Billy's side and began to check the pockets of his jeans. Doctor Backsaw retrieved from them a wallet, car keys, and a map. Dr. Laughnon opened up the map and shone the light on it. "Well, you planned to lure me into this cave, and dare I say it, leave me here to die while you wandered out with the aid of this."

Billy could no longer be silent. "I wanted you to fight for survival. To search, never sure when the nightmare would vanquish hope. Your test subjects felt such horror." Billy began to laugh defiantly. "Only your ending will be more gruesome, dying with judgment awaiting."

Doctor Laughnon moved forward and with the back of his hand, slapped Billy in the face. "Long after the blood dries, death finds its prey." He turned to his colleague. "Take this map and bring him far into the cave. Bury him for eternity," Dr. Laughnon made a choking motion at his throat. The other doctor nodded, moved in front of Billy, and began dragging him by the legs. Dr. Laughnon searched the walls of the cave and found another opening that coincided with the map. "There's a wide enough crevice. Drag him through there and follow the map. Go a good distance before you leave him. I'll wait here."

Billy's head banged along the cold, musty ground. He followed the beam of the flashlight along the ground when he noticed something that commanded his full attention. With blood trickling down from his nose, he focused his watery eyes on the light. Now he was sure he had not seen a mirage. Near the opening to the interior cave wall, where Dieter had disappeared years ago, was a fresh indentation in the ground that appeared to be the size of an adult running shoe. "Um, Doctor, are you sure we're alone?"

Dr. Laughnon ignored him. Instead, he barked at Backsaw to move at a quicker pace. Just as Backsaw found the opening and began to back through it while dragging Billy by his feet, the cave exploded with the razor-like sound of layers of guitars slicing through the air. Billy's mouth gaped open in disbelief as Backsaw released his ankles to shield his ears.

"What's going on?" Dr. Laughnon screamed, only to find his voice overwhelmed by the sound.

Billy began to laugh hysterically as Dr. Laughnon moved toward him. "What game are you playing?"

"It's 'Schism,'" Billy yelled. "This cave has a soul!"

Dr. Laughnon snorted like an irritated bull. He yelled to Backsaw to uncover his ears. When the music stopped, a voice bellowed from deep within the cave.

"Nothing is real. You must forget. This is not real." The voice repeated the mantra.

Dr. Laughnon, now on all fours, moved past Billy, pushed aside Backsaw, and shone his light into the opening. The voice continued with perverse precision. "Nothing is real."

"Someone else is in here. We have a map. Follow the voice!" Dr. Laughnon yelled.

"Are you sure? What about this one?" Backsaw asked, pointing to Billy.

"He won't be able to move on his own until well past sunset. Let's find his accomplice and dispose of them. He can wait and worry about his demise."

Billy recognized the voice and now grew fearful for John. "Leave him alone. He doesn't know anything. John, run!" he yelled with all his capacity.

From within the cave, the mantra from the voice stopped, and a chant began in the form of a song, "Escape is for the believers.

Escape is for the believers."

Billy grimaced. *John did not have the map.*

The two men soon disappeared through the opening, leaving Billy alone in the utter darkness of the cave. On his back, with the salty taste of his own blood trickling to his mouth, Billy began to hum. Before closing his eyes, he whispered: "Save him, Dieter."

Outside, the sun's descent neared completion, and the evening shadows emerged like the backdrop of nature's eternal play. Billy commenced a pattern of humming and listening to any sounds emanating from the opening in the cave wall. Far off in the distance, Billy could hear shuffling and thuds against walls that echoed. In the calm state of humming, he began to linger in and out of consciousness, no longer able to feel his fingers. Only his thoughts could roam free. Wandering within the endless world of his mind, Billy did not hear the footsteps approaching. An angelic voice found its way through the cave's opening and seemed to ride the last ray of light from the plunging sun. Billy's eyes began to tear. Foreign emotions introduced themselves. Unprepared, he began to whimper.

"Cass," he whispered. "Cass?"

CHAPTER 37

No Light Can Escape

"Yes, Billy, it's me. Stay calm. You are not alone," Cass whispered to Billy as she shone her light over his body, examining him. Within seconds, voices filled the cave. Through his blurred vision, he made out Carrie and Riley on all fours, moving toward him.

Billy smiled. "Dr. Woodson, you make cave calls, too, now?"

Carrie ignored Billy and watched as Cass examined him. "He can't feel anything, Carrie."

"He injected me with a nerve blocker. It will wear off, but they plan to return." Billy sputtered. "I'll be okay, but someone needs to help John. He saved me. He is alone without a map."

"Where exactly?" Carrie asked.

"He got the doctors to chase him farther into the cave. He was waiting for them all along. I guess he got here before me." Billy's voice grew excited. "We have to help him. They'll kill him if they catch him."

Carrie looked over to Cass. "Stay here will Billy and make sure he remains stable. Just in case someone else shows up." Carrie rolled up her sleeve and pointed the flashlight at the wall, looking for the opening. "Riley, stay here and protect the opening. Billy can't defend himself in his condition."

Riley protested. "Carrie, you're whacky if you think I'm going to let you go in there alone."

"My son has dragged me along with him into caves before. I've done some amateur spelunking, which I'm sure is more than anyone else here," Carrie protested. "Billy, do you have the map, or did they take it from you?"

"They have a map." Billy coughed as the blood from his nose, trickled into his mouth. Cass put her hands behind his head to prop him up. "But it won't help them much." Billy leaned forward and slid off one of his sneakers, taking off his sock to reveal a folded paper hidden within it. "This is the real map, Dieter's map."

"A second map!" Riley threw his hands up. "Your friend sent you two maps."

Billy's head tilted from shoulder to shoulder. "The one they have is not real. The map is a copy of the original, except for the detours I made up. I can only imagine where they will end up."

Carrie grinned. "You planned to lose them in there?"

Billy nodded. "In case something happened, I didn't want them getting out. But, guys, it has been radio silence. Map or no map, those caves are a death trap, vertical drops, and confined spaces. Carrie, you need help in there."

"I've dealt with male doctors with attitude my whole career. I'll go slow and follow the map, light, or voices. If Riley stays back at the opening over there," — Carrie pointed to entrance into the next section — "I'll be covered."

Cass propped Billy up onto her lap and began wiping the

blood off his face. "You won't be mobile for a spell, and natural light is diminishing. We can catch up while I protect you." Cass winked as a slight smile broke through the dried blood on Billy's lips.

Carrie and Riley scurried along the earth to the opening. Carrie tested her flashlight and maneuvered through the opening. "Riley, if things go haywire, I'll flash the light in your direction. Whatever I do, don't follow me. Make sure Billy is protected. Promise me."

Riley nodded and dipped his head as Carrie crawled through the opening. She had crawled twenty feet, which seemed like a thousand. Barely able to move on all fours without scuffing her head, she crawled only five or six feet at any time before stopping to listen. With three scurrying men in these caves, she expected their resonances would guide her.

A blood-curdling scream cut through the air, freezing Carrie in her tracks. Within moments of the cry, a sickening thud followed. Riley shined his light at Carrie's feet and breathed a side of relief upon seeing them. While echoes can create illusions of time and space, the scream seemed close. Unsure what to do next, Carrie shone her light forward, looking for a sign. Then a voice filled the tunnel. "Help us, please! We won't hurt you." The voice was unfamiliar but gave Carrie something to follow.

She moved farther and farther in, honing in on the tracks she saw before her. Whatever signs of life existing became sparse. Carrie suspected that one of the men had likely met a grim fate. Long ago, she broke off communication from Riley. She never intended for him to follow her. He survived his demons, she thought: he'd earned the right of safety. The voice calling for help stopped. Somewhere along the way, Carrie had taken a detour away from it.

Frustrated and confident she lost them, she paused. Her back began to ache, and sweat poured down her cheeks. Coughing from the air heavy with soot, she considered turning back. Then a flicker of light danced upon the wall. She moved closer to the light, which now flickered steadily. A voice, faint and crackling, reached her ears again. "Help, he's not moving. Help me!"

Carrie moved forward briskly, but when her left hand slid forward, she almost lost her balance before catching herself. She positioned her light to detect the floor of the tunnel giving way to space a few feet ahead. Cautiously, she moved forward and peered over the ledge. Just below, she spotted a man staring up as he grimaced with discomfort. With her light shining in his direction, she saw a body of another man lying face-first amidst a pool of blood flowing from the top part of his body.

"Help me. Who's there? Please, help me!"

Carrie leaned forward and shined the light directly on the face of the man. "Who are you?"

"I am a doctor. My colleague and I were exploring these caves when we took a wrong turn and fell off that cliff up there." He pointed to the edge of another cliff almost opposite from Carrie, though ten or fifteen feet higher up.

"Is he dead?" Carrie pointed her light to the man lying prone as Dr. Laughnon moved toward her.

"Yes. He broke my fall."

"Where is the other man?" Carrie asked. "The man you were chasing."

Dr. Laughnon stopped. "Who you are referring to? Who are

you?"

"Dr. Carrie Woodson."

"Well, Carrie, please come help me."

"Where is the man you were chasing?" Carrie persisted.

"I don't know who you are referring to. Please lower something down so I can climb out."

"I have so much information all about you, Mr. Laughnon, including your experiments." Carrie looked around the chamber, finding no trace of John.

"As a fellow doctor, you understand the research's value." Dr. Laughnon continued moving and positioned himself just beneath Carrie, about eight to ten feet below.

"I suppose I have no choice." Carrie reached forward and began extending her arm and immediately pulled it back. "One question, though. I've struggled to do my own research, and I wondered where your test subjects came from."

"Oh, Dr. Woodson, the world is filled with those on the fringes, whether orphans, refugees, or the intellectually challenged. People are disposable in quests for ethereal knowledge. Now, please give me your hand."

Carrie maneuvered partway over the ledge and extended her arm. Dr. Laughnon crouched low and leaped only to find Carrie smiling as she pulled back her arm, leaving him to fall back to the ground below. Carrie moved back away from the ledge, staring down on him. "My son was once a refugee escaping men like you with no regard for life. He refuses to speak of the horrors he witnessed." She motioned with her hand. "This will make a fine burial site for you. Almost like a great pharaoh's tomb. Trapped here with only your thoughts, your sins.

I suspect as you approach death, you will scream—not because you are in pain or close to death but to drown out the voices of all those whose souls you caused to scream. Souls that my dear friend can hear. And don't call me Carrie." She turned to crawl back to safety when the ledge began to give way, leaving her left leg dangling over the edge. Just as she began to pull her leg up, a hand grabbed her at the ankle. Dr. Laughnon's leap had been most timely and opportune.

"Now, Carrie, save yourself and me, or else I drag you down."

Carrie panicked as she began sliding backward. Then two arms grabbed her at the elbows and pulled her toward safety with Dr. Laughnon in tow. She gritted her teeth and, with the full force of her right leg, stomped backward, landing a direct blow on Dr. Laughnon's hand at the expense of her ankle. The agonizing moan of Dr. Laughnon as he fell towards the chamber's floor distracted her from the overwhelming pain. He rolled around the floor, howling in misery, with one arm broken and a crushed hand. Once away from the ledge, she caught her breath and said, "Riley, thanks."

"It's not Riley, Carrie. It's me."

She looked up and through the rays of a flashlight, witnessed John grinning. "Thank goodness, I found you." She laughed. "I mean, it would make me look good if I said I found you, right?"

"For sure, Carrie. I heard the commotion and literally squirmed my way towards your voice. How is Billy?"

"He says you saved him. He'll recover once he sees you are safe."

"I'm sorry for taking off on you, but I suspected Billy was in danger and would be here. When I ventured into the cave looking for him, I expected he was already far into the caves. Then I heard voices in the entrance area, and by the time I got back to the opening, they'd already hurt him. Luckily, I have Tool's music on my phone." John's hands shook with excitement.

"I take it you had these bastards chasing you until they met their demise." Carrie stopped moving. "I just don't understand how you survived without the map from Billy's apartment."

"Carrie, there's something I want to show you before we see Billy." John tugged at his waist and pulled his belt out from his jeans and handed one end to Carrie. "Follow me and hang on to the belt, so I don't lose you."

With John leading the way, Carrie followed, coughing and sputtering along the way. Turning back frequently, he seemed too pensive and anxious to speak. Carrie tugged the belt to get his attention. "You need a rest, Carrie?" Just as the last words fell out, distant screams filled the air, more desperate and more chilling with each wail.

"No. I just assume this must be traumatic for you—facing Dr. Laughnon."

"I never faced him but heard that voice again. The one that shut my memory down like he must have done to so many others he brainwashed." John coughed and nodded to her. "I don't mind his screams at all, though. It means the other screams will stop. Sounds kind of cold, I suppose."

"Not at all, John."

"Carrie, do you feel guilty over what just happened. Is that why you're asking me?"

"Whenever I reflect upon what just happened, I'll just eat a chocolate chip cookie, and I'll be fine." Carrie crawled on her elbows closer to John. "I stopped now because I know, John, I know."

John's mouth gaped open with his head tilting to the side. "Know what?"

"You've been here before," Carrie said. "You didn't need a map, did you?"

"Why? Is it because I seem too comfortable around the cave, like it's my second home? I'm sure you're wondering." John smirked. "You are too smart. Be patient. I will explain everything." John extended the belt, turned, and continued crawling. He came upon an opening that descended at a steep incline into a smaller chamber relative to the one they left Laughnon and Backsaw in. John lifted himself to his knees, his head skimming the roof of the natural room. His light illuminated a spot in the corner where the ground formed in a distinct rectangular, raised formation.

Carrie gasped. "It's a grave!" John nodded to her as she shivered. His eyes met hers. She knew instantly. "Dieter!"

"Yes. Years ago, after everything that happened. Kate and I were passing through this area. We stopped just near here for gas and a bite when I recognized we were on the outskirts of Billy's hometown. I remembered that black hole story, so I needed to see it." John sighed. "I owed him that, to see it for myself. Kate thought I was crazy, though she is an adventurer at heart. We wanted to find the truth about Billy's past."

Carrie stared at the grave as John continued. "We spent a full day exploring. We had a decent rope and combed the caverns for hours."

"There wasn't, was there?" Carrie pointed at a collapsed wall behind the grave.

"We discovered this chamber and remains. The thing is, there was a backpack, leaving no doubt. In the inside pouch, decently preserved, was a comic book page. *The* comic book page." John said. "Kate and I gave Dieter a proper grave." He crawled past the grave to the pile of earth and rocks behind it. "I suspect another opening once existed, possible the path out, but, the archway collapsed on the kid. Just my guess."

"You told no one?"

"The boy died so long ago. They never cared to find him then. This is the place where he belonged. Here he can be the light amidst the darkness of all these tunnels and chambers—a guardian for the lost souls wandering through the black." John smiled and squeezed Carrie's hands. "Like what you do."

Carrie squeezed back and bit her lips. "So, you sent Billy the letter with the map? But what does the map lead to? I doubt you would want him to find this."

"Carrie, I had to do it because I understood how much he loved Kate." John slouched and shook his head. "I swore Billy's mom to secrecy and got his address. One morning, I left early without telling Kate and dropped off the envelope. I let him be a martyr and repaid him with hope and a belief. Kate and I found another way out. The escape route on the map I sent leads you all over the place, only to bring you back to where you come in by," John said. "I figured it would be safe if Billy ever explored. He would never find the grave or become hopelessly lost. It wouldn't surprise him if Dieter pulled another magician's trick." He laughed. "Carrie, you promise you won't tell him, right? Ever. He needs to believe. Because he followed when no one else would, he needs to always believe."

"Secrets are just truths hidden from disbelievers, anyway." Carrie grinned. "We have some worried people waiting to see us. I'm sure your wife will be relieved to have you back."

John smiled. "When Kate returns, we will have quite the reunion."

"Returns?" Carrie wondered.

"I sent her on a mission. To pull the plug on the Thoth Institute. She is quite the activist. Heaven help them." John reached over and grabbed Carrie's hand. "I will need your help."

Carrie smiled. "Time no longer exists in my world, young man. Whenever you need me."

As they turned to make their way back to the opening, the caves trembled with a shrill howl and horrifying scream. Carrie frowned. "I just got a craving for a chocolate chip cookie."

The duo made their way through the maze of tunnels. A light flashed in their direction, and a voice shouted, "They're okay! They're okay!" Riley excitedly pulled John and Carrie back through the opening and into the main entrance chamber. He squeezed Carrie's shoulders. At first, Carrie recoiled, but then she leaned forward, pulling Riley back toward her in exhaustion and fully embracing his comforting hug.

By now, the sun had set as a faint glimmer of moonlight cast ghostly halos around the occupants. John smiled at Cass before his light set upon Billy, who now leaned forward on his knees against Cass for balance. The two friends exchanged tear-soaked gazes.

"I heard the song playing for me again, my friend. I am part of it." John crawled forward and hugged Billy. "Good thing you never read that Hawking book. He was wrong."

"About black holes?" Billy asked.

"I mean, you don't find God by searching," John stated. "God is looking for us in the dense forest that is silence and finds us all by following the sound of our song. We are lost to him when we stop singing. That is the trick. The only trick I know."

Billy whispered in John's ear, "I suspected that long ago. We are the music we play and hear. We always were."

John laughed and opened his hand. "I see my hand is empty now. You have taken the pebble."

Billy placed his hands on John's shoulders and winked. "More importantly, you suppose Kate will forgive me now?"

CHAPTER 38

The Guardian of the Song

Months flowed to the gentle hum of time.

The Thoth Institute became the subject of numerous investigations, complete with various conspiracy theories about the disappearances of Dr. Laughnon and Dr. Backsaw. As Carrie cynically suspected, when the truth of about the research conducted at the Thoth Institute came out, the search for Laughnon and Backsaw became half-hearted. The story needed to remain contained to two rogue scientists. Besides, the duo had hidden their intent and covered their tracks that day, so few knew their plans. They never anticipated being unsuccessful in their attempts to silence the past. The last trace of them was a car belonging to the Institute, abandoned about half a mile from the caves in the town of Galt. The caves, whose entrance was hidden by those who last exited them, remained off-limits.

No one dared explore the caves again. Carrie surmised that adults found it easier to believe the theory that light is incapable of escaping. In reality, they feared the light lurking and hiding within the depths of darkness. As light can illuminate and differentiate shadows from reality, some prefer that the light remained covered by an ill-fitting cloak stitched with fear. The reward for those who seek the source of illumination is to become blissfully baptized by it.

Maris stared out the window from his room. His eyes danced with each leaf that eloquently fell. Sequestered in his room to complete his homework, his mind escaped the mundane world of academics every so often. On the horizon, he noticed a car coming down the road. "We have a visitor. Wait, I am wrong, visitors. They are finally here."

Marie poked Carrie, who had dozed off on the couch beside her. Carrie bolted upright. "This is a historic moment," Marie said, laughing uncontrollably. Carrie Woodson having guests over for dinner was one thing. Weekend guests were a miracle. Marie smiled at Carrie.

Carrie made her way to the door, only to be brushed aside as Maris raced ahead of her and opened the door even before the bell rang.

"You must be Maris. I have heard so much about you." Cass smiled and extended her hand. Maris shook it like a skilled statesman, while his eyes focused on Billy.

Maris immediately realized his impoliteness. "Sorry, it's just that—"

Cass laughed. "It's okay. I know you're excited to meet him." She leaned forward and whispered, "I'm excited to be with him, too."

Maris blushed and extended his hand to Billy. "Is Riley with you, too?"

Cass said, "Riley is back in New York with Amber. He went back to university to obtain a degree studying artificial intelligence. He sends his love."

Billy grabbed Maris's hands with both of his and winked at Marie. "*The* two humans who elevate Dr. Carrie Woodson to humbleness!" Billy laughed while Carrie rolled her eyes.

"How was your visit with John and Kate? Did you convince them to join you?" Carrie asked. "The last time I spoke with John, he mentioned he would try to make it."

Billy laughed. "Well, they extend their hellos to all of you. They extend sincere apologies, but something happened."

Carrie stopped smiling. "Is everything…"

"Oh, Billy, we are still recovering from your last drama." Cass looked at Billy, who nodded back. "Kate is expecting any day now."

Marie clapped her hands together. "That is wonderful news."

Cass smiled and poked Billy. "Billy will be an excellent godfather!"

"Well, I'm glad everyone else is happy," Maris interjected, moving in between the adults as the guests entered. "I'm still not satisfied."

Billy looked over to Carrie, who filled him in. "He's still ticked about *Time's Musicians* ending."

"I kind of figured that's what it was," Billy smirked. "Maris, your mom told me you've started drawing and working on your own comic book."

Maris frowned. "Yeah, but it's still sucky. Yours was, like, the best ever."

"Oh, I used to worry mine sucked, too. Trust yourself, and it will be great. Besides, you are a lucky dude."

"Yeah, I hear it all the time. I've got two of the greatest moms in the world and lots of friends. My ears are going to burst if I hear it again." Maris chuckled, winking at Carrie.

"Your sweet, gentle mom also is this great superhero." Billy's eyes repeatedly blinked for effect.

"Oh, I heard the story of how she raced into the cave and saved everyone." Maris sighed.

"That's nothing. Wait here." Billy reopened the front door and sprinted back to his car, parked in the driveway. Maris was able to decipher what looked like a magazine in Billy's hand. As Billy entered, Maris's voice rose excitedly. "A comic book!"

"So, *Time's Musicians* continues!" Carrie exclaimed.

Billy ignored Carrie and headed straight to Maris. "This is the first edition, Maris. Consider it a gift to a loyal fan."

Maris's eyes seemed to explode into bright shades of blue. "Why me? I mean, thanks."

"Oh, the superhero is based on... Well, I've known many people who deserve their own comic book, but this is special to me." He glanced over to Carrie. "I, too, look forward to entering her world of adventure. It's the sequel."

Maris stared at the cover, his mouth opening wider as he flipped the pages. His focus shifted between the book and Carrie. Marie chortled, "Oh, we will never hear the end of this."

Carrie gingerly made her way to Maris, her eyebrows furrowed. "Hand this to me, please." Armed with the comic book in her hands, her head began bobbing. "Finally."

Marie peered over Carrie's shoulders and read, "The Guardian of the Song." The cover depicted a female superhero, dressed in azure with an oversize head, a flowing maroon cape, and holding a chocolate chip cookie in one hand with a cat at her feet.

Carrie beamed as a distinct melodic sound originated from her lips. Billy smirked. Carrie was indeed humming.

Made in the USA
Columbia, SC
21 September 2020